Galloway had broken in!

Adam crept toward DJ's bedroom. He stopped and held his breath so he could listen.

A sound. Almost like something brushing against a window.

DJ must be inside, but was she alone? He heard her moan softly, and a second later came another crash. The floor reverberated and DJ cried out in pain.

Adam threw his weight against the door as he propelled himself into DJ's room.

Inside, dresser drawers lay scattered across the floor and the bed had been pulled from the wall. Counting on Galloway to aim high, Adam dropped to the floor and rolled behind the headboard.

Too late, he heard a footstep behind him. He pivoted and found himself staring into DJ's narrowed eyes.

"What in the hell do you think you're doing?" She didn't *sound* frightened.

"I thought you were in trouble," Adam said. "Is everything okay?"

"It was until you broke the door. I'm rearranging my furniture." And she started to laugh.

ABOUT THE AUTHOR

Sherry Lewis won critical acclaim for her first Superromance novel, *Call Me Mom.* She followed that success with *This Montana Home,* and in *Keeping Her Safe,* her third book for Superromance, she once again proves that her forte is "fast-paced action romance with...wonderful characters."

Sherry can't remember when she *didn't* want to be a novelist, but she only began her writing career a few years ago. She's now also published several books in a mystery series. Sherry says she draws her inspiration from the places she visits when she travels and when she's behind the wheel on long drives. She also loves music and reading.

Sherry makes her home in Utah and is the mother of two daughters, Valerie and Vanessa.

Books by Sherry Lewis

HARLEQUIN SUPERROMANCE
628—CALL ME MOM
692—THIS MONTANA HOME

Don't miss any of our special offers. Write to us at the following address for information on our newest releases.

Harlequin Reader Service
U.S.: 3010 Walden Ave., P.O. Box 1325, Buffalo, NY 14269
Canadian: P.O. Box 609, Fort Erie, Ont. L2A 5X3

KEEPING HER SAFE
Sherry Lewis

Harlequin Books

TORONTO • NEW YORK • LONDON
AMSTERDAM • PARIS • SYDNEY • HAMBURG
STOCKHOLM • ATHENS • TOKYO • MILAN
MADRID • WARSAW • BUDAPEST • AUCKLAND

ISBN 0-373-70744-4

KEEPING HER SAFE

For my Knight in Slightly Rusted Armor
who taught me what true love is

PROLOGUE

LARRY GALLOWAY paced to the end of the interview room, pivoted at the barred windows and started back to his seat. In another ten minutes, he'd be standing before a parole board, smiling prettily and looking sorry in front of a bunch of worthless jackasses who had the power to either keep him in prison or set him free.

He wasn't worried—not really. He could get out. He'd done it before. He just had to say the right things and wear the right expressions. Just play the game and tell them what they wanted to hear. They never needed to know how he really felt.

His attorney, Winston Jacobson, scowled up at him from his seat near the door. "Sit down, Galloway. You look nervous."

Nervous? The word didn't even begin to describe Larry's present mood. He'd spent eight years in prison for nothing more than teaching that stupid woman a lesson. Mary, that stupid woman who had been so much like Chrissy, he'd *had* to teach her.

Mary had screwed him over, plain and simple. She'd had no business talking to the guy down the street. No business at all. But Larry had seen her, and he'd confronted her.

Oh, she'd tried to whine her way out of it. She'd tried to confuse him by crying and begging him not to hit her. And then she'd lain there looking pathetic and weak and stupid and pretending he'd hurt her when that prissy cop arrived—the same way Chrissy had done all those years ago, damn her. *Damn her to hell!*

Larry snorted to himself, then shot a glance at Winston to see if he'd noticed. No, he still had his stupid nose buried in that idiotic magazine—*Today's Celebrity.* Larry snorted again and turned away.

"I said sit down," Winston said without looking up.

Larry didn't want to sit. He wanted to think, dammit. Turning at the window, he started back across the room.

Winston glanced up from under his too-thick eyebrows. *"Sit."*

Moron. Larry sat and worked up an innocent smile. Good practice for the parole board. "I'm sitting."

Winston closed his magazine and tossed it to Larry. "Read."

Oh, yeah. Read. Read about movie stars and other witless people who made millions of bucks for nothing. *Nothing.* Larry flipped a few pages and felt the heat rising up his neck as he looked at the smiling faces of the ugly, stupid people on the glossy pages.

He flipped again, but this time he stopped and stared at the picture in front of him. Dark hair cropped short and shot with gray now that she was older. A smile that had once charmed him into making a fool of himself. And those dark eyes that had hidden her lies and treachery.

Chrissy.

He read the first page and felt his control start to

weaken. His temper simmered, his fists clenched, the cords in his neck strained.

She was calling herself Christina Prescott again. *Damn her to hell.*

She obviously hadn't suffered the way Larry had wanted her to for what she'd done. Well, he'd found her again after all this time. And now she would pay plenty.

He scanned the article and turned the page. The picture there made his heart race and his throat go dry. Chrissy and Devon. He smiled slowly. The way to get back at her was spelled out for him right here in this stupid magazine.

Yes. That's exactly how she'd pay. He'd take back what she'd stolen from him—how long ago? Must be thirty years by now.

Larry would make himself the sorriest SOB to ever sit in front of a parole board if that's what it took to get out—especially now that he had a plan. He wanted to laugh aloud, but even stupid Winston might start to wonder about him if he did that.

Humming softly to himself, Larry settled back in his seat to read the article. And to plot sweet revenge.

CHAPTER ONE

ADAM MCALLISTER tossed the day's mail onto the kitchen table, stretched to work the kinks out of his shoulders and slipped his jacket off over his holster and side arm. Draping the jacket over the back of a chair, he glanced at his answering machine. No messages. Good. Nothing would ruin his weekend plans with Seth.

Smiling a little, he removed the elastic from the morning's edition of the *Salt Lake Tribune* and scanned the front page. But he'd already heard most of the big stories on the car's radio, and had heard more than enough about the election while he'd accompanied Milo Harrison along the campaign trail.

He tossed the paper onto the table beside the mail and started to unbutton his uniform shirt as he walked down the hall toward his bedroom. But before he'd gone even halfway, his stomach decided to complain about the number of hours it had been since he'd eaten.

True, he'd had dinner—if you could call it that—at Milo's campaign fund-raiser, but that had been hours ago. He didn't want to get dressed again and go back out, but unless some good fairy had stocked the kitchen in his absence, his cupboards were bare.

Trudging back to the kitchen, Adam tugged open the refrigerator door and checked inside. No surprises there. Nothing but a bit of wilted salad his mother had dropped by days before, two cans of beer, half a six-pack of cola and something else he didn't even try to identify.

He hesitated for a moment, debating whether to have a beer. Normally, he'd have to pass. Regulations prevented him from drinking anything alcoholic within eight hours of reporting for duty, and he rarely had more than that amount of time between shifts. But with his weekend free, he had almost seventy-two hours to call his own, and right now, the beer looked more inviting than a soda or a dead salad.

On the other hand, he wanted to have a clear head when he and his brother started for Idaho in just a few hours. He didn't need a headache while he and Seth argued over who should drive. Frowning a little, he ignored the beer, pulled a soda from its pack and swigged a mouthful.

Sweet. Far too sweet. And it didn't take away the hunger pangs. If anything, it made him almost more desperate for something to eat.

Scowling, he wiped his mouth and glared at the can in his hand. He lifted it for another drink just as the telephone rang into the stillness of his empty apartment. He flicked a wary glance at the cordless phone. A call after midnight could only mean one of two things—a family crisis or Seth calling to cancel their trip.

He snagged the receiver from its base and growled, "Hello?"

"Well?" Chuck Tobler's voice charged through the wire much the same way he barged through everything else in his path. Adam added a third choice to his list of late-night telephone callers—his supervisor at Dodge Detective Agency.

"What happened today?" Chuck demanded. "Anything I need to know about? Why haven't you called in to log off shift yet?"

"Long day," Adam said. "I just got home a minute ago."

"And—?"

"*And* the fund-raiser was uneventful. No trouble."

"No antiabortion protestors?" Chuck sounded almost disappointed. He'd agreed to take Adam's place for the weekend, and Adam knew he'd want some kind of excitement to perk up the long days.

Adam hated to disappoint him, but he couldn't lie. "None."

"What about those environmentalists from southern Utah?"

"Not a sign of them," Adam said. "It was a quiet day. Busy, but quiet."

"Well, I'm glad to hear it," Chuck said without conviction. "I don't want anything to go wrong this weekend."

"Don't worry," Adam assured him. "Milo has a quiet weekend planned."

"What about *Mrs.* Harrison?"

"She'll be fine. She might drink a little to work up courage for public appearances, but she won't cause trouble for Milo."

Chuck let silence hang between them for a second or two, and Adam could almost see him rubbing his hand across his chin as he thought. "Tell me," he said at last. "Do you think Kenny could handle the Harrisons?"

"*Kenny?*" Adam shook his head thoughtfully. At

twenty-two, Kenny Masters was still young enough to think he knew everything—a dangerous way of thinking in the security field. "I thought *you* were going to cover while I'm gone."

"I am," Chuck said. "I'm talking about a permanent change of duty."

Pushing back an unwelcome twinge of apprehension, Adam leaned against the counter and shifted the phone to his other ear. "Why? Is something wrong?" He'd been out of the law-enforcement field awhile now. Maybe his skills were growing slightly rusty.

"No, you've done a great job," Chuck said, as if he could read Adam's mind. "You'll rise to the top in no time. But I've got a new assignment for you. You'll like this one—it's right up your alley."

Adam wouldn't lie—he'd like a new assignment. The Harrison campaign detail hadn't been as bad as he'd feared, but he hadn't signed on with the agency to spend his days walking half a step behind a pampered politician and his wife. "What kind of assignment?"

"I just got a call from home office," Chuck said. "From Thomas Dodge himself, as a matter of fact."

"Thomas Dodge? I didn't think he worked anymore."

"He usually doesn't," Chuck admitted. "But he's got a personal interest in this case, and he told me to assign you to cover it."

"Me? Why?"

"Because of your experience on the police force."

An all-too-familiar bitterness started to work its way through Adam. He still resented Victoria for having pushed him to leave the force and hated himself for having given in to please her. If he'd had his way, he'd have gone back to police work when he'd walked away from the job he'd taken with Victoria's father to make her happy. But hiring freezes along the Wasatch Front had kept him from going back to the job he loved.

He'd taken the next best thing—or so he told himself. But working armed security for Dodge kept his hands tied and left him frustrated most of the time. If he were running things, he'd give his first-line people more authority to deal with offenders, and he'd cut the red tape to a minimum. And if he played his cards right, he could work up into a management position that would give him the say he wanted.

"Tell me," Chuck said, "have you ever heard of Christina Prescott?"

"No. Who is she?"

"She's an author. Lives here in Utah part of each year. You see her books everywhere—are you sure you haven't heard of her? My wife reads all her stuff."

Adam shrugged his indifference. He'd never understood why anyone would sit down with a book if they didn't have to. "The name still doesn't ring a bell."

"Well, it will," Chuck assured him. "She's hired us to keep an eye on her daughter and granddaughter."

Bodyguard work? The assignment didn't sound so intriguing now. In fact, it didn't sound much different from what he'd done for the Harrison campaign. "What kind of an eye?"

"Apparently there's some guy who's being paroled from the Utah State Penitentiary sometime this week. His name's Larry Galloway—a two-bit loser who's been in and out of institutions for the past thirty years. For some reason, Ms. Prescott is convinced he'll show up at her daughter's place. She's paying us to watch out for him and to keep him from bothering her family—that sort of thing.''

That made the assignment sound a touch more appetizing. ''What will I be watching out for? Any specifics?''

Chuck's chair creaked, and Adam could almost see him leaning back in it. ''Your guess is as good as mine. I don't know whether they're in real danger or whether Christina Prescott's paranoid and Dodge is humoring her because of who she is.''

''You mean because of her money.'' Adam had run into people with too much money and imagination before. If Ms. Prescott's daughter was in danger, he'd be glad to help. But he didn't want to waste his time baby-sitting some spoiled rich girl for her paranoid mama. He'd done enough of that during his marriage to Victoria.

With ability born of practice, he forced down his rising resentment and managed to keep his voice sounding normal. ''What's the connection between Galloway and Prescott's daughter? Is he an old boyfriend? Ex-husband?''

''I don't think so,'' Chuck said. ''We don't have his rap sheet yet, but I've skimmed our preliminary report, and what I've read so far makes him sound a little old for that...but you never know. Dodge didn't give me details, so I'd be ready for anything.''

Adam made a face and sank onto a chair by the table. ''Well, that's helpful.''

''Yeah, isn't it? From what I gather, Ms. Prescott is convinced Galloway will violate parole. She wants to make sure we're there when he does so we can put him back behind bars.''

"She wants him sent back to prison? Sounds vindictive to me.''

"You said it, *I* didn't,'' Chuck replied with a thin laugh.

His reaction didn't surprise Adam. Chuck was a company man through and through. He knew how to kiss up to his superiors better than anyone Adam had ever met.

"What did Galloway go to prison for?'' he asked.

"This time? Assault with a deadly weapon. Five counts. He's been on the inside for a little over eight years. I'll have his mug shot and preliminary report delivered to you tomorrow by courier. You can see for yourself.'' Chuck rolled open a file drawer and rustled some papers near the telephone. "Okay, here's where you report for duty—do you have something to write with?''

Adam grabbed an envelope from the stack of mail and pulled a pen from his pocket. "I do now.''

"Ms. Prescott's daughter's name is Devon Jo Woodward, but she goes by DJ. She owns a garden shop on the west side of Salt Lake City somewhere, The Treehouse.'' He rattled off an address, flipped a few more papers and did something to the telephone. "It looks like she's thirty-two and divorced, and she has a four-year-old daughter named Marissa.''

A four-year-old? Adam tried not to groan aloud. He'd spent enough time around his brother Luke's children to know four-year-olds were too young to understand reason but too old to accept instructions without question. He couldn't pretend that he looked forward to spending time around some self-centered woman with too many credit cards and a demanding child. For a heartbeat he considered asking Chuck to leave him with the Harrisons.

"Are you there?" Chuck demanded.

Scratch that idea. Chuck sounded annoyed.

Adam grunted a reply and forced himself to pay attention.

"Ms. Prescott's making arrangements for you to stay in a spare room in DJ's basement."

"Wait a minute—I'm supposed to *live* with them?"

"I thought you said you were paying attention."

"I am," Adam lied. "For how long?"

"I don't know. Until Ms. Prescott feels her daughter's safe, I guess. Or until we have Larry Galloway behind bars again."

Wonderful. An open-ended assignment.

"Dodge wants you to move on this right away," Chuck said. "You start first thing in the morning. Go straight to Ms. Woodward's house. She'll be expecting you. Oh— I'll be sending a laptop computer with the courier, too."

Adam shook his head, slowly at first, then faster as Chuck went on. "I'll do it, but not tomorrow. I've got the weekend off, remember? I'm going to Boise with my brother."

"Not this weekend," Chuck said. "Your leave's been canceled, courtesy of Thomas Dodge."

At first, Adam thought maybe he hadn't heard Chuck right. This was his first weekend leave in six months, and he had plans for every minute of the time.

Irritation tightened his stomach and tensed his shoulders, but he tried to keep his voice reasonably calm. "I cleared this weekend with you more than three weeks ago."

"I know, but Dodge insists on you for this assignment."

"Somebody else can do it until I get back."

"He *ordered* me to put you on this detail." Chuck clipped out the words, a warning that his patience was wearing thin. "It's important, Adam. You're the only man we've got with the background to do the job right." Adam could hear Chuck breathing on the other end of the line. He didn't sound like someone who cared much about Adam's plans.

"Assign somebody else to the case for the first few days," Adam said. "I'll take over first thing Monday when I get back."

Chuck huffed out a deep breath. "I wish I could, but this assignment's different from what we usually do. We're sending you in under cover."

Adam leaned back in his seat and stared at the receiver. "Under cover? Why?"

"Because Ms. Prescott doesn't want DJ to know who you are and why you're there. She wants you to pose as a friend of hers—you're a writer, and you're doing research on a new book."

Adam barked an angry laugh. "A *writer?* That will never work. I don't know the first thing about writing. Hell, I don't even *read.*"

"You'll have to find a way to *make* it work."

"Easy for you to say," Adam grumbled.

Chuck drew in a deep breath and let it out slowly. "Look, Adam, the bottom line is this: Dodge expects you to take the assignment and make it work." When Adam didn't speak, he continued. "I'll have the courier drop off everything by ten in the morning. Do yourself a favor—make sure you're there.'' He disconnected without giving Adam a chance to respond.

Adam closed his eyes and struggled to control his exasperation. He'd been backed into a corner and left with no options.

He flicked off the telephone and dropped it to the table, then spent another minute or two glaring at it as if it were responsible for his disappointment. Shaking his head in self-disgust, he drained the last of his soda and lobbed the empty can toward the trash container in the corner.

After tugging his shirt over his head, he pulled off his shoes. He grabbed the cordless phone from the table and punched in Seth's home telephone number as he walked down the hall toward the bedroom.

Clinging to resentment wouldn't accomplish anything. Traveling to Boise with Seth would have been a pleasant change of pace, but the trip wasn't important or necessary to Adam. It wasn't worth the price he'd have to pay. Any further argument would only jeopardize future promotions.

Adam had lost everything in his divorce—his house, his wife, his security. His new career with Dodge Detective was the only thing he had left—he couldn't risk losing that, too.

DJ WOODWARD pushed back her hair from her eyes and scowled at the mock-up of the ad she hoped to finish in time to run in the Sunday newspapers. She'd been fussing with the layout since well before closing, but she still couldn't get it the way she wanted.

Sighing, she tried once more to focus, but worry over the store's financial picture had kept her awake the past few nights, and for days, she'd been having

trouble concentrating. She leaned back in her chair
and stared at the ceiling. One dim lamp at her desk
provided enough light for her to work in the early-
autumn dusk, but heavy shadows reached eerie fingers
out from the corners of the store and laid a dark blanket over everything else inside.

The evening matched her mood—dark, melan-
choly, pathetic. As she forced herself upright again,
she caught a glimpse of the sunset over the Great Salt
Lake through her office window. She allowed herself
a minute to watch the sky glowing pink, yellow and
lavender where the sun still touched the clouds, finally darkening into a solid base of indigo at the edge
of the horizon.

Her inventory of shrubs and trees stretched toward
the skyline. Backed by the fading sunlight, everything
looked new and clean and beautiful, and for half a
second, hope filled her. But it faded again just as
quickly.

The store's financial demands had almost drained
her bank accounts. She couldn't remember the last
time she'd had a full staff, and if this week's ad didn't
generate business, she didn't know how she'd pay for
the shipment of snowblowers scheduled to arrive at
the end of the month. She was floundering, and staring at sunsets wouldn't do any good.

Turning away from the window, she scowled at the
ad again and pushed aside a sudden urge to quit for
the day and rush home to Marissa. She couldn't allow
herself that luxury—not until she had everything under control.

With a sigh, she pulled off the pictures and type
one more time and started all over again. She reached
across the desk for a cutout of a daffodil bulb just as

the telephone rang. Startled, she knocked a stack of bills onto the floor.

Laughing at herself, she scooped up the mess and reached for the receiver, expecting to hear Marissa's tiny voice or Brittany, her baby-sitter's, bored teenage one. Instead, her mother's slightly husky voice reached across the miles from London. "Brittany and Marissa told me you were still are work. What on earth are you doing there?"

"What on earth are *you* doing?" DJ asked. "Aren't you supposed to be conducting workshops at your seminar?" She wedged the receiver against her shoulder and tucked her feet beneath her on the chair.

"Not until tomorrow. But you didn't answer my question. What are you doing there at this hour? It must be..." Christina paused for a second, then sighed. "What time is it there?"

DJ could almost visualize her mother standing in a hotel room, staring at her watch and struggling to calculate the time in her head. Give Christina Prescott something creative to do and she'd run circles around everyone else, but figuring international time zones still threw her for a loop. "It's a little after seven— in the evening. And yes, unfortunately, I'm still working."

"That's what I thought." Christina's voice sounded faintly accusing. "You should be home with Marissa. It isn't good to leave her alone so long with the baby-sitter."

DJ held back a sigh of annoyance. Of all the people she knew, she'd expect her mother to understand how difficult being a single mother could be. DJ's father had died when DJ was two and her sister, Laura, four-teen, and Christina had never remarried. Until she'd sold her first novel eight years ago, she'd worked at demanding jobs with long hours. DJ had spent her share of time with a baby-sitter, and Laura had turned surrogate mother—a role she'd never completely surrendered.

"Brittany's responsible, and I can't go home until I finish my ad. But enough about that. What's up?"

"I didn't know something had to be 'up' for me to call." To DJ's surprise, Christina sounded slightly offended.

"Only when you're overseas, Mom. Actually, this is a wonderful surprise. I really didn't expect to hear from you until you got back to New York."

"I know," her mother admitted. "But I've been thinking about you a lot lately. And after the conference is over, I'll still be gone another two weeks. It's a long time to be away from home. I just needed to make sure everything's all right—"

"Everything's fine," DJ lied.

"You're sure?"

"Absolutely."

Christina let a short silence fall between them, and DJ expected her to laugh, apologize for being an alarmist and hang up before the bill grew too large. Instead, she cleared her throat and changed the subject. "Then I need to ask a big favor. I *know* this is going to be an intrusion, but I really don't know where else to turn."

"What's wrong?" DJ asked. "What do you need?"

Christina laughed the way she always did in uncomfortable situations. "I have a friend who needs to spend some time in Utah. He's researching a book set along the Wasatch Front, and he needs a place to stay. I told him about the extra room in your basement.''

"What *about* the room in my basement?"

"I told him he could probably stay there with you."

"You're kidding."

Christina didn't respond. She wasn't kidding.

DJ sighed. "You want me to entertain a guest? A strange *male* guest?" She shook her head quickly. "No." She couldn't afford it, either financially or emotionally.

"Now, sweetheart." DJ recognized Christina's mother-soothing-child voice immediately. As an adult, it left her irritated. "Don't get upset. He's really a very nice man."

"Whether or not he's nice isn't the issue."

Christina didn't seem to hear her. "His name's Adam McAllister. He'll only stay for a few weeks."

"And you want him to move into my house? Why can't he stay with Laura and Bob? Or at your place— it's empty."

He needs to stay in Salt Lake, not forty or fifty miles away. Besides..." Her mother hedged a little.

DJ's stomach knotted. "You didn't already tell him he *could,* did you?"

"I told him I'd ask."

DJ laughed without humor. "I don't believe it."

"Is it okay?"

"No!" she almost shouted, then reined in her temper and lowered her voice. "It's my busiest season at the store. I don't have time to cook and clean up after anyone, and I *don't* want some strange man prowling around my house."

"He's not a strange man," Christina insisted.

"And you won't have to cook for him. He can take care of himself—if you don't mind him using your kitchen...."

She let her voice drift away, and DJ could picture her shrugging on the other end.

Lifting the mouthpiece to her forehead, DJ stared at her desktop. It did no good to argue with her mother when she was in this mood. Once Christina Prescott decided something, she moved ahead at full steam, and nothing could change her mind.

But DJ knew only too well what having a writer underfoot meant, and she didn't have the time or the patience to deal with Adam McAllister and his book right now. She didn't have time to remind him to eat when he lost himself in a story. She didn't have the patience to listen to him agonize over endless plot twists and story lines. She didn't have the energy to put up with some strange old man hogging the bathroom and kitchen.

"It won't work," she said again.

"He won't be any trouble."

DJ shook her head. "There are plenty of other houses in Salt Lake—"

"Not where Adam could stay."

"You want me to let some strange man into my house—" she said again.

"No," Christina argued. "I want you to let a friend of mine stay there—a perfectly harmless man who needs a place to stay. The best part is, Adam can get his book done *and* I won't have to worry about you being there alone."

DJ slumped a little farther in her chair. Surely her mother wouldn't waste expensive transatlantic minutes to rehash *that* argument. "I'm not alone, Mom. I've got Marissa."

"Marissa's a child. She's too young to offer any protection. Don't argue with me. You're alone on that street every night after your employees go home. It's all but deserted. It's not safe for a woman and child to live alone like you do. I've never been comfortable with the whole setup."

And she told DJ about it at every opportunity. "The neighborhood's fine," DJ said.

"It's *not* fine. Not anymore. It's changing—and not for the better."

"It's fine," DJ said again. "I'm not afraid." She'd never been nervous like her mother and older sister. She didn't prowl in the dark, checking the doors and windows. She didn't stare into the night as if she expected something to appear out of the shadows, or jump at every sound.

Christina sighed heavily, a clear signal that the real argument was about to begin. "You know I don't ask for favors often. And I wouldn't ask this time if I had any other choice. Besides, I know you've been strapped for cash lately, and Adam's willing to pay rent for the chance to sleep in your basement for a while."

DJ dropped her head to her desk and cursed silently. "I'm not 'strapped.'"

"No? Then why isn't Marissa taking her dance classes anymore? Why did you sell the Cherokee and keep that old Toyota? Why did you change your mind about taking Marissa to Disneyland?"

"Okay," DJ snapped. "So things are a little tight."

"Have you done anything to collect the back child support Jeff owes you?"

"No. And I don't intend to. He didn't want Marissa in the first place, remember? I wouldn't be doing her any favors by dragging him back into her life."

"Then let me help out a little."

"No, Mom."

"We could consider it a business loan."

DJ shook her head and kicked her feet back to the floor. "I'd send it straight back to you. I can make it on my own."

Christina sighed again. "Honey, I know you want to do this. I know you're trying to build yourself back up after the divorce—"

"It's not that, Mom." But they both knew it was. DJ's house and store represented hard-won independence, and she had no intention of leaving either. The figures in her bank balance danced in front of her eyes and urged her to reconsider letting Adam McAllister stay. She wanted to refuse—she certainly *ought* to refuse—but reality forced her to admit that having a boarder might be the only way she could stay afloat through the winter months.

"How much rent?" she asked at last.

Christina named a ridiculously high figure, and DJ could almost hear her gloating on the other end of the line.

DJ argued with herself for a few seconds longer, but it was a losing battle and she knew it. She needed the money too much to let her pride stand in the way. "I'm not going to have a lot of time to socialize with him," she warned.

"You won't need to socialize," Christina assured her. "Just be fairly pleasant—or at least, don't be overtly rude. You probably won't even notice he's there."

DJ didn't believe that for an instant. The layout of her small house wouldn't allow for a lot of privacy. But she didn't want to discuss it anymore; she didn't want the conversation to disintegrate into a full-fledged argument.

She drew in a deep breath and made an effort to steer her mother to a less touchy subject. "Did you get a chance to talk to Laura before she and Bob left for Lake Powell?"

Christina hesitated long enough to make DJ wonder if she'd try to keep the argument going. But her mother finally sighed softly and said, "Yes. I talked to her for a few minutes right before they left. Has she called you?"

"No. But they'll be on the houseboat for two weeks, so I'm not expecting to hear from them."

"You *see?*" Christina demanded. "That's another reason I'll feel better about having Adam stay with you."

DJ groaned aloud. "Mom—"

Christina sighed softly. "Humor me, sweetheart. I'm nervous about you being there alone. Promise me you'll take care of yourself."

"Of course I will. But I'm the one who should worry—you're the one who's half the world away."

"I know." Christina sounded almost sad, but when she spoke again, she sounded more like herself. "All right, sweetheart. I won't keep you any longer. I know you're busy and this is costing me a fortune. Give Marissa a kiss for me when you get home, and be nice to Mr. McAllister."

"I'm always nice," DJ joked, then sobered again. "So, when will my houseguest be arriving?"

Christina hesitated a second before she answered. "Tomorrow morning."

"*Tomorrow?*" DJ rolled her eyes and stared at the ceiling. "Couldn't you have given me a couple of days' notice?"

"I just found out about it myself."

"Well, he'll just have to take what he gets. I'm not even sure I'll have time to put clean sheets on the bed."

"I'm sure you'll make everything lovely," Christina said. "I wouldn't worry about it for a minute. Now, tell me, do you have my itinerary handy in case you need to reach me?"

"Yes, I do," DJ said for probably the hundredth time since her mother had started planning the trip. But that note of sadness had touched her mother's voice again, and DJ couldn't help but ask, "Are you all right, Mom?"

"Yes, of course. Just a little tired, that's all." Christina laughed, but it sounded forced. Unnatural. "You know how emotional I get when I'm tired."

DJ's annoyance faded. "Then get some rest. And *don't* forget to eat."

"I won't forget." Her mother paused for another long second. "I love you, DJ."

Before DJ could respond, the line was disconnected. She stared at the receiver until the dial tone filled the empty room. She tried to tell herself she'd imagined the dejection in her mother's voice, but she knew before she replaced the receiver that she wouldn't rest until she'd talked with her again.

Leaning her forehead on the heel of one hand, she made a mental note to call her mother in a day or two, then reached for her ad and tried not to think about how much a telephone call to Europe would cost. Everything would work out fine. Somehow, she and Marissa would get by. With the help of Adam McAllister's rent, DJ would make ends meet and she'd keep the store going another month or two. She believed it. She had to. She wouldn't even consider the alternative.

ADAM LEFT THE freeway on the Sixth South exit and followed the ramp into Salt Lake's city center. A brisk breeze stirred the air inside the truck's cab, buffeted his face and tugged at his hair, but it did nothing to relieve his tension.

He'd spent half the night thinking about his aborted trip to Boise and resenting Thomas Dodge, Christina Prescott and DJ Woodward for causing the change of plans. He thought bitterly of his lost career and realized he had only himself to blame. His marriage to Victoria hadn't been worth the sacrifice, but he hadn't been willing to admit the truth about their relationship at the time.

He glared at a stoplight and stomped on the brakes. He knew better than this. Dwelling on the past and hoping for the impossible wouldn't get him anywhere. At least he had a job and a paycheck.

Giving himself a mental shake, he maneuvered through the early-morning traffic and followed the Fourth South viaduct over the railroad tracks into the city's west side. But no matter what he told himself, the foul mood seemed to ride beside him in the truck's cab.

As he searched for DJ's address, he stared out the window and took in his surroundings. He hadn't been in this area for years, and what he saw surprised him.

He'd expected to find DJ Woodward living in some preppie locale with inflated property values. Instead, he found her address in the middle of a run-down area full of old houses and vacant buildings with graffiti on the walls.

The Treehouse sat at the end of a street only two houses long, one of which appeared vacant. Fields of trees and shrubs stretched away from the store in every direction. Several customers strolled through the tree lots, and two young men stacked bags of fertilizer in a shed behind a sagging gate. One young woman drizzled water from a hose over flower boxes in front of the store while another dragged a cart into the parking lot behind a woman in a business suit.

Circling the parking lot slowly, Adam parked in the shade of an old tree and cut the truck's engine. From here he could see the store, and he could also study the red-brick house next door—DJ Woodward's home.

In contrast to its nearest neighbor's, the lawn had been recently mowed, the flower beds were virtually weed-free, and the house trim was freshly painted. Terraced rose gardens descended from a redwood deck along the south wall, and planter boxes lined the picture windows and the wide front porch. Huge old trees with slowly reddening leaves bordered the street, and others marked the location of the Jordan River in back.

He studied the layout and grudgingly admitted the place didn't look bad. The house looked comfortable, if a little small. Modest, but livable. The Treehouse was larger than he'd expected, but it wasn't showy or flashy—again, the opposite of everything he'd pictured for the daughter of Christina Prescott.

As he watched, the front door of the house opened and a small girl with a high ponytail stepped outside. She clutched a rag doll under one arm and dragged a teddy bear across the porch with her other hand. A shaggy black dog followed her toward the steps and flopped down in a spot of sunlight while the child arranged her toys.

When the door opened a second time, a young woman in jeans and a sweater stepped onto the porch. She'd pulled her long blond hair into a clip so that it bounced with every step she took. She crossed the porch, settled onto the front steps beside the child and adjusted a pair of sunglasses on her nose. Totally oblivious to him, she leaned back to let the weak autumn sun touch her face.

She had to be DJ Woodward, but she looked like little more than a child herself. A self-indulgent child who sat in the sun while others ran her store and generated her income. Too much like Victoria for comfort.

He was going to hate this assignment. Next time he spoke to Chuck, he'd have a few things to say about being sent on a job that amounted to nothing more than glorified baby-sitting.

Heaving a sigh, he told himself to get out of the truck and introduce himself. Get it over with. Procrastinating wouldn't change anything.

He'd just have to concentrate on the job and put his personal feelings aside. He could do that. He'd done it before—just not with a woman who'd remind him of Victoria every time he looked at her.

As he reached for the truck's door handle, a knock sounded on the window by his ear and a shadow darkened the glass. Years of experience prompted an in-

stinctive reaction. He reached for his side arm half a
second before he remembered he hadn't been author-
ized to carry it on this assignment. He'd left his
weapon zipped inside the duffel bag on the floor.

The shadow shifted a little, and he found himself
staring into the hostile glare of the woman with the
cart he'd noticed leaving the store a few minutes earlier. She'd abandoned the cart a few feet to one side,
and she stood, hands on hips, glaring at him as if he'd
committed some crime.

He pushed open the door and stood to face her. She
wore a pair of overalls, a plaid flannel shirt and steel-
toed work boots with thick soles. She looked like a
wood sprite—the kind of person who'd be at home
deep in a forest somewhere, saving the earth.

She tossed a dark braid over her shoulder and held
his gaze without backing down an inch. "Can I help
you with something?"

He shook his head and flicked another glance at the
house. "No, I—"

"What are you doing lurking out here?" she interrupted before he could even finish his thought.

Silently acknowledging a grudging admiration for
the way she confronted him, he locked his truck's
door and dropped the key into his pocket. "I wasn't
lurking."

Her eyes flashed. "You've been sitting right here,
lurking, for twenty minutes."

Biting back a smile, Adam glanced at his watch
and started slowly toward the house. "I've been here
for ten minutes, and I *wasn't* lurking."

She ran a little ahead of him, then turned and
walked backward, facing him. Her expression grew
serious, and she met his gaze with a challenge in her

deep brown eyes. "You were watching the house. Why?"

Adam stopped in his tracks and looked again at the blond girl on the porch, then turned his gaze back to his interrogator. The two women were as different as night and day, and he infinitely preferred this one. "I wasn't watching the house." It was true—in a way. Pushing gently past her, he started walking again.

She chased after him. "*Excuse* me. Just what are you doing here?"

He glanced back at her, but this time he didn't break his stride. "I have business with Ms. Woodward."

"What kind of business?"

He supposed there was no harm in telling her the basics. She'd find out soon enough, anyway. "My name's Adam McAllister. I'll be staying with Ms. Woodward for a few days."

This time, she stopped walking so abruptly he nearly ran into her. "*You're* Adam McAllister?"

He nodded.

To his surprise, she laughed. Her dark eyes sparkled suddenly and her face became even more appealing. "Why didn't you say that in the first place? I'm DJ."

Adam stared at her for a second, then chuckled softly and shook the hand she offered. It felt warm and firm in his. Capable. Competent. And very soft.

"I've been expecting you—but I must confess, I thought you'd be older. Closer to my mother's age."

And he'd expected her to be younger. Or older. Or less attractive. Flushing slightly, he tore his gaze away from hers and dropped her hand.

She pulled her hand back quickly and started walking again. "Well, now that we know who we are, I guess I shouldn't keep you standing out here all day. Mom didn't call until last night to tell me you were coming, so I haven't had time to do much to your room."

Adam adjusted his stride to match hers. "Don't worry about me. I can do whatever needs to be done."

She tucked a stray lock of hair behind one ear and shrugged lightly. "No trouble. There's a small table in your room you can use for your computer, but I don't have any phone jacks downstairs, so if you need a modem, you'll probably have to work in the kitchen."

"No—" He raised a hand to stop her and tried to come up with an answer that wouldn't make him sound computer illiterate. "I probably won't even use one while I'm here. Besides, I don't want to get in your way."

She took his measure slowly with those deep brown eyes of hers. "It's a small house. We'd have to work pretty hard to avoid each other."

A warm tingle raced up his spine and his mouth grew suddenly dry. Half-a-dozen replies rose to his lips, but each one sounded slightly suggestive. He tried to look away, but her gaze held his captive.

Luckily the child looked up at that moment, saw them approaching and shot to her feet. "Mommy, Mommy, Mommy!"

DJ blinked rapidly and turned toward her daughter. Still shouting, the child raced down the steps and along the driveway. The dog yipped as it ran after her—it looked nearly as excited as Marissa.

Adam watched as DJ swept the little girl off her

feet and twirled her, then reached down to pat the dog's head. She glanced at him over her shoulder and smiled, a gentle smile that spread all the way to her eyes.

He tried to smile back, but he couldn't force his lips to move. Maybe he'd have been better off if DJ had turned out to be the type of woman he'd been expecting. He could have ignored her eyes. He could have disregarded her throaty laugh and the slightly husky note in her voice.

But *this* woman— This woman was going to be dangerous; he could feel that already. He'd known her less than fifteen minutes, and already she'd made him all but forget his reasons for being here.

CHAPTER TWO

DJ WRAPPED HER arms around Marissa and swung her into the air again. She hadn't expected Adam McAllister to look like *that*—dark hair, gray eyes and an intriguing, brooding sort of expression.

She drew in a deep breath and tried to focus on Marissa as Brittany disappeared into the house, but she was entirely too aware of Adam behind her.

"Mommy, you're home!" Marissa cried. "And it's not even time for lunch!"

"I'm only home for a minute, sweetheart. I have to go back to work."

Marissa pushed out her lip in a pout, but DJ pretended not to notice. She nodded toward Adam and allowed herself another tiny peek. "This is Grandma's friend. Remember, I told you he'd be staying with us for a little while?"

Marissa leaned her head on DJ's shoulder and stared at him. She bit one curled finger and nodded soberly.

"His name is Adam," DJ said, then turned to face him fully. "This is my daughter, Marissa. She's a little shy around strangers—especially men—so don't take it personally if she doesn't seem very friendly."

Adam offered what he probably thought passed for a smile. "Hello, Marissa."

The child ducked her face into DJ's shoulder, then peeked back up at him.

He half smiled again. "I don't suppose you know where my room is?"

To DJ's surprise, Marissa almost grinned. "It's down'tairs."

"Good. I like downstairs."

"I don't. It's dark down there. And scary."

Adam frowned at her. "You aren't afraid of the dark, are you?"

Marissa nodded.

"Well. We'll have to help you get over that, won't we?"

DJ started to shake her head. Marissa had defied every one of DJ's efforts to rid her of her fear of the dark.

To her surprise, Marissa nodded. "Are *you* scared?"

He chuckled. "Not of the dark."

"Then what?"

He glanced at DJ, and her heart stuttered. "Of girls with big brown eyes and long dark hair."

Marissa's eyes widened. "Like *me?*"

"Just like you," Adam admitted, but he let his gaze travel over DJ so slowly she thought her heart would stop completely.

She rolled her eyes and nodded toward the house. "Why don't I show you around so you can get settled."

He nodded without looking away. "Sounds good."

Marissa squirmed out of DJ's arms and raced up the porch steps. "I can do it, Mommy. I know where the room is." She held out one tiny hand toward Adam. "Come on, Mr. Man. I can show you."

This time, Adam had to look away, and DJ finally managed to draw a steady breath. But when she climbed the stairs, Adam remained just a step behind. She caught his scent and the heat from his body, and she suddenly felt too close and a little uncomfortable. She could feel his eyes on her as she walked, and for the briefest of seconds, she wondered whether her mother had engineered this meeting for some other reason than the one she'd given.

As soon as the thought formed, DJ forced it away. Her mother had spent most of DJ's life on her own. She'd never believed a woman needed a man to survive. Besides, Christina spent so much time caught up in the fantasy world of her books, she probably hadn't even noticed what Adam McAllister looked like.

DJ reached for the front door at the same time Adam did. Their fingers brushed, and heat spiraled from the point of contact up DJ's arm. She jerked her hand away and forced herself to smile as she stepped inside, but for the first time ever, she wished she could waltz through life as oblivious as her mother.

ADAM WEDGED his last suitcase into the back of the closet, then paused to listen to Marissa's footsteps running down the hall and into her bedroom overhead. From sound alone, he'd decided his bedroom lay directly under hers, which meant DJ's must be over the storage room he'd looked into earlier when he checked the locks on the basement windows.

He'd taken less than an hour to unpack his things and plug in the laptop computer, but it had taken him nearly as long again to figure out how to turn the damned thing on. He'd spent the next two hours reading and rereading the preliminary report on Larry Galloway and studying his mug shot while he waited for a chance to check security in the rest of the house.

He'd found one interesting entry from thirty years ago on Galloway's report—an arrest and brief incarceration for assault against a woman named Chrissy Galloway.

Christina Galloway. Christina Prescott. Connection? Or was the similarity in names merely a coincidence? He shook his head and let his breath out on a heavy sigh.

Maybe he was grasping at straws, trying to find something—*anything* to tie Galloway to his client. Why did Christina insist on keeping the connection a secret? Why didn't she warn DJ about Galloway's release from prison? Why keep the truth from her security people? Why tie Adam's hands and keep him in the dark? To make matters worse, Chuck had told him she was in Europe on a book-signing tour. He'd have to find the answers on his own.

He looked back at the report. Galloway had done time more than once in his life. In fact, his last sentence had been a singularly harsh one—a fitting penalty for such an all-around nice guy, Adam thought grimly.

He tossed the report back into his duffel bag and zipped it closed, then glanced impatiently at the ceiling. DJ had long ago gone back to the nursery, but he couldn't check out the house with Marissa and the baby-sitter, Brittany, upstairs.

He paced to his door and pulled it open a crack. As if on cue, Marissa's footsteps suddenly changed direction and raced toward the back stairs. Scarcely able to believe his luck, he stepped into the shadows and listened while Brittany descended the steps behind Marissa.

"All right," she said in a bored voice. "We'll play for half an hour, then you have to take your nap. Promise?"

"Promise."

Adam quirked an eyebrow at the child he couldn't see. He'd heard that kind of promise from his nieces and nephew more than once, and he knew how unlikely Marissa was to keep hers. She'd have half-a-dozen reasons why she couldn't take a nap when she came back inside, and she'd use those huge brown eyes of hers to make each one more convincing than the last. But that wasn't his problem.

Moving quietly, he crept through the laundry room to the foot of the stairs and watched as Marissa and Brittany stepped outside, banging the door closed behind them.

Perfect. He had half an hour—that should give him plenty of time to check security upstairs. He moved silently up the steps to the landing. Standing to one side of the door, he watched as Marissa raced across the lawn to her swing set and Brittany settled herself comfortably on the lawn, then he hurried up the rest of the stairs two at a time.

He looked into the kitchen to make certain DJ hadn't come home unexpectedly, then crept down the corridor toward the bedrooms. He checked the bathroom window quickly, disturbed by the soft wood of the frame and the weak lock. But the window itself was only a narrow opening high in the wall, and he didn't expect Galloway to make that his choice of entry.

Slipping out of the bathroom, he ducked into the

first bedroom he encountered. A single bed with a dark blue cover held an assortment of soft stuffed animals and well-loved dolls. A tiny desk just Marissa's size filled one corner, and a shelf of books stretched along one wall.

Opposite the bed, a sliding-glass door led onto a redwood deck overlooking the side yard. He swore softly and crossed to the door. All that glass might make the room light and airy, but it sure didn't provide much protection from intruders.

He checked the lock, relieved to find that the door was still fairly new and the lock sturdy. But no lock would keep Galloway from breaking through this door if that was what he had in mind.

Standing at one edge of the door, he craned to see outside and tried to determine whether Marissa and Brittany could see the deck from the backyard. He couldn't see either of them, so he decided to take the risk and check outside while he had the chance.

He unlocked the door, slid it open and stepped onto the deck. It ran the length of the two bedrooms and provided a pleasant view of DJ's garden and the huge red-leafed trees that lined her property. Even better, the deck stood several feet above ground level—high enough to prevent anyone from reaching it easily.

Slightly relieved, he walked to the edge and looked over. But when he realized the terraced rose garden he'd noticed earlier provided convenient steps almost to deck level, he groaned aloud. How in the hell was he supposed to protect DJ and Marissa in this environment? He might as well open the door and invite Galloway inside.

He stood for a moment, battling frustration and calculating his options. His chances of keeping anyone safe in this house weren't high. Retracing his steps, he slipped back inside and locked the door behind him.

He listened for a few seconds to make sure nobody had come back into the house, then he stepped out of Marissa's room and into what had to be DJ's bedroom.

He paused on the threshold and looked around. If someone had asked him, he wouldn't have predicted DJ Woodward slept in a room like this. He couldn't have said what he'd expected, but it hadn't been this. The room looked comfortable. Feminine, but not overly so. Certainly nothing like the bedroom Adam had shared with Victoria.

Victoria had favored pastels and flowers everywhere. Pink, lavender, blue and yellow had covered every chair and draped both windows. He'd felt almost claustrophobic in that bedroom, and he'd often wondered whether he truly belonged there. With every year that passed, the feeling had grown, until he realized what Victoria seemed to have known all along—they didn't belong together.

DJ's room was the opposite of Victoria's. It held a queen-size bed covered with old-fashioned quilts like the ones his grandmother had made. A lacy white ruffle dusted the floor, a woman's robe lay across the foot of the bed and the air held a pleasant musky scent he'd already noticed on DJ.

On either side of the bed, tables made of dark, gleaming wood held brass lamps shaded in soft teal. Across the room by the sliding door, an easy chair and ottoman provided a comfortable-looking place to sit. A stack of books on a nearby table told him what she did when she sat there. She'd tossed a pair of jeans across the back of the chair and abandoned a pair of shoes in front of the closet. Tiny shoes compared to Adam's feet. Delicate. Nothing like the boots he'd noticed earlier.

He felt like a voyeur standing here, gawking at her things. But he had a job to do. If Galloway was an ex-husband or old boyfriend, or even an unhappy employee, he'd probably strike this room first.

Adam started across the room toward the glass door. But before he'd gone even halfway, he heard a voice behind him.

"What are you doing here?"

Thinking frantically, he wheeled around to face Marissa. She stood just inside the room with her tiny brows knit, her mouth drawn into a frown and her hands propped on her hips.

He managed what he hoped looked like an innocent smile. "I'm looking for a telephone."

Her scowl deepened. "You're not allowed to use the one in my mommy's bedroom. You have to use the one in the kitchen." Pointing the way, she stood back as if she expected him to leave.

Still smiling, he started back across the room. "Oh. Thanks. I'll go there."

But as he neared the door, Marissa seemed to change her mind. She firmed her stance and glared up at him. She showed no fear, and Adam didn't know whether to admire her for it or to worry.

"Who said you could go in my mommy's bedroom?" she demanded. "She doesn't like people to play in there."

"I wasn't playing," he said honestly. "I got lost, I guess."

She crossed her small arms across her chest and

glared up at him. "How can you get lost in my house? I don't."

She looked so serious, he couldn't keep from smiling. "I haven't ever been here before."

"You're a big man. You're not s'posed to get lost."

He hunkered down to face her. "Really? I didn't know that. Nobody ever told *me* big men can't get lost." Trying to look thoughtful, he rubbed his chin. "Do you suppose I'll be in trouble?"

"I don't know. Maybe."

"What will happen to me if I am?"

"You'll get grounded."

He frowned and worked up an expression of horror. "I will? For how long?"

She shrugged. "I don't know. Maybe a year."

He bit back a smile and shook his head. "A whole year? Are you sure?"

She studied him for a long moment, then smiled. "You're funny."

"I am?" Adam didn't have to pretend surprise at that. His relationship with his brothers' children had always been a little stilted. He didn't think any of them would classify him as even slightly amusing.

She giggled. "You're *very* funny."

Unbelievably touched, he tapped her chin with one finger. "Thank you. Now, suppose you tell me what *you're* doing back inside."

Her smile faded, her eyes widened and a look of sheer horror crossed her face. "I have to go potty!" she cried. Pivoting away, she raced into the bathroom and closed the door behind her.

Laughing softly, Adam watched until she'd disappeared. But the instant the door closed, his expression sobered. He straightened and hurried to the kitchen, cursing Chuck, his assignment, Thomas Dodge and his rotten luck the whole way.

Whether or not Marissa told DJ about finding him in her bedroom, he'd had a close call. Too close. If he had another slipup like that one, he'd expose his cover.

He'd have to watch himself in the future. Keep a better eye on the little girl. He couldn't afford a mistake.

DJ ROLLED OVER IN bed and slapped the snooze button on her alarm clock. It couldn't be time to get up. Not already.

She squinted at the clock. Six o'clock. Groaning, she fell back on her pillow and closed her eyes. She'd sleep just ten more minutes. Then she'd get up and fix breakfast for Marissa.

She covered her eyes with the crook of her elbow and tried to slip back to sleep, but her mind began to tally the day's responsibilities, and yesterday's accomplishments began to take their toll.

Every muscle in her body ached, and her eyes burned with fatigue. She'd worked later than usual the night before, stacking fertilizer, shelving insecticides and moving late-season stock to a more convenient spot for the sale scheduled to begin in a few short hours.

She needed rest. A day off. Downtime. But she wouldn't get it today. If the advertising gods decided to smile on her, she'd be too busy to even think.

Forcing herself to sit up, she began to stretch, but when her muscles screamed in protest, she moaned softly and lowered her arms to her sides. How would she make it through the day? She couldn't even move.

She shoved her fingers through her hair and rubbed her face with her hands. Either her imagination was working overtime or she was hungrier than she'd thought. She almost believed she could smell fresh coffee. In fact, she could have sworn she heard the gurgle of the coffeemaker. Still bleary-eyed, she reached for her bathrobe.

Somehow, reality forced its way through her sleep-fogged brain. She stopped moving and stared at the door. Adam. He was in her kitchen, and he'd made coffee. Some part of her wanted to be angry. The more rational part blessed him and hoped he'd made enough to share.

She slipped on her robe, ran her fingers through her hair again and stepped into her slippers without even glancing at the mirror. Adam McAllister might be young and good-looking in his own sullen way, but she didn't care what he thought of her.

Stumbling slightly, she peeked into Marissa's room and closed the door as she made her way toward the kitchen. Sure enough, Adam was there, with his back to the door as he worked on untwisting the coated wire on a loaf of bread. He turned and flashed a hint of a smile. "Good morning."

She mumbled something she hoped sounded like a greeting and leaned against the doorframe.

He wore soft, faded jeans and a worn T-shirt. His feet were bare, and she could tell by the shadow of whiskers on his chin that he hadn't shaved yet.

He towered over her by at least a foot. His thick, dark hair brushed the tops of his ears and danced across his collar, and his slate-gray eyes looked as if they could reveal the answers to countless mysteries if only he would unshutter them for a moment.

He trailed his gaze over her slowly, as if taking inventory of her puffy face, tousled hair and ratty bathrobe.

She still didn't care. "Please tell me you made a full pot of coffee."

"As a matter of fact, I did. Do you want some?"

Nodding, she started toward the cupboard, but he waved her toward the table.

"Sit down. I'll get it. You don't look awake."

She didn't even think of arguing. Dropping into a chair, she propped her elbows on the table and her chin in her hands while she waited.

He pulled two mugs from the cupboard and held them up for her approval. "Cream? Sugar?"

"Black."

After filling the cups, he crossed the room to place one in front of her. He leaned across the table and met her gaze steadily. He was *much* too close. "Do you want some toast?"

Her nerves and hair tingled, as if he emitted some low-wave frequency only she could feel. She nodded. She didn't seem capable of anything else. "Thanks."

"No trouble." He stood quickly and moved away again.

She drew in a deep breath, suddenly aware that she'd been holding it while he stood beside her. What on earth was wrong with her?

As if he could feel her watching him, he glanced over his shoulder. "You're up early."

"Actually, I'm running late." She sipped coffee and studied him carefully, trying to decide if she found him attractive. Yes, she supposed she did, even though she didn't want to.

Marriage to Jeff had taught her a lesson—one she wouldn't forget. Men were high-maintenance. They required too much. She'd only been able to maintain her marriage to Jeff as long as she had by giving up parts of herself, but she didn't intend to do that again. Other than Marissa, she hadn't gained enough to compensate for what she'd lost.

Adam pulled open the refrigerator and rummaged inside. She wondered idly whether other women considered him good-looking, with all that dark hair and those eyes and the tuft of hair peeking over the neck of his T-shirt. Well, of course they did. He probably had a bevy of female fans with knees that lost their starch when they saw his photo on a book jacket. Nevertheless, he seemed totally unaware of his appeal.

He emerged from the refrigerator, holding aloft a tub of margarine. "What time do you usually go to work?"

"I try to be in the store by seven. Obviously, I'm not going to make it today."

"You didn't get home until after nine last night," he said. "Do you always work that late?"

She sipped again and forced herself to stop admiring him. "No. I'm usually home in time to fix dinner."

He nodded, but she could see him mentally filing away her answers, the same way her mother did. "Even that makes a long day."

"We're having a huge sale today. If I'm lucky, we'll do well enough to help catch up on a few things. Once the store is on its feet, I'll be home a lot more."

To her surprise, he laughed bitterly as he placed a plate of toast in front of her. "There's a fine line between investing enough time in your career to get it off the ground and giving it too much. That's what my ex-wife says, anyway. But don't ask me. I got it wrong."

DJ lowered her cup to the table. "She resented your writing?"

An emotion she couldn't read flashed across his face. "Yes."

"It can be consuming. At least, it is with Mom." Just thinking about her mother brought a smile to her face. "You know how she is. She can get so far into a story, you wonder if she'll ever touch base with reality again."

He didn't respond.

"I shouldn't say that, though," DJ added quickly. "I don't know anything about how you work. I wouldn't want to offend you."

"Yes," he said again. "Well, don't worry about it. I probably don't work much like your mother."

She bit into the toast and chewed thoughtfully for a few seconds. She tried to remember details of the conversation with her mother about Adam, but if Christina had given her details, DJ didn't remember them. "Which conference were you at when you met Mom? Was it Bouchercon? Malice Domestic?"

He wedged half a piece of toast into his mouth and shrugged to indicate he couldn't speak yet.

DJ sipped again and became aware of the silence. Of the tiny crumbs of toast on his lips. Of his hands just inches from hers. She wondered, irrationally, whether his hands were smooth or callused. How one would feel against her cheek.

The moment the thought formed, she forced it away and pushed to her feet. Oh, no. She was *not* going to let herself think like that. She hadn't felt an attraction for any man in years, and she didn't like feeling one now.

Adam flicked crumbs from his lips with the tip of his tongue and looked as if he intended to speak.

Without giving him a chance, she pointed to the wall clock and started toward the door. "Look at the time. I've really got to get moving. Thanks for the coffee."

He arched one eyebrow in surprise. "You're welcome. Sure you don't want more?"

"No, thanks." She glanced back at him, but she didn't allow herself to look at his eyes or his smile. What had her mother been thinking when she'd sent him here? Did she know how attractive he was? Had she intended for DJ to fall for him?

It didn't matter, DJ decided. She had a good life— her *own* life. She worked hard. She took care of her daughter and she'd finally healed enough to put Jeff and her marriage behind her.

She didn't need a man in her life, and she certainly didn't have room for one. Christina could play games if she wanted—DJ didn't have to play along.

But would Adam? DJ stole another glance at him. He seemed oblivious, and not at all the type to welcome Christina Prescott's interference in his personal life.

Breathing a sigh of relief, she turned away again and forced herself to think about the day ahead. But Adam's early-morning image kept popping into her mind as she showered, and the deep rumble of his voice seemed to follow her as she dressed.

No doubt about it, she would have to watch herself around him in the future.

DJ WALKED SLOWLY as she led her elderly customer through the rows of potted perennials. "What about lupine? It would look good in an old-fashioned garden, and it will grow well in the kind of light you're describing." She struggled to sound patient, but she'd been working all day, and the fatigue that had plagued her since early morning now threatened to get the best of her.

The man studied the flower for several seconds, then shook his head, just as he'd done over two dozen other varieties. "It's not what I want."

"As I told you earlier, I can special-order the bleeding hearts if you'd like."

"I don't want to wait."

"I could have them for you in two days. Maybe even by tomorrow."

But the old man shook his head again. "If you don't have them, you don't have them. I'll try somewhere else."

DJ forced a smile. "If you don't find them, please give us a call and we'll place that order for you."

The old man turned away without even bothering to thank her for her time. She rubbed her forehead and tried to push away the dull headache that had grown steadily worse since morning.

She scanned the tree lot, looking for an empty area where she could hide for ten minutes. But before she could even manage that, Ramon Cordoba broke into her thoughts.

"Hey, DJ," he shouted from the doorway of the nursery. "Ed Hansen's on the phone for you."

She tried not to groan aloud. She considered asking Ramon to take a message, but Ed represented one of her major suppliers, and she'd been trying to reach him for days.

She rubbed the back of her neck and shouted back. "Ask him to hold on for just a minute."

Ramon gave her a thumbs-up, and turned back into the store.

"Don't let him hang up," she called after him. It was unnecessary, really. Ramon was one of her best employees and she relied heavily on him. She lived in fear that he'd quit working for her after he graduated from college in the summer.

Pushing aside a wave of depression, she reminded herself not to think about losing Ramon. She had other fires to put out first.

She walked to the end of the raised bed of flowers and turned on the spigot. Filling her hands with water, she splashed her face and decided to get two more Tylenol from her office after she dealt with the elusive Mr. Hansen.

Inside, she slid into the checkout stand beside Heather Robbins and squeezed herself into an out-of-the-way corner before snagging the receiver. "Hello, Ed."

"Is that you, DJ?" Ed's gravelly voice cut through the store's background noise.

"Yes."

"I was about to hang up."

Ed started every conversation the same say—with DJ on the defensive. But she refused to rise to his bait today. "I've been calling for two days. I'm sure you know why."

"Two days?" Ed sounded shocked. "I only got one message. When did you call?"

DJ refused to let him distract her. "I need those snowblowers you've back-ordered, Ed. I've got a pre-season sale scheduled for next weekend."

"You don't have the blowers yet?" Ed tried to sound shocked and dismayed, but DJ didn't fall for the pretense. He knew everything about every order from all of his customers almost before the order was placed.

"No, I don't."

He sighed heavily. "I wish you'd let me know sooner. I don't have any left in stock."

DJ's stomach lurched. "I *did* let you know sooner."

"When?"

"Wednesday. I talked to your secretary on Wednesday afternoon. She gave you my message Wednesday afternoon."

"No, she didn't."

But she had, and DJ knew she had. This wasn't the first time Ed had played games like this with her.

"This is tough," Ed continued without giving her a chance to respond. "There's nothing I can do at this stage of the game."

"Oh, come on, Ed. That's ridiculous. I know you got my message. I know you ignored it. And I know you've sold my snowblowers to someone else."

"That's quite an accusation, DJ. I'm not sure I like the sound of it."

"I want my order."

"Well, I don't know...." He let his voice trail off and pretended to ponder. "I might be able to get a few for you in a week or two."

"That's not good enough. I need them by Thursday of next week."

"Can't do it."

"I *need* them, Ed. I ordered them for this sale because you said you had plenty in stock."

Ed sighed heavily into her ear. "I know that, DJ." His voice sounded patronizing, and her anger swelled. "But I had no idea the salespeople were overselling. Don't overreact."

"I need my order, Ed," she repeated, determined to keep him from sidetracking her into an unproductive argument.

"The only way I could possibly get the blowers for you now would be to take them from someone else."

"Fine. Then do it."

"I can't do that, DJ. You're being unreasonable."

"I'm asking for the merchandise you promised me. I've already sent the ad to press."

"I can try," Ed said after a long hesitation. "But I can't guarantee anything."

DJ didn't respond.

"All right," he said, as if her demands took a heavy toll. "Let me see what I can do. I'll call you in a day or two."

"Not good enough," she insisted. "Call me back later today." But he'd already disconnected before she could finish speaking.

She held the receiver away from her ear and glared at it. "I don't believe it. That smarmy little weasel hung up on me."

Heather turned toward her and opened her mouth to respond, but the voice that spoke came from just behind DJ's ear—too close for comfort, and too familiar after such a short time. "Anything I can do?"

She brushed the hair back from her forehead and turned to face Adam. She tried to work up a smile, but she probably managed only a grimace. "No. But thanks, anyway."

He gave her a slow once-over. "I hope you don't mind, but I decided to come and see what your place looks like."

DJ tried not to cringe, but she couldn't help thinking he hadn't seen her looking decent yet. This time, her hair was a mess, her overalls stained, her shirttail half out and her face muddy. "You want to see the store?"

"If you don't mind."

Embarrassed, she turned back to Heather and gestured toward the phone. "If Ed Hansen calls back, page me. And keep him on the line. Tell him I'll sue if he hangs up again."

Heather nodded, but she didn't look overly anxious to relay that message. No matter. That was mild compared to what DJ intended to say.

She turned to Adam and gestured with one hand. "Here it is," she said. "My store.

"Do you have time to show me around?"

She blinked once. Twice. And she wondered if she'd heard him right. A dozen customers wandered the aisles, lines of people waited at the checkout stands and Adam wanted a guided tour. "It's a little busy right now. You're welcome to look around, and I can show you the rest some other time."

"I wasn't asking for myself. I just thought it might do you some good to take five minutes away."

She hesitated. The allure of five minutes without demands appealed to her far more than it should have.

Nodding, she slipped from behind the checkout

stand, but he stood so close she had to brush against him. The skin on her arm tingled and her heart beat a little faster. *Ridiculous,* she told herself. She was acting like a high-school girl with a crush on the football captain. Pulling herself together, she led him down a long aisle crowded with lawnmowers and weed trimmers to the back door.

"This is nice," he said when they stepped outside.

"Thank you."

"You own all this?"

"The bank and I are partners at the moment."

He nodded slowly and studied everything he could see. "What made you decide to get into this line of work?"

She laughed. He sounded just like her mother. "Why?" she asked. "Am I going to show up in one of your books?"

He looked at her for a long moment, then shrugged and let his gaze wander away again. "No."

She'd intended the comment as a joke. Obviously he hadn't taken it as one. She started walking. Slowly. And tried to decide what to tell and what to omit.

"My husband and I got divorced a couple of years ago. After he left, I needed a job. I didn't know what I wanted to do, but I knew I *didn't* want to wind up in an office somewhere, answering telephones in my business suit and panty hose—which is exactly the kind of job Jeff would have considered acceptable."

He arched one eyebrow. "Jeff?"

"My ex-husband. We were complete opposites." She managed a weak smile. "Opposites might attract but they don't work well together long-term."

He looked thoughtful. "No," he said at last. "I suppose they don't."

"Anyway," she said with a weak laugh, "I looked around, finally found a job here and fell madly in love with the place. When the owners decided to retire to Arizona, I begged the bank for a loan and bought it."

He walked beside her without speaking for several feet, then snapped a carnation from a plant on the raised bed and held it out to her. "What about your ex-husband? What does he do?"

Glancing at him, she hesitated only a second before she accepted the flower. "He's an attorney."

Adam still didn't look at her, but this time DJ sensed his interest. "Criminal law?"

"No. Real-estate law. Prestigious stuff—in Jeff's opinion, at least. He was with Peebles, Bateman & Lawrence here, but he got an offer from a huge firm in San Diego after the divorce, so he moved there."

Adam looked at her out of the corner of his eye. "Do you see him often?"

"Never." The word came out harsher than she'd intended, but she didn't elaborate. Adam didn't need to know how much Jeff's complete absence from Marissa's life disturbed DJ. Or how bitter his comments about her new career had left her. She'd said too much already.

He didn't speak again for a long time, and the only sound was of their footsteps on the concrete walk, mixed with snatches of conversation from people they passed. To DJ's surprise, the silence felt almost companionable, and some of the tension eased from her shoulders.

"Has there been anyone else in your life since Jeff?"

She slowed her steps and waited until he looked at her. "Why do you ask?"

"Just curious."

Too curious. She started walking again, debating whether to answer the question or not. "No," she said at last, and tried turning the tables on him. "What about your ex-wife? What does she do?"

He squinted at the tops of the trees. "Nothing."

DJ stopped altogether. "Nothing? What do you mean, nothing?"

"She doesn't work," he said.

"But she must do other things."

He shrugged. "She does other things."

"Like what? Does she volunteer with charities? Belong to clubs?"

"No. But she does shop a lot."

She turned toward him again, surprised at the answer. "You married a professional shopper?"

He lifted a shoulder and dipped his head to one side.

She allowed herself a tiny smile. "Sounds like Jeff's kind of woman. Did you have any children?"

He glanced at her. "No." He turned to face her squarely and folded his arms across his chest. "You're ahead. You've asked me more questions than I've asked you."

"I didn't know we were keeping track."

"Oh, but we are."

"And you're behind? All right, go ahead. Ask me something else."

He nodded toward the tree lot. "How far back does your property go?"

"How—?" She broke off and studied him for a second, then gave up trying to figure him out and answered the question. "Just as far as the river. The land's fairly narrow here, but it widens out on either side."

"And the other boundaries?"

"The river on the west. The street on the north. The school on the south, and the fence on the east."

He followed as she pointed and took in everything with such a serious expression, DJ couldn't fight her smile. "Is this for your research?"

He nodded thoughtfully. "Yeah."

"Why don't you tell me about your story? Then I'll know what to show you."

"Just show me everything."

She shrugged and started walking again, but she couldn't help thinking that her mother met some awfully intense people in her travels. "Okay," she said, trying to lighten the mood. "This is where we keep the annual and perennial flowers. Rosebushes are on the south benches, and we keep plants that are less hardy in that covered area just outside the nursery." She pointed as she talked and stepped onto the narrow gravel road that separated the tree lot from the rest of the nursery grounds. "Which way do you want to go?"

"You choose."

She turned toward the south lot without breaking stride. "We keep the evergreens back here."

"Great."

They walked in silence for several minutes more, until the sound of someone running toward them through the gravel caught her attention. She stopped to wait, hoping for good news about the missing snowblowers.

But Ramon closed the distance between them, puff-

ing a little. "Telephone again, DJ. It's the guy from
Jackson & Perkins."

Surprisingly disappointed that this meant the end
of their walk, she smiled up at Adam. "Duty calls."

"Go," he said. His face revealed nothing, not even
a touch of disappointment.

"All right. Make yourself at home. And if you need
anything—"

"Don't worry about me. I can find my way
around." To her surprise, he smiled. His face changed
completely, and his eyes unshuttered for a moment.
They changed from slate gray to almost blue, and
something that looked almost like desire flickered
there for a second before they shut her out again.

The transformation left her speechless. She'd considered him attractive before, but that smile— He
looked like a different man.

She tried to smile back, but her lips felt stiff and
heavy. Suddenly self-conscious, she turned and
started away, but the walk back to the nursery seemed
to take forever.

She didn't look back, not even when she reached
the door. She couldn't decide whether what she'd
seen in Adam's eyes left her disturbed or flattered.

CHAPTER THREE

ADAM STOOD IN the listless autumn sunlight and watched as DJ walked away. A light breeze whispered through the leaves on the trees, and the mossy scent of rich soil filled the air. After just a few hours, he could sense how completely DJ belonged here. The store and its surroundings reflected her essence, and he found it and the woman strangely comforting.

Pushing aside the unwelcome sensation, he turned away and hurried down the gravel path. He hadn't checked the perimeter yet, but the little he'd seen of the grounds convinced him Galloway wouldn't have to work very hard to get inside if he wanted to.

He hated knowing so little about his assignment. He could protect DJ and Marissa better if someone would just tell him who Galloway was and why DJ's mother feared him. The only thing he knew for certain was that Galloway had been in prison too long to be an ex-employee of DJ's. And unless DJ lied well, he didn't think Galloway was an ex-boyfriend, either.

So who was he and how would Adam ever learn what he needed to know?

Crossing his arms on his chest, he ducked between two rows of trees and walked toward the fence. He paused several times to look at the leaves on the trees or touch the bark and to check for employees or customers nearby. Finally satisfied that he was alone, he studied closely what purported to be DJ's security.

Just as he'd expected, the fence was rusted in places, sagging in others and bent so far out of shape it looked as if an elephant could have crawled underneath. How did anyone expect him to maintain proper security with a setup like this? Chuck should have sent a whole crew to do this job.

Already, he hated lying to DJ—but only, he told himself, because the assignment would be so much easier if he could tell her the truth. Then, he could carry his weapon and maintain a visible watch at night. In fact, if it weren't for this stupid cover, he could do a dozen things, take countless steps to keep DJ and Marissa safe. Instead, he had to stand around and wait for Galloway to make a move.

He shook his head in exasperation and went back out to the gravel drive. Every few feet, he repeated the inspection process, checking for loose fence posts or gaping holes that would lure Galloway. By the time he'd covered the entire southern end of DJ's property, he'd decided DJ couldn't possibly be anticipating trouble. If she had, she'd have taken steps to protect herself, her daughter and her property.

Contemplating the possibilities, he followed the gravel drive around its final curve and back to the front of the store again. He passed a shed heaped almost to the ceiling with bags of fertilizer.

Even the shed needed repairs. Its walls consisted of nothing more than chain-link fence covered with clear plastic. Gaping holes in the plastic left the bags exposed, and the gate that must have once provided an adequate lock, sagged on its hinges.

Somewhere nearby he heard DJ's voice. It rose and

fell in syncopated rhythm, first rushing, then slowing, then moderating in tempo. She laughed, and almost without realizing it, Adam smiled in response.

She was a different sort of woman from any he'd known before. Fiercely independent without sacrificing her femininity. Competent. Capable. Witty. Obviously intelligent enough to run an operation this size. And attractive.

He tried without success to picture Victoria in DJ's place, but no matter how hard he tried to form the image, it wouldn't come. Victoria's priorities had been different. She'd had no interest in working outside their home, and Adam hadn't argued with her choice until she'd started to complain about his salary.

As the years passed, it had become increasingly evident she wanted more than Adam could ever afford to buy her. And the tension between them had started to mount.

The arguments had gone on for at least two years. He'd suggested that she find a job. She'd questioned his ability to provide for her. He'd suggested a budget. She'd called him cheap.

Honesty forced him to admit he'd responded in kind. She'd suggested he take a job with her father's business. He'd refused. She'd insisted that he leave the police department because of the dangers involved. He'd refused. Until she'd found the one argument that could persuade him—children.

She'd refused to discuss starting a family for the first few years of their marriage. She'd argued that she didn't want to raise children alone, and with Adam's hours, she would have been the only parent home most of the time. And if something happened to him in the line of duty, their children would never know their father. They'd be the ones who would suffer for Adam's stubborn pride.

So, he'd relented. He'd accepted the job she'd picked out for him, but she'd refused to get pregnant even then, and Adam had been miserable working for his father-in-law.

The breeze picked up, scattering a handful of dried leaves across the ground and calling him back from painful memories. DJ laughed again, and the sound seemed to dance across the breeze toward him.

For one brief moment, he almost gave in to the urge to step inside and find her. He'd enjoyed their few minutes together, and he wanted to continue their conversation. Scratch that. He *needed* to continue their conversation. Interrogating DJ was part of the job. But she sounded relaxed and happy, and he didn't want to spoil the moment for her with questions.

Increasing his pace, he passed the shed and turned toward the east tree lot. He couldn't allow himself to seek her out for her company; he was here to do a job, nothing more.

TIRED AND TOO full from dinner, Adam dropped onto his bed and propped a pillow against the headboard. He'd spent the rest of the afternoon checking DJ's property and her limited security, but every fence he checked, every gate he inspected, every door, every window, every lock had left him more concerned than ever about DJ and Marissa.

On top of that, he'd spent an even longer evening trying to make small talk with DJ and avoiding the subject of books while he'd tried pumping her for information about Larry Galloway. But he'd come away empty-handed and more than a little frustrated—both by the lack of information and by the way he found himself reacting to her. After the divorce, he'd sworn off women—at least women who wanted a full-time relationship—and he couldn't imagine DJ wanting anything else.

He shifted position, groaning a little as he did, and aimed the remote control at the small television set across the room. A sitcom popped onto the screen, accompanied by the wild shrieks of a laugh track.

Adam made a face at the television and flicked the power off, but within seconds, he realized what a mistake he'd made. Silence hummed through the room.

He thought about calling Seth, but he couldn't risk having a conversation with him where DJ could overhear it. He tried to imagine what they'd be doing right now if he'd gone to Idaho as planned, but that didn't make him feel any better.

Propping his arms under his head, he stared at the ceiling. But within seconds, thoughts of DJ began to intrude. And no matter how hard he tried, he couldn't rid himself of the image of her standing outside her store, hair blowing in the wind, eyes dancing with laughter and darkening with caution. Adam hadn't been able to ignore her—not the way he should have ignored her.

He rolled onto his side and punched the pillow into shape. What was the matter with him? He knew better than to let himself think this way about a woman. It could only lead to one of two things—sex or commitment. Adam couldn't afford to indulge in the first—not on assignment—and he didn't want the second. Not by a long shot.

He rolled onto his other side and started to readjust

the pillow when something heavy crashed onto the floor overhead. *Galloway!* He'd broken in!

Without pausing to think, Adam jumped from the bed, crossed the room in four strides and jerked open the door. With his heart drumming in his veins and his mind racing, he ran through the laundry room and raced up the stairs two at a time.

Which room? DJ's or Marissa's? Should he rush Galloway or take a more cautious approach? Slowing his steps, he pressed his back against the wall and cursed himself for not grabbing his weapon. If Galloway was armed, Adam's bare feet and empty hands wouldn't protect anyone.

Soundlessly he rounded the corner and crept toward the bedrooms. He couldn't see any light coming from Marissa's room, but a thin ray of light illuminated the carpet in front of DJ's. He stopped moving and held his breath so he could listen.

Nothing.

No, wait. A sound. Soft. Almost like something brushing against a window.

He crept a step closer.

It stopped, then started again.

He closed the distance to the door and pressed his ear against the wood.

DJ must be inside, but was she alone? He heard her moan softly, and a second later came another crash. The floor reverberated and DJ cried out in pain.

Adam threw his weight against the door. He heard the satisfying sound of wood ripping from hinges as he pulled himself into DJ's room.

Inside, dresser drawers lay scattered across the floor and the bed had been pulled out from the wall. Even the chair had been moved since yesterday.

Counting on Galloway to aim high, Adam dropped to the floor and rolled behind the headboard.

He caught his breath and strained to control his breathing, suddenly aware of a heavy silence. Inching along the headboard, he started toward the opposite side of the bed. He had to spot Galloway's position before Galloway got a bead on him.

Too late, he heard a footstep behind him. He pivoted toward the sound and found himself staring up into DJ's narrowed eyes.

"What in the hell do you think you're doing?"

She didn't sound frightened. In fact, she sounded almost angry. Before he could think of a reply, she folded her arms and glared at him.

He stood to face her. "Are you all right? Is anyone else in here?"

"Am I—?" She broke off and shook her head, then pointed toward the sagging bedroom door. "Why did you do that?"

Adam shifted position and tried like hell to come up with a reasonable explanation for breaking into her room. "I thought you were in trouble," he said at last.

She cocked her head a little and closed her eyes as if she were seeking help from somewhere else. "I'm rearranging my furniture."

He glanced around the room again, more slowly this time. "It sounded like something broke—"

"I dropped the end of the bed. It's heavy."

He looked back at her. "Then everything's okay?"

"It was until you broke the door."

He looked away again. "I'll replace it."

She laughed sharply. "Oh, well, then. Fine. You

came rushing up here and broke down my door because you thought I was in trouble?"

He couldn't do anything but nod.

Her eyes glinted. Her cheeks flushed. And he half expected her to launch into a lecture on the political incorrectness of rescuing damsels in distress—real or imagined.

Instead, she started to laugh.

He stared at her, scarcely able to believe her reaction. But when he took another look at the room— at the drawers on the floor and the dresser in the middle of the room, the bed on the diagonal and himself cowering behind it—he couldn't help but laugh with her.

He knew how foolish he must look to her, but he couldn't make himself care. Not at the moment. Standing in the middle of this ridiculous scene, he felt better than he had in years.

He leaned an elbow on the headboard and cupped his chin in his hand. "Do you mind my asking why you're rearranging your furniture now?"

She dropped onto the foot of the bed and smiled up at him. "I'm too tired to sleep."

"Trouble?"

"No. Not really. Just the usual."

The answer might have done more to set his mind at ease if he'd had any idea whether "the usual" concerned Galloway. He glanced around again and quirked an eyebrow at her. "I'll be glad to help you finish, if you'd like."

Her smile faded a bit and she shook her head. "No. Thanks. I'm used to doing it alone."

"Not with me trying to sleep in the room downstairs," he said.

Her impish grin returned. "That's true."

"Then you'll let me help?"

She considered the offer for such a long time, he could sense the amount of effort it cost her to accept. "All right," she said at last, and her gaze met his. "Thank you."

The expression on her face touched something inside him he didn't want reawakened, so he glanced away quickly. But he couldn't maintain his distance.

He turned back, fully intending to say something else. When their eyes met this time, his memory flickered and died, leaving him with no idea what he'd been about to say.

She stared at him with eyes so dark they looked nearly black. Her mouth parted slightly, softly, as if she, too, wanted to speak.

He let his gaze travel from her eyes to her lips and down to the point in the hollow of her neck where her pulse jumped. And he felt an unexpected urge to pull her into his arms and hold her there. He imagined himself lowering his lips to hers—just for an instant—and brushing her mouth with his own. He could almost feel her pressed against him.

He blinked and tried to drag his eyes away. This was *not* what he wanted in his life. But he couldn't do anything to break the silence that grew around them. It rolled outward in waves, until it blocked everything else.

Drawing in a sharp breath, Adam forced himself to turn away. He tried to ground himself by taking a drawer into the hall and clearing floor space so they could move the rest of the furniture. He tried to calm the thudding of his heart and to appear as if he hadn't almost lost his senses. He tried to put the image of her eyes and lips from his mind, but he knew he'd never be able to look at her the same way again.

DJ CARRIED HER FIRST morning cup of coffee down the hall and stared at the broken door to her bedroom. Quite honestly, she didn't know what to make of Adam McAllister. He'd come bursting through her door like a madman one minute and stared into her eyes as if he wanted to make love to her the next.

She'd needed every ounce of self-control she could find to ignore him while he'd helped her move her furniture into place. And she'd stayed awake far too long thinking about him even after he'd gone back downstairs to bed.

This arrangement would never work. He'd have to go. Now. If they had any more episodes like the one last night, she would have a hard time sending him away. But if yesterday was any indication of things to come, she couldn't afford to let him stay. He stirred feelings that were better left alone.

Shaking her head slowly, she pivoted back toward the kitchen. How would she tell him to leave? What excuse could she offer? He hadn't actually *said* anything. He hadn't made a play for her or tried to initiate sex. Maybe she'd only imagined that spark of interest in his eyes. Maybe it was something else—like heartburn.

She pushed her fingers through her hair and sighed loudly. She couldn't waste any more time agonizing over Adam McAllister. She had a thousand things to do today—her rosebushes needed trimming, the flower beds needed weeding, the lawn should be mowed at least once more. Marissa needed some time and attention, and she wanted to call her mother again to make sure everything was all right.

"*Mommy,* what *happened?*"

DJ turned back to find Marissa in front of her own bedroom and pointing toward DJ's with a horrified expression on her sleepy face, her hair tangled into a rat's nest.

"What are you doing awake so early?"

"That man woke me up."

"Which man? Adam?"

"I don't know. Maybe."

"How did he wake you up?"

Marissa glanced up at her in surprise. "He was outside in the rose garden. Didn't you see him?"

"No, I'm afraid I didn't." She hadn't even heard him leave the house.

"How did you break your door?" Marissa asked again.

DJ pursed her lips and tried to think of a reasonable explanation. She couldn't. "Adam sort of broke it last night."

"He broke it? How?"

"He—" She paused and managed an embarrassed laugh, then started again. "He thought Mommy was in trouble, so he came in to help."

"And he broke your door?"

DJ nodded.

"*Were* you in trouble, Mommy?"

She shook her head quickly. "No, sweetheart. I was changing my bedroom around and I dropped something...." She let her voice trail away as the significance of Adam's actions hit her squarely. She smiled softly. "Everything was fine."

When Marissa walked closer to the door and

reached out to touch the splintered wood, DJ grabbed her by the other hand and guided her away. "Don't touch it, sweetheart. You might get hurt." She hefted the child to her hip and kissed her cheek. "Do you know what today is?"

Marissa beamed. "Sunday! You stay home today."

"You're right." DJ kissed her other cheek noisily.

Marissa giggled and wriggled from DJ's grasp to the floor. Still grinning, she tugged on the hem of DJ's sweater. "Can we go to the zoo today? P'ease?"

"I can't today, sweetheart. We have too much work to do. But I'll make you a deal. I'll take you next week if you'll help me clean up the rose garden today. Okay?"

Marissa didn't look happy. "What do I have to do?"

"You can hold the garbage bag while I clean out the flower beds."

"Yucky."

"But necessary." DJ touched her fingertips to Marissa's soft cheek. "Is it a deal?"

Marissa nodded.

"Good. Now, what do you want for breakfast?"

"Pancakes."

"All right. That's what we'll have." DJ carried Marissa into the kitchen and settled her at the table. She cooked breakfast quickly and chatted as she worked, but the memory of Adam bursting through her door to rescue her kept replaying through her mind the entire time.

He didn't even know her, but he'd been willing to put himself in danger to help her. And the more she thought about it, the more she realized she might not mind having him stay in the basement, after all.

FEELING HIS WAY through the dim morning light seeping in through the basement windows, Adam crossed the laundry room and started up the stairs toward the back landing. He'd spent half the night studying Larry Galloway's mug shot and preliminary report again, noting Galloway's history of ever-increasing violence and trying to find the connection between Galloway and DJ.

His thoughts always returned to the same question. Why did Christina Prescott insist on keeping vital information secret from DJ and her own security people? Why tie Adam's hands by keeping him in the dark?

By morning, his frustration level had doubled. Obviously Christina Prescott didn't intend to tell him anything useful, so he would have to pump DJ again—more directly this time.

He'd still have to approach her cautiously, though, and in just one day, he'd already realized that catching DJ alone might be the hardest part of this assignment. Someone always seemed to be with her—if not one of her employees, then a customer. If not a customer, Marissa or the baby-sitter.

Well, he'd just have to put himself in her path often and work his way into her confidence. And hopefully, he would be able to find out *something* before Galloway appeared.

He climbed the last of the stairs into the kitchen. The window over the sink was partway open, and the air—autumn-crisp and cool—drifted into the room and fluttered the window coverings.

A pot of coffee warmed on the burner and mixed with the fresh air to fill the room with a rich, earthy aroma. A clean mug and spoon waited for him in the

middle of the kitchen table, and early-morning sunlight flickered across the tile floor, making the room
feel homey. Warm. Inviting. But only her breakfast
dishes drying in the drainboard gave any indication
DJ had even been here.

Adam glanced at his watch and scowled. It wasn't
even seven o'clock, and she'd already gone. He'd
missed her. He'd have to get up even earlier tomorrow.

Crossing the room, he poured a cup of coffee and
leaned against the counter to think. Outside, a cat
crept across the wide back lawn toward the trees and
somewhere nearby church bells began to peal.

Sunday. DJ's day off. So where was she?

He shoved his fingers through his hair and started
to turn away just as DJ and Marissa stepped into view
carrying a collection of garden tools across the back
lawn. He studied DJ intently and wondered what kind
of woman she really was.

She looked different this morning, more…fem-
inine, somehow. She'd left her hair loose so that it
fell across her shoulders and down her back and
caught the sunlight as she moved. She wore a gray
sweatshirt that looked far too big, faded jeans that
molded to her figure and a pair of white sneakers, but
even in such ordinary clothes, she looked almost ex-
otic. Compelling.

Marissa walked at her side, almost a mirror image
of her mother. They shared the same mannerisms, the
same easy smile, the same barely harnessed energy—
like wild horses.

He drained the rest of his coffee, flipped off the
coffeepot and left his cup on the counter. Trying to
think of an acceptable excuse to hang around, he set

off down the stairs and out the door. He caught up with them on the north side of the house just below the terraced rose gardens.

Strolling casually, he tried to look as if he were doing nothing more than enjoying the morning. He needn't have bothered. DJ didn't even seem to notice him until he spoke.

"Good morning."

She pivoted to face him and laughed stiffly when she recognized him. "Good morning. I thought you'd be working on your book."

"Not yet. I woke up a little late this morning. I didn't even hear you moving around."

"You just got up?" She glanced at Marissa, and her brows knit in confusion for a heartbeat, then relaxed again. "When do you write the most—at night? Or are you a morning person?"

"I'm definitely a morning person." At least, he'd become one if he tried to keep up with DJ. But he didn't want to discuss himself, and he most definitely didn't want to discuss his writing habits, so he nodded toward the tools at her feet and tried to guide the conversation away from either topic. "Looks like you're planning to do a little gardening."

"We're pruning the dead roses from the bushes this morning," DJ said with a glance at Marissa. "Aren't we, sweetheart?"

The girl hugged her mother's leg and nodded up at him.

Adam smiled at her. "Do you like to garden?"

Marissa nodded again without taking her eyes from his face.

"Really? That surprises me. I thought maybe you liked to play."

DJ shot him an amused glance. "Play? *Marissa?* What makes you think that?"

Adam shook his head and made a face that earned a giggle from Marissa. "I don't know. It just came to me out of the blue."

"I *do* like to play," she said softly. "Even better than working. But Mommy says she'll take me to the zoo next Sunday if I help her today."

"The *zoo?*" Adam shook his head and whistled through his teeth. "Lucky girl."

Marissa nodded solemnly. "On Mommy's next day off."

He hunkered down to Marissa's level and whispered, "You know what? You're lucky. I haven't been to a zoo in years, but I don't even know how to garden."

Marissa frowned. "You don't?"

"No. I don't suppose you could teach me?"

Marissa nodded solemnly. "Can we teach him, Mommy? He could go to the zoo with us."

DJ hesitated for an instant, then nodded. "I suppose we could. What should we have him do first?"

Marissa didn't even miss a beat. "He could hold the garbage bag."

DJ's lips twitched, but she struggled to keep her expression serious. "He could? But I thought that was *your* job."

"He can do it."

"And what will you do?"

"I could take Holly for a walk."

This time, DJ didn't even try to hide her smile. "I see. Well...I suppose it *would* help if you could keep the dog out of the flower beds."

Marissa nodded eagerly. "And she needs a walk or she'll get sick."

"You're right. I don't know why I didn't think of that." DJ ruffled Marissa's hair. "All right, go ahead. But stay where I can see you."

"We will, Mommy. Don't worry." Marissa raced to the end of the driveway, then turned back for an instant to study Adam before she ran down the sidewalk in a flash of tennis shoes and pink denim.

"Don't worry," DJ said with a soft laugh as she looked back at Adam. "Why is it those words always strike terror in my heart?"

"Because kids are still young enough to think they're in control."

She brushed her bangs back from her forehead and smiled. "You're right. You might not have kids of your own, but you must have had *some* experience with children."

"Two nieces and one nephew," he replied, and waited for her to ask the inevitable questions about his own childless state.

To his surprise, DJ didn't speak again. And when he dared glance back at her, she'd turned away to watch Marissa's progress.

Silence stretched between them for an uncomfortably long time. He finally forced himself to say something. "She's a cute girl."

DJ smiled back at him. "Thank you."

He gestured toward the garden. "What about those roses? Are you going to show me what to do?"

She frowned at him with mock seriousness. "You need me to teach you how to hold a garbage bag?"

"I could be a *little* more help than that."

"You really don't know anything about gardens?"

"No." He shrugged and grinned. "But how hard can it be? I know you dig in the dirt, and I've always been good at that."

She laughed—an easy sound that sent a wave of comfort through him—and brushed hair from her cheek with the back of her hand. "I'll bet you have. Just follow along behind me and do what I tell you."

After checking on Marissa and the dog again, she climbed to the highest level of the terraced garden. Adam watched, anticipating the outline of her waist and hips beneath the sweatshirt.

She turned back and caught him standing there, and her expression left no doubt in his mind that she knew exactly what he'd been doing. Her cheeks flushed a delicate shade of pink. "Well, come on."

Ducking his head to hide his grin, he followed her up the narrow rock walls and through the damp, spongy soil. She moved easily; he felt slightly off-balance and decidedly less than surefooted.

The fragrance of roses filled the air as if it emanated from her. DJ breathed deeply, pulling in the scent with her. She met his gaze and grinned almost shyly. "I love roses. They're probably my favorite flower."

Adam picked up a smashed beer can and came to a stop behind her. "I can tell you spend a lot of time working with them."

"Can you?" She looked pleased. "How?"

"Footprints. They're all over." He stooped to pick up another can from the rutted soil. "Looks like you had a party out here."

She frowned and held out a hand for one of the cans. "These aren't mine."

Adam's hand froze, but he tried not to let his face betray him. "They're not?"

She shook her head slowly and studied the can before she dropped it into the garbage bag. "No. Probably some homeless person who needed a place to sleep."

Adam hoped the explanation was that innocent. Just the idea of Galloway getting this close made him nervous as hell.

DJ didn't look even slightly concerned. She crouched beside a bush and snipped several drooping blooms from its branches. "Mom didn't tell me what kind of books you write."

The sudden change of subject caught him off guard, and he blinked in surprise. "Didn't she?"

"No. So what do you write?"

He thought frantically. What could he say? What did he know about? "I...uh..." He laughed and said the first thing that came to mind. "Police..."

"Police procedurals?"

Maybe. Sounded good. He just wished he knew what they were. "Yeah."

"Is that what you like to read?"

"Mostly."

"What else?" She held out a handful of dead leaves and twigs, a few weeds and a plastic ring from a six-pack of soda or beer.

He held open the garbage bag while she dropped the trash inside. "That's it, for the most part."

"So who's your favorite author—besides yourself, of course?"

What a question. He could feel the heat creeping up his neck. "I try not to have any favorites."

She leaned back on her heels and studied him as if he'd landed from another planet. "Are you serious?"

"Absolutely."

She grinned and turned her attention back to the garden. "It's a tactful answer, but I don't believe you for an instant. What about my mom's books? Do you read them?"

He couldn't say yes. One question about the books would give him away, but how could he maintain his cover as Christina Prescott's friend if he said no? Frustrated beyond words, he hesitated a second too long.

To his surprise, she laughed. "I didn't think so. Does she know?"

"I don't know. She probably suspects."

"And she likes you, anyway?" She shook her head in mock amazement, then sobered. "She probably wouldn't care, you know. She's not the type to hold a difference in taste against you. Has *she* read all *your* books?"

He shook his head and allowed himself a smile. "I don't think she's ever read a word I've written."

"I didn't think so. Police procedurals aren't really her type of books. She's more the cozy type—nice, innocent murders committed by the next-door neighbors." She grinned suddenly. "I'll admit, I haven't read your work, either. Are you going to hold that against us?"

He couldn't help but laugh. "Not in a million years."

"Good. I'd like to look at them—do you write under your own name?"

He didn't know the right answer to that—didn't authors usually write under their own names? He nodded slowly and muttered something vague enough to leave her free to interpret the sound in whatever way she chose.

DJ clipped a few more roses and held out another handful of trash, and for a moment he thought she was about to say something more. But her expression suddenly sobered and she focused on something over his shoulder.

Half expecting to find Marissa in some sort of mischief, he glanced behind him. He did see Marissa walking toward them, but a man was approaching just a step or two behind her.

Adam stood slowly and studied him. Medium height, medium build and dark hair. And he knew that if he got close enough, he would see a cold pair of dark eyes.

Larry Galloway. He'd aged a bit and his face had grown heavier over the years, but even at this distance Adam recognized him easily from the mug shot locked in his suitcase.

Adam's shoulders tensed, his easy mood evaporated, and his nerves pricked just under the skin the way they'd always done when he'd dealt with offenders like Galloway.

Every impulse urged him to grab Marissa and stand in front of DJ to shield her. Every instinct told him prison hadn't changed Galloway a bit—he was still a very dangerous man. But Adam couldn't do a thing.

He'd been ordered to say nothing to DJ. He'd been assigned to watch Galloway and, if possible, catch him violating parole. He forced himself to stand still and wait. Sooner or later Galloway would reveal his reasons for being here. And when he did, Adam would be ready for him.

CHAPTER FOUR

DJ WATCHED ADAM push to his feet and glare at the stranger on the driveway. Tension radiated from him, and a surprising level of hostility crackled in the air. His face looked taut and angry, just as it had when he'd come crashing through her bedroom door to save her.

She wondered whether he'd always had a hero complex or whether her mother had charged him personally with DJ and Marissa's safety. She'd long ago learned not to be suspicious of everyone who came her way, and she hoped that this time Adam would contain his urge to leap into battle over some imaginary problem.

Standing quickly, she moved through the flower bed toward the bottom terrace level. To her dismay, Adam followed.

Marissa stopped near the end of the driveway and cupped her hands around her mouth. "Mommy. This man wants to talk to you."

"I'll be right there, sweetheart."

"Who's that?" Adam asked under his breath. "A friend of yours?"

"I don't know who he is," DJ admitted.

"Do you want me to see what he wants?"

"No." She smiled and tried to use a more mellow tone. "He might be a customer."

Adam nodded, but he didn't look convinced. He followed her onto the grass and moved swiftly to her side. "I'm serious, DJ. Why don't you let me talk to him?"

This time, she didn't bother to hide her irritation. "Why? Because you're a man and I'm a woman?"

At least he had the grace to flush with embarrassment. "No. It's just—"

But he broke off and shook his head, as if he didn't know how to explain.

DJ turned away again and crossed the lawn toward the driveway. The stranger wore jeans and a baseball cap, a black T-shirt and matching cowboy boots. He looked harmless.

Until he smiled down at Marissa and hooked his thumbs in the waistband of his jeans. "You have an awfully cute daughter."

DJ might not instinctively fear everyone, but she wouldn't allow her annoyance with Christina and Adam to make her reckless. She put one hand on Marissa's shoulder and spoke softly. "Sweetheart, why don't you take Holly inside for a few minutes, okay?"

Marissa frowned at her. "Do I have to?"

"Yes, you do. But just for a few minutes."

Marissa hesitated another second, then seemed to think better of protesting any further. Calling to her dog, she led the way inside.

As soon as the door closed behind her, DJ turned back to the stranger, only to discover that Adam had taken up an almost-threatening stance at the man's side. She sighed softly and wished she could think of a way to send Adam inside with Marissa and Holly.

She tried to ignore him and turned her attention to

the stranger. "Is there something I can help you with?"

He studied her for several long seconds without answering. His eyes flicked over her face and hair, and she felt another small twinge of concern. "Are you Devon Jo Prescott?" His voice was deep. Gruff. Gravelly. And the sound of it sent shivers down her spine.

She pulled back and stared at him. *Devon Jo?* Where on earth had he heard that name? She hadn't used it for years. In fact, she'd *never* used it that she could remember.

She nodded slowly. "I am."

"I guess you don't recognize me."

She narrowed her eyes and studied him. "No," she admitted. "Should I?"

"I thought you might," he said. He glanced at Adam, then back at her. "Can we talk for a few minutes? Alone?"

Before she could even open her mouth to respond, Adam pushed his way between them. "I don't think that's a good idea."

DJ had no intention of going off alone with some strange man, and she resented Adam's implication that she might, or that she needed him to tell her not to.

"It's a personal matter," the man said without even sparing Adam a second glance.

DJ shook her head. "I think it would be best for us to stay right here. Tell me, how do I know you?"

"The name's Larry Galloway."

It meant nothing to her. She frowned a little, trying to remember. "Have we met before?"

Something unsettling flickered behind Larry's eyes;

his smile withered, but his voice remained friendly. *"Galloway,"* he said again. "Larry Galloway."

It seemed so important that she recognize him, DJ probed her memory again, hoping to find some clue, but her mind remained stubbornly blank. "I'm sorry. Where—"

Adam sent her a sideways glance. "You don't know him?"

"Not that I remember."

Adam firmed his stance and crossed his arms. "Why don't you tell her who you are and how she knows you."

Larry barked a laugh—one humorless note. He turned halfway away and worked his baseball cap over his head for a few seconds before he faced DJ and tried to laugh again. "I've gotta admit, this is strange. Not what I expected at all."

Larry's evasive tactics combined with Adam's defensive ones grated on DJ's nerves, and a headache started throbbing low in the base of her skull. "Can you tell me something that might help me remember?"

"All right. You *were* awfully young last time I saw you, so I'm not surprised you don't recognize me. But I thought for sure you'd know my name. Didn't your mother tell you about me?"

"My mother?" DJ glanced at Adam, then back at Larry. "How do you know my mother?"

"You really don't know?" Larry asked. "You don't remember anything?"

Adam took another step toward Larry, but DJ put a restraining hand on his arm. "I don't remember anything, so please, just tell me who you are."

"This, uh…" Larry paused, then snorted. "Hell, I

don't know *what* to say. This wasn't how I pictured meeting you again after all these years. I expected you to remember.''

"Remember *what?*" Adam demanded.

This time, DJ didn't resent his interference. Larry's cat-and-mouse game had worn her patience thin.

Larry drew in a deep breath and let it out slowly. "I'm not trying to cause trouble, I just didn't expect to have to introduce myself." He fiddled with his cap again, readjusted the waistband of his jeans, then sighed heavily. "All right, look— I don't know any other way to say this, so I guess I'll just blurt it out. I'm your father, Devon."

DJ drew back as if he'd hit her, and her stomach clenched. Whatever she'd been expecting him to say, it hadn't been that. "What kind of sick joke are you playing? My father is dead."

His expression sobered instantly. "Is that what she told you? She told you I was dead? Where is she? She'll have to tell you the truth now."

DJ shook her head and backed a step away. "She's on a book-signing tour if it's any of your business. Look, I don't know who you are, and I want you to leave. Now."

"What about Laura? Ask her, why don't you?"

She could feel Adam watching, but while he'd been so anxious to play hero a few minutes ago, *now* he did nothing but stare in stony silence.

"She's away, too, but I don't need to ask her anything. You are not my father." She spoke slowly, deliberately, so Larry wouldn't misunderstand a single word. "My father died when I was two years old. His name was *not* Larry Galloway."

"I've got all the documents right here to prove what I'm saying. At least look at them."

DJ shook her head and took another step away. "I told you to leave. If you don't, I'm calling the police."

But Larry didn't look even slightly concerned. Instead, he reached for her as if he intended to keep her from leaving. "Wait. At least look at what I've got. If you don't believe me then, I'll leave. I swear I will." Without waiting for an answer, he pulled a folded manila envelope from his back pocket.

DJ didn't want to touch anything of his. She shook her head again, cautious now about saying something that might anger this man who was so obviously delusional. She silently willed Adam to go inside the house and telephone the police, but he remained rooted to the spot.

He nodded toward the envelope in Larry's hand. "Take a look inside. See what he's got."

"No." The word exploded like a gunshot, but Adam didn't listen. He took the envelope from Larry's grasp and pulled a worn Polaroid snapshot from inside. He studied it for countless seconds and his expression grew more guarded, more sullen, more solemn by the moment. Without a word, he handed the photograph to her.

She didn't want to look at it, but Adam insisted. In her hand she saw a handsome, youthful version of Larry Galloway, smiling at the camera and holding a beaming child in his arms. DJ closed her eyes and fought back the wave of nausea that washed through her. She knew that child. She'd looked through her mother's old photographs too many times not to recognize herself.

She lowered the picture slowly. "Where did you get this?"

Larry smiled. "I've had it since the day your Grandma Galloway took it. It's worn, but it's the only picture I have of you. To tell you the truth, it's the only thing that's kept me going."

DJ held it out to him. It proved nothing. *Nothing.* "I don't know who you are or what you're trying to do," she said. "But it's not going to work."

He nodded toward the envelope again. "There's more. Go on. Look at the rest."

"I don't want to look at anything else," she insisted. Her voice sounded too high, too frantic, and she forced herself to calm down before she spoke again. "This is a cruel joke, and I refuse to have anything to do with it."

She expected Adam to hand the envelope back to Larry, but he didn't. Instead, he pulled out a folded document and studied it before he held it out to her.

Her eyes focused on the document slowly. It looked like a birth certificate, but it said her name was Devon Jo Galloway, and named Lawrence Andrew Galloway as her father, not Peter Prescott.

Her heart raced, her mouth dried and the world around her seemed to blur as tears of anger filled her eyes. She touched the seal, praying it wasn't real, but the embossed lettering certainly made it feel authentic.

She fought down the nausea that swamped her and shoved the offending document back at the vile man who'd brought it. "This isn't real. It *can't* be. Who are you? What do you want?" As if he intended to calm her, Adam touched her shoulder lightly. She jerked away from the contact, too angry to think, too confused to want anything from him.

Larry looked at her with sad eyes. "It's true, Devon. You were the most beautiful baby I ever saw, and you were mine, my first child."

Covering her ears with her hands, she backed away from him.

"What about Laura?"

"She was Prescott's, but you were my very own daughter."

"Stop it. Don't say another word."

"Laura and I waited together for the nurse to bring you into the nursery. Seemed like they took forever. I drank tons of coffee, and I thought Laura would jump out of her skin waiting." Larry laughed a little and tried to meet her gaze.

She refused to look at him. She couldn't. She wanted to throw up. She wanted to purge herself of this horrible feeling. "If you're not off my property in thirty seconds, I'm calling the police."

Half expecting Adam to start toward the telephone, she glanced at him, but he stood beside her, watching without moving, listening without reacting.

Larry stepped into her line of vision. "You were the noisiest baby in the nursery. In fact, the nurses had to bring you into your mother's room so the other babies could sleep."

Bile rose in DJ's throat. She'd heard that story many times before, from her mother and Laura. And somehow this man had heard it, too—in some writing class her mother had taught, or at a seminar. Somewhere. Anywhere.

She didn't care who Larry Galloway was, what he wanted, when he'd met her mother or where he'd come from. She just wanted him gone. Pivoting away, she started up the steps toward the front door.

But Galloway called after her again. "All right. I guess I don't blame you for not believing me. It's a shock. I understand that. Hell, *I'm* shocked to find out you don't even know who I am." He fell silent for a moment, then went on. "Do yourself one favor, Devon. Ask your mother for the truth. Or ask Laura. You might be surprised by what they tell you."

She tried in vain to block out the sound of his voice, but she could hear Adam mumble something and Larry respond. And then silence.

"I've written down a phone number and given it to your friend, here," Larry said at last. "If you change your mind, give me a call." And then, blessedly, his footsteps retreated and followed the driveway to the sidewalk before they finally faded away.

She tried to take a deep breath, but her lungs failed her. She tried walking up the remaining steps to the front porch, but her knees refused to hold her. She tried to focus on the house in front of her, but the tears wouldn't stop.

She dashed them away with the back of her hand, but they came again and forced her to give up the effort to look in control. Sinking to the steps, she let herself cry as she hadn't cried in years.

Adam climbed the steps and stood beside her. "Is there any chance he's telling the truth?"

"No. It can't be true."

"Are you sure?"

"Of course I'm sure. I don't care how many documents he forges or how many old photographs he produces, I refuse to believe him."

He dropped to the step beside her. "You'll ask your mother?"

"Of course I will. And when she denies his story, I'll call the police and press charges. He gave you a phone number?"

Adam nodded and offered her a scrap of paper, but she didn't want to touch it yet. Doing so might make Larry Galloway and his ugly story real somehow.

She closed her eyes and tried to pull herself together, but the suddenly too-sweet scent of roses hung heavy in the air, and this time the fragrance made her want to retch.

Adam shot her a sideways glance full of genuine concern. "Are you all right?"

"I'm fine," she lied. She could hear the anger in her voice, and she tried to push it away. She had no right to be angry with Adam. He'd played no part in this nightmare other than to hand her the picture and falsified birth certificate. Irrationally, she resented even that, as if Larry Galloway and his cruel joke would have evaporated without Adam to give them substance.

When he looked as if he might speak again, she stood quickly and turned away. She didn't want to talk. She didn't want to listen. Her mind raced, alternating between shock and disbelief. Just now, she didn't want to see Adam or hear his voice. She wanted only to be alone.

ADAM PACED THE length of his bedroom, debating whether to leave the house long enough to call Chuck from a pay phone or to stay here in case DJ came out of her bedroom. He cursed under his breath and battled the urge to slam his fist into the wall out of sheer frustration.

He knew that birth certificate and photograph were genuine as surely as he knew his own name. And no matter how vehemently DJ denied it, he suspected she knew, too. Why else had she grown so pale and shaken? Why had she locked herself away in her bedroom all day with Marissa?

Somewhere along the line, Christina Prescott had changed her name, and DJ's. But why? Christina must have taken her new name after the divorce. He could understand her reasons. He'd met men like Galloway over the years. Cold. Ruthless. Capable of almost anything. Galloway might be able to control himself for a little while, but one of these days he'd slip. He'd step out of line—even hurt someone. And Adam hated the thought of a man like that disturbing DJ's life and hanging around Marissa.

Wheeling away from the wall, he began to pace again. Now that he'd met Galloway, now that he'd looked into his eyes and seen the barely suppressed anger there, Adam wouldn't hesitate to act when the need arose.

He cursed aloud—once for the rotten luck that had landed him on this assignment, once because he had to work for a woman capable of lying to her daughter about something so critical, and once more just for the hell of it. He hated this assignment. He hated listening to DJ pace the floor overhead. He hated knowing how much she hurt. And he hated caring.

He wasn't supposed to care. He was supposed to remain detached. Professional. But he couldn't forget the look on DJ's face when Galloway had hit her with that bombshell—even Adam had felt as if the man had gut-punched him.

So what would DJ do now? Would she call her mother and try to discover the truth? Would Christina Prescott verify it if DJ asked? She had gone to great lengths to keep that truth from DJ.

Dropping to the foot of his bed, he propped his elbows on his knees and rested his chin in his hands. For now, he supposed, nothing had changed.

After a moment, he lifted his chin and listened to the silence of the house around him. DJ had finally stopped pacing. She must have gone to sleep. Good. She needed to rest.

Adam stood slowly and smoothed the legs of his jeans. He might as well make a quick sweep of the property before he turned in. He wouldn't be able to sleep until he knew DJ and Marissa were safe—at least for tonight.

DJ LEANED HER CHIN on the back of the couch and watched the shadows of the trees dance across the lawn in the moonlight. Marissa had been in bed for hours, but DJ's mood had dipped so low she hadn't accomplished any of her usual late-night tasks.

Larry Galloway's story had haunted her all day. She didn't believe it, of course, but she couldn't put it out of her mind. Why would anybody make up a story like that? What did he hope to accomplish? What did he want?

Maybe he wanted money. DJ had none, but her mother had enough to tempt someone. Maybe he was a crazed fan of Christina Prescott's. Maybe he was a relative DJ knew nothing about. She'd come up with a dozen explanations throughout the day, but she couldn't prove any of them. And the only person who could was in London, England.

She'd agonized all day over whether to call her mother. Christina always overreacted. If DJ told her about Larry Galloway, she would get upset. She'd want to ignore her commitments and abandon her vacation plans and come rushing home. But what could she do here? Nothing DJ couldn't do as well.

On the other hand, Christina might know Larry Galloway. She might be able to set DJ's mind at ease, which would be a good thing. DJ didn't think she'd be able to eat, sleep, concentrate on work or give Marissa the attention she deserved until she had some resolution to the day's episode.

Standing quickly, she started from the room, but a sound near the back of the house caught her attention. She took a step backward, deeper into the shadows, and watched as Adam appeared on the rear landing.

He unlocked the door silently, glanced over his shoulder once and slipped outside. She heard the door shut and the key turn in the lock. A second later, she saw the bobbing light of a flashlight as he walked away.

What on earth was he doing?

She hurried to the front windows again and waited for the light to appear. Seconds later, she caught sight of it sweeping the trees across the street. She could barely make out Adam's shadow by the corner of the house, and she watched, breathless, as he made his way across the front yard and flashed the light through the bushes and across her windows.

At the far corner, he turned toward the rear of the house. DJ rushed into her bedroom and watched, fascinated, as he repeated the process through the rose garden and along the back of her yard. A few seconds later, he let himself into the house and crept downstairs to bed.

She sat on the edge of her bed and pushed her fingers through her hair, oddly comforted by his concern but at the same time confused. Living alone on this street didn't usually bother her, but tonight she felt exposed and defenseless. Much as she hated to admit it, she liked knowing Adam was only a few feet away, that he cared enough about their safety to check the house and yard before he went to sleep. She might not be ready to talk to him about Larry Galloway, but she liked knowing she wasn't alone.

She closed her bedroom door, checked the sliding-glass door and pulled the curtains so she wouldn't feel so exposed. She dug through her nightstand and finally found her mother's itinerary buried inside the drawer. Dragging in a steadying breath, she dialed the number for the conference hotel and asked for her mother's room.

She counted rings while the phone whirred in her ear and prayed that her mother would answer. A second later a familiar voice came over the line. "Yes?"

Her mother's voice sounded solid, familiar and comforting. DJ had to blink away tears of relief. "Mom?"

"DJ? Sweetheart, is that you?"

"Yes."

"What's happened? Is something wrong?"

DJ might have been eight years old again, for all the strength she had. "I don't know, Mom. I need you to tell me."

"What is it? What's happened? Is Marissa all right?"

"Marissa's fine. I just need you to clear something up for me."

"What?"

"I had a visitor today. A man named Larry Galloway. Do you know him?"

"Larry Galloway?" Her mother's voice grew sharp. Tense. "Yes, I know him. He came to see you? What did he say? What did he want?"

"He tried to tell me he's my father."

Her mother responded with uncustomary silence that lasted so long, DJ's heart began to thud in her chest. "Well, he's not, but he's also not someone you want around."

Relief rushed through her, and common sense told her to let the matter drop there. But she couldn't. "He had a picture of us together, Mom. And a birth certificate."

"A *what?*"

"He has a birth certificate with my name on it. Only I'm listed as Devon Jo Galloway, not Prescott, and Dad's name isn't on there, Larry Galloway's is."

Another pause, this one even longer. When her mother finally spoke, her voice sounded far away. "Dammit! Where did he get hold of that?"

"What?"

"Nothing. Just do me a favor, sweetheart. Stay away from him. I'll come home right away and explain everything."

DJ shook her head rapidly, as if her mother could see through the telephone lines. "You can't cancel your speech at the last minute. They're counting on you."

"They'll understand if I explain it's a family emergency."

"But it's *not* an emergency. You don't need to come home. Just tell me now."

"Not over the telephone."

"Why?"

"It's complicated."

"All you have to do is tell me it isn't true," DJ insisted. "Tell me Larry Galloway's not my father. He's *not,* is he?"

"Sweetheart—"

DJ's heart pounded with dread. It wasn't like her mother to skirt an issue or refuse to answer such a direct question. "Who is he, Mom?"

"I'll explain everything when I get there."

"Is he my father or not? That's all I'm asking. If you don't want to tell me, I'll find someone who will. I've still got friends at Jeff's old firm. I'll hire someone to trace that birth certificate—"

"That birth certificate was supposed to be sealed—" Christina broke off suddenly and sucked in a sharp breath.

"What?" DJ's heart seemed to stop beating. She gripped the bedside table and closed her eyes to stop the room from spinning, but she couldn't breathe and she couldn't feel her fingers on the receiver. "It's true? He's my father?"

"Technically, yes," Christina said. "He's your biological father. But DJ, sweetheart, I really don't want to go into all this on the phone. This isn't fair—"

"Fair?" DJ exploded. "You've lied to me for thirty-two years, and you're complaining that I'm asking you something that isn't *fair?"*

"You don't understand how it was," Christina argued. "He's no good. I couldn't let him ruin your life the way he did mine. And Laura's."

DJ paced as far as the cord would let her. "I don't believe this. He says Laura's not even his daughter."

"That's the point! I had to do what I did to protect *you*, DJ. There wasn't any other way...."

DJ shook her head. She couldn't listen. For the first time in her life, she found the sound of her mother's voice intolerable. "I'm hanging up."

"No!" her mother pleaded. "Don't hang up, DJ. Talk to me. Let me explain."

But DJ couldn't talk anymore, and she didn't want to listen. Not right now. "I can't, Mom."

"I'm coming home—"

"Don't!" DJ snapped. "Stay there. Give your speech." Her voice caught, even on those simple words, and tears flooded her eyes. Without allowing her mother a chance to respond, she replaced the receiver long enough to be certain she'd disconnected, then took it off the hook and left it on the table.

She sat back on the bed until she regained her equilibrium, her ears stopped ringing and her tears slowed a little. Then she walked through the darkened house back into the living room, dimly aware of the dial tone fading away in the distance.

A thousand questions raced through her mind. A thousand answering emotions chased them. How many times had her mother soothed her when she'd cried for Peter Prescott, the man she'd believed to be her father? How many times had her mother lied? How could DJ ever trust her after this? How could she forgive?

She hurt so deeply, she felt almost numb. Leaning her chin on the back of the couch, she let fresh tears spill onto her cheeks as she watched the shadows of the trees dance across the lawn in the moonlight. She didn't want to cry anymore, but she couldn't stop. In one afternoon, she'd lost everything—her father, her mother, her world as she knew it.

She closed her eyes and tried to clear her mind. Crickets chirped in the moonlight and kept time with the throbbing in her head. Roses filled the air with their cloying fragrance, making it hard for her to breathe. And Larry Galloway's image rose before her eyes, reaching for her, trying to pull her into his arms, trying to make her love him.

After a moment, she got up again and closed the window. She could see light spilling across the side yard from Adam's bedroom window. It looked warm, comforting; and it almost dared her to run down the stairs and hammer on his door. She wanted to cry and shout and scream, and she wanted him to wrap his arms around her and take away this pain. But he couldn't. Nobody could.

She stood by the window and stared into the night for what felt like forever. Trees swayed in the wind, leaves skittered across the driveway and the moon disappeared behind a cloud.

A second later, Adam's light blinked out and left the world nearly black. DJ leaned her head against the window and sighed softly into the silence. She didn't even know herself anymore. She'd never felt so frightened.

She'd never felt so alone.

CHAPTER FIVE

ADAM DRUMMED HIS fingers on the table and glared at the laptop computer. It blinked at him, almost daring him to type something. He scanned his one-page, handwritten set of instructions and pressed the F1 key. Instantly, the computer whirred to life and the screen changed before his eyes.

Not so bad, he supposed. He pressed F1 again. The screen blanked, flashed a logo and changed colors. But there it stopped, and that annoying little dash blinked at him, waiting for attention like a cat expecting to be fed.

Adam rubbed a hand across the stubble on his chin and scowled back down at his instructions. Maybe if he read them aloud they'd make more sense. "'To call up the report form,'" he read, "'hold down the control key, press the Alt key, then the 5.'"

He wiped his palms on his pant legs and studied the computer, trying to locate the keys he needed. He found the "5" key almost immediately, but it took another few seconds to locate the other two. At this rate, he'd still be writing his first report at his retirement party.

Following instructions, he pressed the keys in order. The computer whirred to life again and painted the report outline onto the screen. "So far, so good," he muttered, and tried to make sense of the next step.

Before he could figure out how to insert his name and rank into the appropriate slot, a soft knock sounded on his bedroom door. "Adam? Are you in there?"

Brittany? What was she doing down here? He tossed his pillow over the instruction sheet and crossed the room to open the door. "What is it?"

"You have a telephone call. She says it's urgent."

"She?"

Brittany nodded. "It's DJ's mom. Christina Prescott."

"Christina Prescott? Are you sure it's for me?"

"Positive." Brittany wove her fingers through two of the beltloops on her jeans. "She, uh, doesn't want DJ to know she called."

Abandoning the report and the computer, Adam pulled his door shut and followed Brittany up the stairs to the kitchen. She nodded toward the receiver she'd left on the counter and pretended to return her attention to a stack of books on the table, but he knew she would hang on every word.

Great. No privacy. He snagged up the receiver. "Hello? Christina?" He tried to sound like an old friend.

"Is this Adam McAllister?"

"Yes. How are you?"

"Not good. I'm told you know what happened there yesterday." She sounded worried, and she had every right to be.

"Yes."

"Tom Dodge assures me you know your business. I hope he's right."

"I believe so."

She sighed. "Tell me what happened."

He flicked a glance at Brittany. "That's a little difficult to do right now."

"Someone's in the room with you?"

"That's right."

Another sigh. "I don't care. Tell me what happened there yesterday."

Keeping his voice low, he turned away from Brittany to muffle the sound. "DJ and I were working in the rose garden when Larry Galloway stopped by to see her. He had a document and a picture—did Dodge tell you about those?"

"No, but DJ did. She said Larry told her he's her father."

"He did. Is it true?"

"Yes." The word came so softly, he almost didn't hear it, but it hit him with as much impact as if she'd shouted.

"Tell me about it. Why the secrecy?"

"I can't."

"If I'm going to do what's necessary, I need to know everything."

"No."

"Ms. Prescott—"

"No," she said again. "I don't want DJ to know. Ever. Right now, there are only three people in the world who know the whole story. I don't see any reason to change that."

"Things are different now," he reasoned.

"No." The word came out clipped and angry. "I refuse to discuss it."

Adam knew she'd made a decision she wouldn't back away from unless he could give her a compelling reason. Obviously, Larry's reappearance in DJ's life wasn't compelling enough. But if not, why had she hired him? "All right," he said at last. "I won't push you—for now."

She drew in a shaky breath and waited a few seconds before going on. "I suppose I'll have to assume that he didn't do anything you could send him back to prison for...."

"That's right."

"What did you think of him?"

Adam hesitated. He shouldn't offer a personal opinion. Regulations required him to stick to the facts. But he glanced over his shoulder at Brittany and paced another few steps away. "I wouldn't trust him—if that's what you're asking."

"Not exactly. I don't want DJ or Marissa hurt. Tell me honestly: Is Larry still violent? Is he capable of hurting them?"

He couldn't go that far. "He hasn't done anything to give me that impression."

"I'm not asking what he's done. I'm asking what you think."

Adam hesitated again.

This time, Christina didn't wait for a response. "I'm coming home." Her voice trembled and he could hear a slight catch in it. "I'm catching the first plane out of here."

He lowered his voice another notch and leaned over the receiver. "I don't think that's a good idea."

"Why not?" she practically shouted at him.

"For exactly the reasons we just discussed. I think Galloway's volatile. I think he's dangerous. But considering what I now know about your past relationship with him, I'd guess you're more likely to be a target for his anger than either DJ or Marissa.

Chances are, if you show up here, you'll push him into something he might not otherwise do.''

"My God." She sniffled, and he could hear her pull a tissue from a box somewhere near the telephone. "I can't leave DJ and Marissa there alone with him."

"They're not alone," he reminded her.

"No, of course they're not. But I can't sit here, halfway around the world, knowing that…that *psycho* is there with them. I couldn't live with myself if anything happened to either one of them." She began to cry in earnest—huge, gulping sobs.

Adam gripped the receiver tighter and flicked another glance at Brittany. She'd all but abandoned any pretense of studying, and he had no way of knowing how much of his end of the conversation she'd heard. "I won't let that happen."

"You don't know Larry. You don't know what he's like—"

"I've had experience with others like him. That's why I'm here."

She sniffed again. "I need to be there."

"Like I said, coming here is the worst thing you could do right now." He drew in a deep breath. "Ms. Prescott, I give you my word, nothing's going to happen to them." He knew it was crazy to make a promise like that, but she desperately needed reassurance and he absolutely believed that she'd help DJ and Marissa more by staying in London.

She didn't speak for a long time. He could hear her pacing, picking up an object, setting it back down again and crying softly. "I have to trust you, don't I?"

"Yes."

"You understand, don't you, why I need someone to look after them?"

"I do."

"And you'll watch him? If he does *anything* to violate his parole, I want his butt back behind bars."

"I'll watch."

She let another few seconds elapse. "Do you know how hard it is for me to stay away?"

"I have an idea."

She tried to laugh, but the resulting sound was more like a sob. He could hear someone knocking on a door, and she swore softly. "Oh, God, they're here to get me for a book signing—"

"Go," he said. "Do what you have to do over there. Take care of business, and I'll do the same on this end."

He waited until she disconnected, then replaced the receiver. He just hoped the years he'd spent away from law enforcement hadn't left him so rusty that his promise turned out to be a lie.

DJ PUSHED A CART loaded with trees into a checkout stand and tried not to snap off any branches as she did so. For the first time in memory, she didn't want to be at the store. She had no heart for it today. The customers' questions annoyed her, the employees' chatter irritated her and the noise level inside the store had cranked last night's headache to full volume.

Forcing a smile, she pulled a bottle from an end display and held it out for her round-faced customer to inspect. "You might want to put a little of this around the roots when you plant these trees," she said. "It will help minimize the shock."

The man screwed his face into a frown as he studied the bottle. "What is it? Some chemical? Or is it organic? Will it hurt my wife's cat?"

DJ kept her voice pleasant as she answered, but she breathed a sigh of relief when the man placed the bottle on the cart.

"Have you got somebody to cut these cans for me?" he asked. "And what about newspaper and rope for my trunk?"

Under normal circumstances, DJ would have been happy to follow through on the sale, but she didn't think she would survive one more question. She lifted a hand to catch Ramon's attention, then smiled back at the customer. "Heather will ring all this up for you, and Ramon will help you get it outside. Let us know if there's anything else we can help you with."

She turned away as Ramon approached. Rubbing her forehead, she closed her eyes and tried to will away the throbbing pulse at the base of her skull. But when she opened her eyes again, the light sent a shaft of pain through to the back of her head.

She groaned softly and admitted defeat. She'd tried, but she couldn't concentrate. She was no good to anyone—least of all to herself.

For probably the hundredth time since hanging up on her mother last night, she told herself she would feel better once she'd talked with Laura. Even with the difference in their ages, they'd always been close. If DJ ever had a problem she couldn't discuss with her mother, she turned to her sister. But Laura was still somewhere on Lake Powell, blissfully unaware that DJ's world had been turned upside down by the one person she'd always trusted to keep it secure.

She forced herself to focus on Heather and tried to

smile, but she wondered whether her effort looked as unnatural as it felt.

Heather leaned on the counter and tucked a stray lock of hair behind one ear. "Are you all right? You don't look very good."

"I'm not feeling well," DJ admitted. "I think I'll get out of here for a while. Take a walk and get some fresh air. Page me if you need me, okay?"

Heather nodded, swigged a mouthful of soda and reached for the telephone when it rang in her booth. "Good morning, The Treehouse. This is Heather."

Taking advantage of the distraction, DJ slipped through the checkout stand and out the front door. Just escaping her responsibilities for a few seconds made her feel better.

She stood for a minute in the autumn-crisp air and tried to decide where to go. She didn't want to go home—at least, not yet. She couldn't sleep even if she tried, and she didn't want Marissa to see her frustration and pain. She couldn't walk through the east tree lot—it had been busy all morning with sales of late-season stock, and she'd set a crew moving one-gallon tams in the back lot. That left only the south lot empty if she wanted time alone.

Turning away from the store, she walked slowly down the gravel road. Sunlight played across the ground and leaves danced from the trees in a graceful ballet. Usually she found joy in moments like this, but not today. Today, she couldn't find pleasure in anything.

She let her mind wander, and events from the day before replayed endlessly. She heard the sound of Larry Galloway's voice and relived that horrible moment when he'd told her who he was. She heard her mother's voice, denying and then admitting the truth and pleading for a chance to explain.

Her stomach lurched as reality hit all over again, and she tried in vain to push the memories away. She didn't know what to do next.

She walked until she knew nobody could see her, then stopped in the middle of the road and tipped her head back. She let the autumn sunlight caress her face and shoulders as the silence closed in around her. She mentally calculated the days until Laura and Bob's scheduled return. Ten. She'd counted them so many times last night, she couldn't even imagine why she needed to do it again.

She stood there for a long time, trying alternately to forget and then remember details of yesterday's conversation with Larry Galloway. She lost herself so completely, she didn't even hear the footsteps approaching on the gravel until they were almost upon her.

Straightening, she blinked rapidly and tried to focus. A second later, Adam McAllister rounded a curve in the path. He wore faded jeans and an old sweatshirt and didn't look as if he'd shaved, yet DJ found the combination oddly appealing.

He managed a smile when he saw her. "I didn't expect to find you here. Am I interrupting something?"

She shook her head and stuffed her hands into her back pockets. "Nothing important."

"Good. I'm glad I ran into you." He took a few steps closer. Concern darkened his eyes to a steel gray, and DJ wondered why she hadn't noticed how extraordinary they were before now. "I've been wondering how you're feeling today."

"So have I," she said with a thin laugh. "I'm not sure."

He smiled in response. "You were up late. I heard you walking around."

"So were you. I saw you check outside."

His smile widened slowly, an incredible smile that made her mouth dry. "Yes, I did. I hope you're not offended that I took it upon myself to do that, but it made me feel a little better."

"No, not at all."

"Good. Have you had a chance to talk to your mother yet?"

"I called her last night." She should have said more. After all, he knew nearly as much about Larry Galloway as she did. But she couldn't make herself speak.

Suddenly, he felt too close. His shoulders seemed too broad and his legs too solid. He had strong hands and an even stronger profile, and DJ's reaction to him left her flustered. She turned away and took a few short steps toward the edge of the road. "Well," she said at last. "Larry Galloway wasn't lying. Mom admitted he is my biological father."

Adam didn't move a muscle, but DJ could tell it took an effort for him to remain so still. "I see." He drew in a deep breath, then released it. "How do you feel about it?"

"I don't know." She looked away again. His eyes asked too much of her. "I don't know," she repeated.

He crossed the road to stand behind her. "Did she give you any explanations?"

"She tried to claim she lied to protect me."

"You don't believe her?"

DJ managed a harsh laugh. "Believe her? How can

I? The man's my father, but I didn't even know he existed until yesterday.''

"What reasons did she give for hiding the truth from you?''

"Just that. To protect me. But she won't say from what. She wants me to wait until she comes home to talk about it.''

"Maybe you should.''

DJ shook her head quickly and glared up at him. "Why? No matter what happened between them, there's no excuse for what she did.''

He considered that, tilting his head slightly as if he needed to give her answer some thought. "So, what are you going to do?''

She sighed heavily and shivered in the breeze. "I don't know. I can't concentrate. I can't work. I'm not even sure I can be a decent mother to Marissa until I get my head straightened out. What do you think? How would *you* feel?''

"You want *me* to tell you how to feel?'' He pulled back a little, as if he found the idea unappealing.

In spite of her inner turmoil, she couldn't help but smile at his stricken expression. "No. Not really. I guess I just need a listening ear.''

He looked greatly relieved. "I've got one of those,'' he said, and waited for her to speak again.

But faced with someone willing to listen, she couldn't speak.

"Maybe your mother will call back after she has a chance to think things through,'' he suggested.

"I don't think so,'' she said with a laugh. "I hung up on her last night, and I've left the answering machine on all day. You know how she is.''

He lifted one shoulder but didn't say anything.

"There's nothing she can say that I want to hear, anyway. She hasn't tried to call you while I'm at work, has she?"

He looked startled by the question. "Me? No."

"You can't blame me for being suspicious," she said. "She might have called and asked you to talk some sense into me."

Adam shook his head and grinned. "I'd have refused. Too big a job."

She made a face at him and looked away again. She didn't want to make light of this horrible situation. "I can't decide how I feel about my mother and what she did. I don't want to think about her. I don't want to speak to her. I don't want to hear any excuses."

"Maybe—"

"I have a *father*," she said, raising her voice as if that would make him understand. "After all these years, I have a father. But he's a stranger to me. I don't know anything about him. I don't know what he's like or what he does or whether he's married again. Do I have brothers and sisters somewhere? Nieces and nephews? Grandparents? I don't even know where he's been or why he left in the first place."

"No, you don't."

"I want to get to know him—can you understand that? But if I do, my mother will be hurt."

"You don't think she'll understand?"

"My *mother*? After everything she's done to keep him from me?" She shook her head and looked back at him. "You know her. Do *you* think she'll understand?"

An expression she couldn't read flitted across his face, and he shook his head. "It's hard to say."

DJ sighed and flicked a lock of hair over her shoulder. "You know, I'm really not sure why I care about her feelings after what she's done. But she's my mother—" Her voice caught and tears suddenly filled her eyes. She looked away quickly and hoped Adam wouldn't notice.

"Forget your mother for a minute," he said softly. "What do *you* want to do?"

She took a moment to pull herself together. "I want to know my father. I think I *deserve* to know him."

"What if you find out things you'd rather not know?"

She slanted a glance at him. "Like what?"

"Whatever it was that made your mother lie to you in the first place."

"Maybe I need to find out. Maybe it's time to get the whole story out in the open." She paced away again, then pivoted back to face him. "I'm not a child. I need to know the truth."

He nodded slowly. "Okay."

"I need to know my father."

"Probably."

She glared at him and refused to tear her gaze away from his. She challenged Adam as if he were her mother standing there. "There's only one way to do that," she warned. "I need to spend time with him."

"Do you want me to tell you not to?"

"No!"

"Are you sure?"

"Of course I'm sure."

"Then what's holding you back?"

"My mother." She sighed heavily.

He shook his head slowly. "I don't believe you."

"I don't care whether you believe me or not. I don't want to hurt my mother's feelings."

He dipped his head and lifted one shoulder as if he couldn't wholeheartedly agree. "Maybe you're afraid to find out about him."

She snorted. "That's not it."

"Really?" He moved a step closer. "What if you don't like him? What then? You won't be able to walk away."

She planted her fists on her hips and met his gaze. He looked back, wide-eyed and innocent, but she couldn't rid herself of the feeling that he wanted to lead the conversation somewhere.

"Just what do you think I'm going to find out?" she asked.

"I don't know. Have you asked anyone to check him out? Do you know anything about him?"

The questions hit a nerve, but she refused to let him see that. "When did I have time to do that?"

"Yesterday after he left," Adam said unreasonably. "Or earlier today—"

She blew out a heavy breath and turned away again. "In my spare time? My job isn't like yours, McAllister. I have to work certain hours. I need to be available for my customers, and when I'm *not* working, I have a daughter who needs my attention. I don't intend to make those kinds of calls when she's listening."

"You could still find *some* time to make a few inquiries."

Her patience evaporated and her temper soared past the boiling point. "Don't," she said quietly. "Don't even start that sort of thing with me. You don't have children. You don't have to answer to anyone. You can work when you want, make calls when you want—''

He didn't respond. Instead, he propped one hip against a fence post and crossed his arms over his chest. But she'd worked herself up too far to stop now. "I don't need you coming in here and butting into my life and telling me how I should deal with my problems. I don't need you standing around my kitchen looking like some...some..." She searched the sky for the words, then shoved him with both hands. "Some hairy-faced testosterone-ridden male. I don't have time for you. I don't have *room* for you in my life right now."

He waited a second, then asked, "Is that all?"

"No!" She paced a few steps away. "I'm frightened, Adam. Can't you understand that? I don't know what I want. I don't know who I am anymore. Yes, I want to get to know my father. I think. But you're right, I'm afraid. I'm deathly afraid." Tears stung her eyes and spilled over onto her cheeks. She tried dashing them away with the back of her hand, but she couldn't stop them. "Oh, God!" she cried. "Look at me!"

She turned away from him and wrapped her arms around herself. "I'm confused. I'm scared. I feel lost and alone. I feel as if I've lost everyone who ever mattered to me all at once."

Before she heard him approach, he put his arms around her and turned her to face him. His eyes looked gentle and caring, and he pulled her against him until her cheek lay against his chest. "You still have Marissa," he said softly.

More touched than she could ever have imagined,

she wrapped her arms around his neck and let her tears flow. He held her there for a long time and let her cry until she couldn't cry anymore. He whispered to her—words she couldn't even understand but which carried their message to her wounded heart.

She clung to him, feeling grounded and solid for the first time since Larry Galloway had walked into her life.

He kissed her softly on the forehead and once more on the temple, and said, "I'm not going to leave you alone. If you want to learn more about him, I can help you."

She pulled away slightly and met his gaze. "How?"

"I have contacts."

"Who?"

To her surprise, he grinned and his eyes twinkled with mischief. "Just a few of my hairy-faced, testosterone-ridden friends."

She ducked her head, embarrassed by her outburst. Of course he made contacts doing research. And he was willing to use them now for her. "I'm sorry. I didn't mean—"

He touched one hand to her mouth to still the words. "DJ, you needed to say everything you said. You were confused and angry. You needed to clear everything out so you could start over."

"But—"

"You feel better, don't you?"

She pulled back to arm's length and scowled at him. "You goaded me into getting angry?"

He shrugged and looked off to one side as if he needed to consider his answer. "Yes," he said at last. "I did."

"I don't believe it."

He grinned and made a face of exaggerated horror. "I may not have known you very long, but already I know enough not to try to tell you what to do." He kissed the tip of her nose quickly and released her.

She let her arms fall to her sides. To her surprise, she wanted him to hold her awhile longer. But she knew she couldn't hide from reality in his arms. He was right. She could either wallow in self-pity or take steps to reach a solution.

"I'd feel funny asking someone to check on him. What I *should* do is invite him over for dinner. That would give us time to talk, and I could ask him everything I want to know. Did you keep that number he gave you?"

Adam pulled a scrap of paper from his pocket. "I did."

She took it and clutched it in her hand. "If I do, will you be there? I'm not sure I'm ready to be alone with him yet."

He nodded. "Of course, if you want me there. But what are you going to tell Marissa about him? Have you thought about that?"

What *could* she tell her? Jeff's parents had been as absent from Marissa's life as Jeff himself. Marissa couldn't remember any grandparent other than Christina, and DJ didn't want to spring a grandfather on her without warning. She couldn't help Marissa adjust until she'd accepted the idea of having a father first. The whole concept still seemed unreal. Dreamlike. Or perhaps more accurately, nightmarish.

"I won't tell her anything yet," she said. "Not until I have a better handle on the situation."

"She'll be there during dinner, won't she? You don't think she'll pick up on the conversation?"

"I won't discuss it until she's gone to bed."

"No, but Larry might say something you don't want her to hear."

D.J. squared her shoulders and prepared for an argument. "I'm not leaving Marissa with a baby-sitter while I deal with this. I'm away from her too much as it is."

"All right." Adam ran his fingers though his hair and stared at the trees in front of him for a few seconds. "Why don't I fire up that barbecue grill I saw on your deck? It's still warm enough to eat outside if we start early. Marissa could play on the lawn with Holly, and I could do the cooking and leave you two free to talk."

His reaction amazed her. She relaxed again and smiled. "You don't mind?"

"Not at all."

"What about your book? I shouldn't interfere with your work." It was a halfhearted protest, and DJ had no doubt Adam knew it.

He brushed away her concern. "Don't worry about that. The research is coming along fine. Besides, I have to eat sometime—it might as well be with you."

She allowed herself a relieved laugh. "That's true. Besides, think what a great story line this would make. You could chalk up the whole evening to research."

His expression grew thoughtful. "Yes, I could, couldn't I?" All at once, his eyes brightened. "You know, this is sounding better all the time. It might give us what we both need. When do you want to do it?"

"Tonight. I hate waiting."

Adam half smiled and started to respond just as Ramon's voice blared over the store's loudspeaker and demanded DJ's presence at the customer-service booth.

She groaned a little and stuffed her hands back into her hip pockets. "Sounds as if they need me. I'd better go." She started down the road, but Adam fell into step behind her.

"I'll walk back with you," he said.

She couldn't even pretend not to want his company. "Okay. Thanks." To her surprise, her headache had all but disappeared and she felt almost relaxed in spite of everything she still had to deal with. She wondered how he'd known she needed to release some of her pent-up tension and what would trigger her response.

They walked in silence, and DJ glanced at him every few seconds. He felt solid beside her. Reassuring. And she'd done exactly what she'd hoped to avoid last night—she'd turned to him for comfort for all the wrong reasons.

Yes, he'd held her while she cried. He'd even kissed her. It had been the embrace of a brother—a friend. Nothing more. But it had left her body pulsing with a life of its own.

She looked down at her feet and followed a rut in the road. When it dipped suddenly, her arm brushed against his and her skin tingled at the point of contact. She drew away quickly, disturbed by her reaction to him and more than a little embarrassed.

Even if he reacted to her as a man instead of a brother, she couldn't let herself get involved. A relationship based on need couldn't hope to survive.

She moved a few feet away to avoid accidentally touching him again and kept her eyes straight ahead so she wouldn't be tempted to look at the line of his jaw or the set of his shoulders.

He didn't appear to notice anything. In fact, he didn't look at her again until the nursery came into view. "Let me know when you've talked to Galloway. I can even pick up the groceries while you're working."

"Thanks. I'll call." She started to turn around, then made herself look back again. "And thanks, Adam. For everything."

A smile curved his lips and sent another flash of longing through her. "No trouble. That's what friends are for."

She made herself turn away and hurry through the open glass doors, but when she reached Heather's cash register, she gave in to the urge to look back. To her surprise, Adam stood rooted to the spot, watching her.

In spite of the vow she'd just made to herself, she didn't blush or look away, but returned his smile and held his gaze until the loudspeaker clicked on again. And when at last she could make herself walk away, she warned herself she was inviting heartache. But at that moment, she didn't care.

CHAPTER SIX

ADAM YANKED OPEN the door to the federal building and strode inside. His footsteps echoed from the walls of the foyer and brought Don Meier's head up from his newspaper with a jerk.

Don stood and propped his hands on his duty belt, but when he recognized Adam, he relaxed and smiled broadly. "What are you doing here? I thought they finally fired you."

Adam forced a smile and tried to look as if he'd stopped by for a casual visit and not like he wanted to throttle Chuck for sending him on assignment without a full briefing. "You wish."

Don laughed. "Yeah, I do. It'd be the only way I'll ever get top score on the firing range again." He stood, stretched, and readjusted his belt. "What's up? I heard you were on some top-priority detail."

"I am," Adam admitted. "And if anyone asks, you haven't seen me. I need to talk to Chuck. Is he here?"

Don nodded toward the elevators. "I just saw him heading downstairs. I think he's on his way out."

"Damn."

"You want me to call him back?" Don started to lift his radio from his belt, but Adam stopped him.

"Don't call. I'll find him." Opting against using the slow-moving elevators, Adam raced to the stairwell and bounded down the steps two at a time to the basement level. There he followed the corridor around a couple of twists and outside into the parking lot.

Chuck had made it halfway across the lot, but he wheeled around when Adam shouted, and waited with his fists on his hips while Adam closed the distance between them.

"What the hell are you doing here?"

"I need some answers."

Chuck turned away. "Then call in like you're supposed to. You're putting the contract on the line by coming down here."

Adam followed him. "I want to know what's going on, Chuck, and I want the truth."

Chuck glared up at him without breaking his stride. "Have you jeopardized the assignment? Does DJ Woodward know who you are?"

"No, I haven't. No, she doesn't. But why in the hell didn't you tell me who Larry Galloway was?"

Chuck's step faltered. "Why? What happened? Did he show up?"

"Yeah. He showed up early yesterday morning. Came waltzing right up to the house and asked to talk to her. We were just damned lucky I was outside when he came along, or I'd never have known about it."

Chuck halted beside his car and slipped the key into the lock. "No kidding? I never figured he'd actually show. I thought you were there for nothing."

"Yeah?" Adam asked skeptically. "Well, so did I."

"So what happened? Did you keep him away from her?"

Adam gave a harsh laugh. "No. The best I could

manage was to stand there like a nosy tenant until he left.''

"You got rid of him, then?''

"For the moment.''

Chuck pulled open his door and pressed the automatic unlock button. With a jerk of his head to indicate that Adam should get inside, he dropped his cell phone onto the dashboard and slid into his seat. "What did he want?'' he asked when Adam joined him.

"*Want?* He came for a reunion.''

"A what?'' Chuck stared at him, squinty-eyed, as if he couldn't process Adam's words.

The mock confusion won no sympathy from Adam. "Damn it, Chuck, you sent me in there blind. Why didn't you tell me he's DJ's father?''

Chuck's eyes widened with genuine shock. "Her father? Are you sure?''

"Yeah. I'm sure.'' For some reason, Adam couldn't make himself tell Chuck about Christina Prescott's call. "He had a birth certificate with him.''

Chuck leaned back in his seat and rubbed a hand across his chin. "DJ didn't know about him?''

Reluctantly, Adam conceded that Chuck might be as surprised as he had been. "No. She thought her father was a man named Peter Prescott. She's been told he died when she was two.'' He shifted in his seat and leaned his head back. "I'm going on record, here. This detail stinks and I have no idea how to handle it.''

"What do you mean, you don't know how to handle it? You've got your assignment. Do your job. If you catch him violating parole, you call SLPD immediately. Until then, keep him from getting too close.''

Adam shot him a look of disbelief. ''How? I'm supposed to be a writer, remember? What excuse do I give for hanging around all the time? And if Galloway gets pushy, how do I convince him to back off—pull a pencil on him?''

Chuck's face reddened. ''Don't get sarcastic with me. I didn't accept this contract or assign you to it. I'm the middleman here, remember?''

Adam drew in a steadying breath and rubbed his forehead. ''You're right. Let me talk to Dodge, then.''

''Why?''

''*Why?* So he can tell me what's going on. Why didn't Christina Prescott tell DJ about her father?''

''You don't need to know that. Your job is to keep Galloway away from DJ and her daughter.''

''I don't like being blindsided.''

''That's unfortunate.''

Adam's temper flared. ''Yeah, it is. What's Dodge's number?'' He reached for the cell phone, but Chuck caught his wrist in a surprisingly tight grip.

''You're not calling Dodge.''

Adam glared at him. ''I can't protect DJ and Marissa unless I know what's going on. I can't do my job this way. I need to know everything about Galloway and why Christina Prescott kept them apart all this time.''

''You're assuming Larry Galloway's telling the truth.''

''Yeah? Well, he is. Christina Prescott admitted it to DJ last night.''

Chuck whistled softly, but he still shook his head. ''You know Larry's an ex-con with a fondness for using weapons. You know our client is paying you to keep Larry away from her daughter and granddaughter. What else do you need?''

"How about what happened between them, and why is Christina Prescott so set against Larry and DJ knowing each other?''

Chuck released Adam's wrist and leaned back in his seat. "What's going on, Adam? This isn't like you. You're the best man I've got because you take your assignments and you complete them. No questions asked. Results guaranteed.'' He shook his head slowly and met Adam's gaze. "You've never jeopardized an assignment before. So what's different this time? Why are you here?''

Adam stared back, uncertain how he would respond if he could force himself to speak.

Chuck propped an elbow on the door handle and faced him squarely. "If your loyalties are unclear, you won't do anybody any good—not DJ, not Marissa, not Christina Prescott and especially not yourself.''

His accusation hit Adam like a blow to the midsection. Clenching his jaw, he ground his next words out through his teeth. "My loyalties aren't in question.''

"Frankly,'' Chuck said, "the way you're acting, I'd just as soon take you off this case. But you're too good a man.'' He looked away and rubbed the back of his neck. He looked tired.

Adam thrust his fingers through his hair. "I still don't like it.''

"You don't have to like it. Dodge wants you on this detail because of your police background. He doesn't give diddly-squat what your personal feelings are.''

Not very comforting, but true. Adam stared straight ahead, working a muscle in his jaw.

Silence stretched between them for several long seconds before Chuck spoke again. ''So, tell me, how do you get along with DJ?''

Adam forced an indifferent shrug. ''She's all right, I guess.''

''She believes your story?''

''Yeah.''

''I hope you've been pleasant.''

Adam flicked him a sideways glance. ''I've been a bundle of charm. You know me.''

To his surprise, Chuck laughed. ''I do. That's why I'm worried.'' He paused again. ''How did she react to Larry?''

Adam could still see her as she'd looked facing Galloway. The top of her head barely reached his shoulder, but she'd faced him like a warrior, straight-backed, her eyes black with anger. And Adam hadn't known whether to shield her or stay out of her way.

Chuck studied him as if he'd spoken aloud. ''What? Why are you smiling?''

Slightly embarrassed, Adam wiped the unexpected grin from his face. ''She didn't believe him.''

''She didn't? Good. I'll tell Dodge.''

''She knows the truth now,'' Adam reminded him. ''Her mother admitted it. Now DJ wants to get to know him. In fact, she's invited him for barbecue tonight at the house.''

''You're kidding?'' Chuck stared at him. ''You're *not* kidding, are you?''

''No, I'm not.''

"Can you find a way to be there?"

"I'm already there. I'm cooking while DJ talks to Galloway."

"You're *what?*" Chuck laughed in disbelief, but he sobered almost immediately. "What's going on with you?"

"Nothing." Adam had intended to reassure him, but even he could tell his answer had come too quickly.

Chuck leaned back in his seat and groaned aloud. "Don't tell me you're attracted to her! Hell, Adam. You know the rules—"

"Quit trying to read something into every move I make, would you? I'm *not* attracted to her. I'm doing my job. I'm keeping an eye on the subject of our investigation, that's all."

"Right." Chuck shook his head and ground the ignition switch a little too far. "I thought you'd sworn off women for good."

"I have."

"Yeah. You barbecue on every assignment."

"You want to tell me a better way to hang around a family barbecue without looking conspicuous?"

Chuck rolled his eyes and jerked his chin toward Adam's door without offering any suggestions. "Get out of here and go back to work. You're wearing me out."

Only too glad to comply, Adam shoved open the door and stood.

Chuck leaned across the seat and stared up at him. "And watch yourself, my friend. I have a feeling you're skating on very thin ice."

Adam didn't even bother to dignify that with an answer. He slammed the door and stalked away from

Chuck's car, but he didn't feel a whole lot better than he had when he'd arrived.

What he'd said to Chuck about DJ should have been the truth, but he was more attracted to her than he cared to admit, and far more worried about her safety than he'd let on.

KEEPING ONE EYE on DJ and Larry Galloway across the deck, Adam sprinkled lighter fluid over the charcoal, struck a match and tossed it into the grill. Flames leaped into the air, forcing him to step back quickly.

He cursed under his breath and told himself to pay more attention to his immediate task. But he hated taking his eyes off Galloway for even a minute.

DJ sat on a lawn chair facing Galloway. She wore a long denim jumper with a crisp white blouse and those god-awful army boots with thick white socks. She'd pulled her hair up with some sort of clip that let several wisps spill back to her shoulders. She looked young and beautiful and entirely too vulnerable to be at the mercy of scum like Galloway.

Adam couldn't see Galloway's face or hear the conversation, but he tracked it by watching DJ's responses. She darted glances over the deck's rail at Marissa playing with Holly on the lawn, and she responded to Galloway's comments with a tight smile, a tiny laugh or a worried frown.

Adam willed the coals to catch quickly so he could rejoin her. He wanted to hear everything Galloway said. He needed names of current associates in case Galloway was spending time with known criminals. He needed to know if Galloway owned a weapon or planned something illegal. Anything could slip out in casual conversation.

Sending Galloway back to prison wouldn't spare DJ what she had to face while she adjusted to suddenly having a father she had never suspected existed, but it just might spare her from being hurt by Galloway's future actions.

Checking the coals again, Adam convinced himself they were burning well enough to be left alone and lowered the lid on the grill. He crossed the deck and dropped into a chair beside DJ's. "We'll be ready to cook in a minute. How do you like your burgers, Mr. Galloway?"

"Rare. And you might as well call me Larry. You're making me feel old."

DJ crossed her legs and managed to look graceful doing it, in spite of the boots. "If you're taking orders, make mine medium and a little better done for Marissa."

"Got it."

"I was just starting to tell Devon about a vacation her mother and me took before she was born. Laura musta been a few years older than Marissa, there." Galloway leaned back in his chair and smiled at some memory. "We drove down to Page, Arizona. Have you ever been there?"

DJ shook her head, but Adam nodded and said, "Once."

Galloway gave a little laugh. "I had a job down there, so I let Chrissy and Laura come with me. We did that town up right, I can tell you. I took Chrissy out every night and bought Laura just about everything her heart desired. Your mother loved that trip, Devon. Absolutely loved it."

DJ smiled softly, but Adam knew she wanted answers to basic questions, not just pretty memories.

"Did she ever tell you about the time we decided to go dog sleddin'?"

"No," DJ said.

Adam forced himself not to speak, but surely the idiot remembered that Christina hadn't told DJ anything. Not even that Galloway existed.

Galloway laughed again and lifted one ankle across his knee. "Funniest story you'll ever hear," he said, and launched into a tale about a dog sled and a pack of malamute puppies.

Adam watched DJ's face. No one could miss the wistfulness there, the longing or the occasional flash of envy when Galloway talked about something she'd missed. No doubt about it, the man was winning her over.

And why not? He *was* her father. No matter what choices he'd made during his lifetime, no matter how hard Christina Prescott tried to undo it, that fact would never change.

"So there Laura was," Galloway said, "running alongside of those pups and falling down all over herself—you know how damned clumsy she is—and those dogs just sat down in the snow and watched that poor girl run." He laughed hard enough to bring tears to his eyes. "Your mother, though. She didn't think it was nearly as funny as I did."

If Adam read DJ's expression right, she didn't think it was funny, either.

Galloway took a moment to wipe his eyes and stop laughing, then turned his attention to Adam. "Do you know her? My ex?"

"Slightly," he lied.

"She can fly off the handle quicker than any woman I ever knew before or since. You didn't inherit her temper, did you, Devon?"

"I don't know," she admitted. "Maybe. You've got to remember, Mom's passionate. That's why she's so good at what she does."

Suddenly sober, Galloway nodded. "I know what she's like. We were together awhile."

DJ leaned forward in her chair. "What happened?"

Galloway looked confused. "When?"

"Between you and Mom. What happened?"

Shaking his head, Galloway pushed to his feet. "Usual stuff, I guess. She got tired of me." He clapped Adam on the shoulder and headed toward the barbecue. "Them coals must be about ready. You want me to do the cooking?"

"No, that's okay. You stay and talk to DJ. I'm sure she has a million questions for you."

Galloway acted as if he hadn't heard. "I'm quite a hand with a grill. I'll fix you up the best burgers you've ever had. Guaranteed."

The man was obviously trying to change the subject to avoid discussing his marriage to Christina Prescott in any but the most general terms.

DJ must have sensed his reluctance to talk about it. She forced a thin smile. "Go ahead. I need to check on Marissa, anyway." Without waiting for a response, she walked to the edge of the deck. Marissa climbed up the rose terrace and ducked under the rail to join her.

Acutely aware of DJ's disappointment and more than a little annoyed with Galloway for causing it, Adam watched her for several seconds, then followed Galloway to the grill.

Galloway grabbed a hot pad and nodded in the direction DJ had gone. "How long have you two been together?"

Adam hesitated before answering. The idea of letting Galloway believe he and DJ were building a life together tempted him. Galloway might be less anxious to take advantage of DJ if he thought someone else had a stake in her future. But if he lied now, the story would probably come back to haunt him. "Actually, I'm just staying in the basement for a while."

Galloway's brows shot up. "Then you're not a couple?"

"No. DJ's mother arranged for me to stay here." No lie there.

Galloway squinted at him through a cloud of barbecue smoke. "What for?"

"Research."

"What kind of research?"

"I'm a writer."

Galloway pressed grease from a burger and watched the flame leap. "A writer," he said at last, but his voice held a strong note of derision. "What do you write?"

"Crime novels. Police procedurals."

Galloway's expression tightened. "Really?"

Adam nodded. "Yeah. I don't suppose you know anything about that."

"Nope," Galloway said quickly. "Sorry."

"You don't know anybody who's ever been arrested, do you? I'm trying to find out about the incarceration process here in Utah from the prisoner's viewpoint."

Something flickered in Galloway's eyes, but it died out again. "Sorry." He pressed grease from another burger and glanced toward DJ. "She turned out real nice, didn't she?" He lowered the grill's lid again and helped himself to a handful of vegetables from the relish tray. "Who'd ever have thought I'd have a kid who'd make good like this? Her own business. Her own house. I'm real proud of her."

"She's something," Adam agreed. And far more unique and wonderful than a man like Galloway could appreciate.

Galloway popped a piece of cauliflower into his mouth and chewed thoughtfully for several seconds. "This is a dream come true, you know that? Thirty years I've waited for this. A chance to set things straight. A chance to find my daughter and make my family whole again." He almost looked sincere. Almost.

"What did happen to keep you apart?"

A shadow flicked across Galloway's face, but he met Adam's gaze with clear, bright eyes. "Her mother's a vengeful woman—don't let anybody tell you different."

Adam moved in front of the grill and spread barbecue sauce on the burgers. "So, where have you been all these years? Why did it take you so long to track DJ down?" He met Galloway's gaze innocently and waited, but he didn't expect Galloway to answer. He'd dodge the question and run away—just as he always did.

"Here and there. Doing a bit of this and that." Just as Adam had expected, he turned away and started toward DJ.

No doubt about it, Galloway didn't intend to discuss his past. Not with DJ, and certainly not with him.

Adam kept an eye on Galloway as he made his way

across the deck, wrapped an arm around DJ's shoulder and reached out to ruffle Marissa's hair. But when Marissa pulled away from his touch and Galloway's expression changed subtly, Adam couldn't fight his growing uneasiness any longer. He didn't trust Galloway. The man had some reason for being here, and he was working so hard to keep it hidden, Adam's instincts told him it couldn't be good.

Whatever had brought Galloway here, Adam would find out eventually.

No matter what Chuck ordered him to do from here on out, he wouldn't leave DJ and Marissa alone. Christina Prescott might want to take her secret to the grave, but Adam *had* to learn Galloway's story if he hoped to protect them. And he wouldn't rest until Galloway was out of their lives.

DJ RESTED HER ELBOWS on the picnic table and watched Larry take another hamburger from the serving tray. He seemed content, happy to be here and oblivious to the emotions clashing within her.

Marissa had long ago abandoned the table for the lawn and a game of fetch with Holly. Adam worked on the other side of the deck, dousing coals and scraping the grill.

Larry swiped at his mouth with a paper towel and smiled around his food. "This is mighty good."

Was it? DJ hadn't been able to swallow a single bite, and her anxiety seemed to increase with each passing minute.

She brushed her hair from her eyes and folded her hands on the table in front of her. She had a moment alone with her father; she couldn't ask for a better opportunity to satisfy her curiosity. But how could she bring up the only subject she wanted to discuss when he seemed unwilling to talk about it?

He stuffed another bite into his mouth and chewed happily until he realized she wanted something from him. Swallowing quickly, he met her gaze. "Is something wrong?"

"We need to talk."

He looked baffled, but he put down his burger and nodded for her to go ahead. "Okay. Shoot."

"I know you don't want to talk about the past, but I need to know what happened between you and Mom. Why did you leave?"

Larry picked at a small pile of potato-chip crumbs on his plate—a nervous gesture that DJ didn't miss. He tipped his head and shrugged. "I don't know. I guess we weren't meant for each other."

DJ waited for him to continue, but he picked up the burger and took another bite, as if he thought his answer would suffice.

It didn't even begin to answer all her questions. "But you—" She broke off and started again. "What about me? Why didn't you come back?"

"I didn't know where you were."

"Did you look?"

"Of course I did. All the time." He reached for an olive from the vegetable tray and popped it into his mouth.

She reminded herself that he didn't understand how she felt. He hadn't been presented with a daughter he'd never known about. Maybe she was expecting too much too soon. Maybe she should relax and get to know him slowly. But patience had never been one of her strong points. She needed answers.

"I'm confused," she told him. "I feel lost. I need

to know about you and Mom. I need to know about *me*."

Larry pondered her words, then pushed his plate away. "All right. I'll tell you what I can."

She closed her eyes in relief, then faced him again and asked, "Why did you leave?"

He shrugged again. "Chrissy and I were different. She needed stability. She needed a house and a car. The same neighborhood, the same school for Laura. But I couldn't stand living that way. I wanted to move around. To learn about new places and things." His voice had risen steadily; now he dropped it and paused. "I guess the bottom line was, we couldn't have what we wanted and stay together."

"So you left."

"I suppose you could say that."

Yes, DJ thought, she supposed she could. A twinge of bitterness zinged through her heart.

Larry must have sensed it because he smiled softly. "I expected we'd stay friends." He paused and allowed himself a wry grin. "Well, maybe not *friends*, but I thought we'd both have a say in raising you. I expected we'd put aside our differences and even do things together once in a while so you didn't have to grow up thinking we hated each other." He looked away and added, "That's a horrible feeling—never seeing your parents in the same room. Hearing one say hateful things about the other. I didn't want that for you. But the minute my back was turned, Chrissy ran. And she's spent all this time hiding you from me."

DJ pondered that for a few seconds. The story sounded believable, but it didn't match the few things her mother had said. "When I asked Mom about you the other night, she said she'd done everything to protect me."

Larry barked a laugh and amusement danced in his eyes. "Did she? From who? *Me?*"

"I don't know," DJ hedged. "She wouldn't give me details."

Larry touched her chin and smiled—a gesture she should have found comforting and familiar. But his touch was that of a stranger.

She searched his face for something that would spark recognition. A feature they shared. An expression or a mannerism. But she found only her own curiosity reflected in his eyes.

He dropped his hand and glanced across the patio at Adam, still intent upon the grill. "Your mom's a good woman in a lot of ways," he said at last. "But she has a real big imagination, and she lets it run wild."

"Then you don't know what she meant?"

Larry laughed sadly. "No. But that isn't unusual. Not between Chrissy and me. I never could make sense of her half the time."

"Did you love her?"

He glanced at her unhappily. "Of course I did."

"Will you tell me about it?"

His expression clouded. "What good will it do to dredge up the past? There was a lot of hurt involved, and it's taken me years to put what your mother did behind me."

"What my mother did?" DJ pulled back a little and stared at him. She'd been under the impression that Larry was at the root of the problem. "What did she do?"

"That's not important anymore."

DJ's temper flared. "Why won't you tell me?"

"It might change the way you feel. Besides, it's all in the past. Better forgotten."

"It's my past, too," she reminded him. "I can't forget what I don't know."

He shook his head, obviously intending to let the matter drop.

"I don't even know who you are. What you did. How you and Mom met. When did you get married? What happened the day I was born? And what have you been doing for the past thirty years?"

A muscle in Larry's jaw tightened, but he kept his expression soft. "I don't want to hold on to the past. Raking everything up again won't do any good for anyone. All that matters is that we've found each other, so let's start over from here, okay? It'll be better that way, take my word for it." He chucked her under the chin again and winked. Without giving her a chance to respond, he pushed away from the table, ducked under the deck's rail and made his way through the rose garden to the lawn below.

DJ stared after him, too stunned to speak. She wanted to run after him and demand that he talk to her. She wanted to shout that it wasn't okay to turn around and walk away or to leave her with all her questions unanswered. But she'd seen the determination in his eyes, and she knew she'd be fighting a losing battle.

Marissa tossed her ball to Holly, but Larry stepped between them and caught the ball in the air. He held it out to Marissa, but she was still too shy with him. She backed away.

If DJ had been a different type of woman, she might have been content to wait for Larry to tell her what she needed to know. But unresolved issues drove her crazy, and questions ate at her until she found the answers.

Jeff had hated that about her. He'd expected her to relinquish control to him and to be content doing it. *Take my word for it,* he'd said more than once. *Trust me.*

But DJ had never been able to do that. She still couldn't. Not even for her father.

CHAPTER SEVEN

ADAM WATCHED Galloway walk away from DJ and cursed under his breath at the expression on her face. Replacing the grill on the barbecue, he crossed the deck to her and tried to look casual and unconcerned. "Well? Did you find out what you wanted to know?" He straddled the bench and sat beside her.

"No."

"He didn't tell you anything?"

"He said that he used to love my mother." She started to look away, then immediately turned back, holding up her index finger as if she were about to make a point. "He *did* say that he doesn't see any point in holding on to the past."

"Well, that was helpful."

She didn't smile.

"So now what?"

"Now I'm going to find out what happened between them."

She sounded more confident than Adam would have expected. He leaned an elbow on the table and propped his chin on his fist. "How are you going to do that?"

This time, she smiled. "I'm going to talk to my sister, Laura, when she and her husband get back from vacation."

A tiny flicker of admiration rose in his chest, but

he pushed it away. He wasn't being paid to admire her. "You think she knows anything?"

DJ met his gaze, and he could see the determination and excitement in hers. "She *must*. She was there."

"And you think she'll tell you?"

DJ nodded. "She'll tell me."

Adam wished he could share her confidence, but he couldn't help thinking that if Laura was going to tell DJ anything, she'd have done so already. He opened his mouth to say so, then clamped it shut again. Voicing his doubts would only hurt DJ, and she'd be hurt enough by the time this was all over.

He looked away and watched Galloway toss a stick for the dog to fetch. Holly scampered across the lawn, and Galloway looked at Marissa as if he expected her to smile or laugh or show her approval in some other way.

But Marissa held back.

Galloway held out a hand for her to hold, but Marissa shook her head and backed away. Adam watched, wary and ready to jump if Galloway did anything even slightly questionable.

"I know I asked you this before," he said softly. "But what if you find out something you'd rather not know?"

DJ laughed without humor. "What wouldn't I want to know?"

"I don't know."

"No matter what happened between them, I want to know about it. I want to know why my mother felt justified in hiding my father from me all these years. Why he left. Why he stayed away—" She broke off and shook her head quickly. Her eyes glinted with tears, and Adam's heart softened.

He reached a hand across the table and touched her fingertips gently. "Then I hope you find out."

She met his gaze, but the sadness in her eyes made his throat constrict. "Do you?" she asked.

"Yes." He caressed her hand with his own. Her fingers felt like rose petals and the top of her hand like a newborn's skin. His pulse beat faster and he had trouble swallowing. "Yes," he repeated uselessly.

She held his gaze for what felt like forever. He couldn't have made himself look away even if he'd wanted to. Everything about her seemed designed to pull him under her spell—her eyes, her lips, her hair, her hands.

He wanted to feel her hands touching him—running along his shoulders, trailing down his chest. He wanted to feel her softness pressed against him. He wanted to bury his face in her hair, her neck, her breasts, and never emerge.

He could hear the sound of his breathing—ragged and harsh—but he couldn't seem to pull himself back under control. He ached for her. He wanted her.

Everything he felt must have been written on his face, but she didn't look away. She held him with her eyes and caressed him with her gaze. He could kiss her without any effort at all—he could lean slightly forward and let his lips touch hers. But he wouldn't want to stop with one kiss.

Somewhere, far away, a child's laugh punctuated the evening air, then sounded again a split second before Marissa launched herself into DJ's lap and shattered the spell.

Adam sucked in a sharp breath and looked away. As Marissa clung to DJ's neck and whispered something he couldn't make out, he watched Galloway walking across the lawn toward them, and the last of his desire faded away.

Standing quickly, he started to gather the remaining dishes from the table, trying to look as if he hadn't almost thrown discretion—and his career—to the wind. He cursed himself silently for letting the woman get to him that way.

He'd vowed never to let a woman get close to him again. The cost was simply too great. Yet here he was, contemplating a kiss with a woman he'd been hired to protect. And if he'd kissed her, what would have happened then?

DJ wasn't the type of woman for a casual sexual romp. She'd been hurt far too much already. She needed love and commitment. Passion and tenderness. Trust.

Adam growled deep in his throat and shoved a handful of paper plates into the garbage. *Trust.* There wasn't any such thing. He'd had enough of empty commitments and the demands on his heart that came with them. He'd learned through experience that trust and love were not the same thing, and he didn't want anything to do with either. Not now. Not ever.

DJ FUMBLED WITH the coffeemaker and tried to focus on her task. She'd stayed up far too late the night before, and for nothing. No matter what questions she'd asked, no matter what Adam had done to lead the conversation into the past, Larry had remained stubbornly evasive.

She'd gone to bed tired, frustrated and far too aware of Adam McAllister for her own good. He'd almost kissed her—she knew it—and she'd wanted it.

But Marissa had chosen that moment to run from Larry, and DJ still couldn't decide if she wanted to hug Marissa for having saved her from making a mistake or cry at the interruption. Another few seconds alone with Adam and she would have thrown herself at him. And in her dreams last night she'd done exactly that. This morning, with Marissa sitting two feet away at the kitchen table, DJ felt more grounded.

Drawing in a steadying breath, she reminded herself that any woman would react the way she did to a man like Adam under these circumstances. He was here when she needed him—like a guardian angel. Unfortunately, her thoughts were anything but angelic.

Surely he'd seen the desire written on her face. He must know she'd almost succumbed to the moment. But she couldn't let herself do that. She couldn't let her frustration, her anger or her fears drive her into Adam's arms. *If* she ever became involved with a man again—*if* she decided to take that chance with Adam—she would have to be certain she made her decision based on love and respect, not need. Until then, she had to remain in control. No matter *what*.

If she were smart, she'd avoid him whenever possible. She would stay out of his path and hope he'd return the favor. She would stop burdening him with her personal problems and let him get back to work on his book. She'd already kept him from it too long.

She poured water from the carafe into the coffeemaker's reservoir just as a board creaked on the landing behind her. She closed her eyes and willed her heart to stop racing. She steadied herself with one hand on the counter and turned to face him. And she told herself to be friendly—nothing more.

He wore those faded jeans that fit so well, a soft brown Henley shirt and no shoes. He crossed the room to stand in front of her. Close. Too close. She could smell his soap, his aftershave—the mint of his toothpaste, for heaven's sake. Did she really feel his breath on her cheek or did she only wish she could? Some emotion seemed to simmer just below the surface, nearly hidden behind the cool gray of his eyes.

She should know better than to let herself feel this way. She'd learned her lesson with Jeff. Jeff had been all sex appeal, and it was only later she'd discovered he had very little depth. She'd paid a steep price for falling in love with him.

She'd almost lost herself in her marriage. Jeff had expected her to change so much, she'd never been certain why he'd married her until almost the end. Until he'd shouted at her for showing up to meet him for lunch in jeans and a sweater.

He'd said ugly things that day. He'd expected more from her, he'd said. He'd expected a little class from Christina Prescott's daughter. And the realization that he'd married her because of her mother's name had killed what little love DJ still felt for him.

Adam seemed to have a great deal more depth of character than Jeff had ever dreamed of, but she'd learned the hard way to beware of men with such magnetism. And she would never again get involved with someone who cared who her mother was. No matter how she tried, she couldn't forget it was Adam's friendship with Christina Prescott that had brought him here.

Marissa looked up from the table and tried to smile, but her cheeks bulged with milk and made the smile lopsided. Her Utah Jazz cap lay abandoned on its crown; a rag doll sat on the table next to it. She swallowed and wiped the milk mustache from her upper lip with her sleeve. "Can we have pancakes, Mommy? P'ease?"

DJ handed her a napkin and looked over her shoulder at Adam. In spite of her resolve, she couldn't ignore him. "Would you like to join us for pancakes?"

He leaned one shoulder against the side of the refrigerator and shrugged casually. "Fine with me. I'll eat anything."

"Coffee?"

He started to nod, but Marissa interrupted. "Hot chocolate," she said seriously. "It's lots better than coffee."

When his lips curved into a gentle smile, DJ caught her breath. That smile transformed him.

"Hot chocolate, then," he said, and joined Marissa at the table. "How's the milk?"

Marissa grinned at him. "It's good." And to prove it, she took another huge swallow, then studied him for a moment. "Do you have any kids?"

His smile faltered. "No, I don't."

Marissa wiped her face with a napkin. "Why not?"

DJ had longed to ask the same question, but she'd managed to hide her curiosity. "Marissa—"

To DJ's surprise, Adam didn't seem to mind the intrusion into his personal life. "My ex-wife didn't think I was home enough to be a good daddy, and she didn't want to take care of kids all by herself."

Marissa's brows knit. "Why weren't you home?"

DJ busied herself with the pancake mix and the griddle, and pretended not to listen to their conversation, but she hung on every word. She wanted to know everything about Adam he was willing to reveal.

"Because my job—" he glanced at DJ "—the job I had then—took too much time."

"You could have kids now," Marissa reasoned.

Adam shook his head. "We're not married anymore."

"Oh." Marissa nodded as if that explained everything. "Are you 'aborced?"

He smiled sadly. "Divorced? Yes."

"So's my mom."

"Yes, I know." He lifted his eyes to meet DJ's.

She flushed, embarrassed at having been caught watching him. "Lots of people get divorced."

"You could have kids anyway," Marissa said, patting his hand quickly and squirming from her chair. "Lots of daddies don't live with their kids. *Mine* doesn't, does he, Mommy?"

DJ hated discussing Jeff with Marissa. Marissa didn't need to know how upset Jeff had been to learn about DJ's pregnancy or how concerned he'd been by what he saw as their daughter's intrusion into their lives. Or that he'd quickly grown tired of diapers, bottles and early morning feedings. So she only shook her head and said, "No."

"See?" Marissa demanded.

Adam nodded, and a ghost of his smile darted across his face again. "Yes, I do."

"Don't you want kids? Don't you like 'em?"

"Very much, but I wouldn't be able to see them much, and I'd miss them a lot."

"Just like my daddy misses me, huh, Mommy?"

DJ smiled. "Just like that." And she excused the tiny lie in the interests of Marissa's peace of mind.

Marissa hummed softly for a few seconds, then her face brightened. "I know what we could do. You don't have any kids, and I don't have a daddy who lives here. So *you* could be my make-believe daddy. Couldn't he, Mommy?"

Where did the child come up with such ideas? DJ tried to laugh as she looked at Adam. "No, Marissa."

Adam didn't appear offended. Instead, she saw amusement lurking behind his eyes. "I don't know," he said slowly. "What exactly would a make-believe daddy have to do?"

Marissa settled her cap on her head and shrugged. "Just dad things."

"Like fix your bike and help you train Holly and stuff like that?"

She nodded. "And ride without training wheels."

"The important stuff," Adam said.

"Marissa—" DJ warned again.

But Marissa ignored her. "Yeah. The 'portant stuff." She reached for her doll and dragged it across the table, nearly knocking over her glass.

Adam caught it and settled it out of her way, then nodded as if he found the whole idea fascinating.

"Stuff Mommy can't do 'cause she has to work and Brittany doesn't want to."

DJ left the bowl on the counter and crossed to the table in an attempt to make Marissa pay attention. "You can't ask Adam to be your make-believe dad."

Marissa's eyes clouded. "Why not?"

When Adam looked up at DJ, he mimicked Marissa's pout. "Yeah. Why not?"

"Because," DJ said, staring straight into Marissa's eyes so she could ignore Adam's, "Adam has to work, too."

He waved her concern away with one hand. "I've got plenty of time to be a make-believe dad—as long as you don't mind."

How could she possibly answer that? Yes, she minded. She wanted to accept his offer more than anything. Marissa had never reacted so well to a man in her life, and DJ knew her daughter could only benefit from the association. But she wanted to spend *less* time with Adam—not more. She wanted to forget the sound of his voice and the color of his eyes, not to find more ways to ingrain them in her mind. She wanted to forget the way she felt in his arms, not torment herself with memories and long for more.

He stood and placed his hands on her shoulders. His smile nearly undid her. "I'm a good guy," he said. "Trustworthy. I get along with my nieces and nephew. I've got references—" His face sobered. "I'm realistic enough to know why you're worried, but I won't help Marissa with anything unless you or Brittany are there. And I won't mind doing a few things with her. It'll give me something to do with my days."

He'd answered almost every concern she could think of, but she couldn't give in. "You have work to do," she reminded him.

"It'll get done."

Marissa slid from her chair and tugged on DJ's pant leg. "Say yes, Mommy. P'ease?"

DJ's common sense warred with the hope on Marissa's face. "I can't believe I'm even considering this," she said. Then, with a thin smile and a tiny nod, she agreed. "All right. But I'm not even certain I know how you two talked me into this."

For the first time since his arrival, Adam laughed

aloud. Every nerve in DJ's body tingled when she heard the deep bass tone, and her senses soared when she looked into his incredible eyes. She knew, with dreadful certainty, that she was being pulled into something beyond her control. But at that moment, she couldn't honestly have said that she wanted to escape.

ADAM PECKED OUT a few words on the laptop computer, glanced up at the screen with a frown and deleted half of what he'd typed. He'd been working at the kitchen table for an hour, and he'd thought he was getting the hang of the stupid machine—until he looked back at what he'd done.

He'd forgotten to hit the damned F9 key to move to another box in the report form, and he'd inserted the answers for three boxes into one. Muttering to himself, he removed the extra answers, pressed F9 and started again.

"Whatcha doin'?"

Marissa's voice startled him. He hadn't even heard her come into the room. Some security. The officer on duty caught off guard by a four-year-old.

He glanced at her and smiled. "I'm working."

She climbed onto the chair next to his and tried to peek at the screen. "On your book?" She'd obviously dressed herself this morning—purple sweater, red jeans, bright blue high-top tennis shoes with a Tweety Bird appliqué. Definitely her mother's daughter.

He bit back a smile. "Yes. On my book."

She nodded thoughtfully and watched him for a few seconds while he hunted for the right keys. "Grandma types faster than you."

"I'm sure she does."

"And she doesn't have all those funny lines on her books."

Adam felt pretty certain she was right about that, too. He pressed the key to save what he'd done and lowered the screen to keep her from noticing anything else. "What are you up to this morning?"

"I'm going to Brittany's school with her. She has a 'portant paper to sign."

"I see. And you need to help her sign it?"

Marissa nodded. "I think so. Will you help me ride my bike when I come back?"

He pretended to give her request some consideration. "All right."

Brittany's hurried footsteps sounded in the hallway just before she came through the door. She frowned at Marissa and held out a hooded sweater. "So this is where you ran off to. You'd better hurry or I'll be late."

Marissa slid from her chair. "I'm helping Adam write his book."

Brittany met Adam's gaze with a knowing one of her own. She'd obviously heard more of his conversation with Christina Prescott than she should have. But if Christina didn't care, Adam wouldn't make waves.

He gave Marissa's shoulders a gentle nudge. "You'd better hurry, squirt."

Marissa looked up at him with huge eyes full of hope. "Can I stay here with you?"

Brittany worked the sweater over Marissa's head and helped her get her arms into the proper holes. "No, you can't. He's working. You're stuck with me. Now hurry."

Adam glanced at the clock. Only eleven-thirty.

He'd have half an hour alone in the house before DJ came home for lunch, and he ought to take advantage of the time to check in. He hadn't called in three days, and he knew Chuck would be chomping at the bit for a report.

He ruffled Marissa's hair and leaned forward to tie her hood. "You want me to help you with your bike, don't you?"

She nodded.

"Well, if you go now, I'll help when you come back, okay?"

"P'omise?"

He smiled and touched the tip of her nose with his finger. "I promise. Now hurry, before Brittany gets upset with both of us and your mom decides not to take you to the zoo this weekend."

"You're coming with us to the zoo. You helped with the roses."

"That's right," Adam said. "I did."

"And we can see all the animals. And have cotton candy. And popcorn. And you can give me a piggyback ride, too."

Adam cocked an eyebrow at her in an expression he already knew would earn a giggle.

She didn't let him down, and her laugh made him smile in response. "Will you?" she asked. "Give me a piggyback ride? P'ease?"

He shook his head in mock exasperation. "I suppose. Now go."

She beamed up at him, allowing a tiny flicker of triumph to show in her eyes, then pivoted away and raced down the hall toward the front door.

Adam smiled to himself. He'd been had—by a four-year-old. He wouldn't even **bother** to deny it. In fact, he'd been on the losing end of the battle with his defenses since the minute Marissa and DJ appeared in his life.

He waited until he heard the front door close, then paced to the telephone and punched in the number for Chuck's office.

Chuck answered on the second ring. "Tobler."

"Chuck. It's Adam."

"Where in the hell have you been?" Chuck demanded. "You're supposed to call me once a day."

"I've been busy with daddy things."

"*Daddy* things? What do you mean, 'daddy things'?"

"Things fathers do for their children," Adam explained.

"I know what a daddy is," Chuck snarled. "What I *don't* know is why you're pretending to be one."

"Because Marissa needs somebody to help her and DJ's too busy at the store. Besides, it's a good way to keep an eye on them."

"So, have you got anything new on Galloway?"

Adam shook his head, as if Chuck could see him from halfway across the city. "Not yet. Anything new on your end?"

"Nothing. Just make sure you're there when trouble starts and not playing house."

"Don't worry," Adam snapped. "Everything's under control. I'll be there no matter what. I have no intention of letting anything happen to DJ and Marissa.

"What's the matter with you?" Chuck asked. "Bad night or something?"

"No. Nothing like that."

"Then why are you in such a lousy mood?"

Adam couldn't tell him he'd spent the night thinking about DJ. Or that he'd spent more time in a week thinking about children of his own than he ever had. Or how tired he was of living alone. Or how desperately he needed to tell DJ the truth.

He could almost feel Chuck's suspicion through the wire, and they played a waiting game, each determined to make the other speak first.

"Keep your eyes and ears open," Chuck said at last. "And be ready for anything. If Galloway hurts DJ or Marissa, you're the one who'll pay for it—I guarantee it."

In more ways than one, Adam thought. But he said only, "I'm not going to let Galloway hurt them."

Chuck made a noise on the other end. "I heard Christina Prescott called you the other day. What happened with that?"

"She just wanted to hear my version of DJ's meeting with Galloway. She was ready to leave the conference and fly home, but I think I calmed her down a bit. At least, she hasn't shown up here yet."

"No, but she's been on the phone with Dodge every day. Sounds like she's a basket case. Are you sure Galloway hasn't done anything we can get him for?"

"I'm sure. Believe me, I'm not going to hesitate to call SLPD the minute he crosses the line."

Chuck spent a few seconds digesting that. "You think he will?"

Adam could be honest with Chuck. "I'm sure of it. I can see it in his eyes. And I'll tell you one thing for sure—if Christina Prescott did come home and show up here, he'd slip up in a heartbeat. He's one angry SOB."

"Just keep an eye on him," Chuck said, as if Adam needed to be told.

"I will." Adam tried to keep the irritation from his voice, but he knew a little must have come through.

"Good," Chuck snapped back. "We understand each other perfectly. Now, get back to work." And he hung up before Adam could say another word.

Adam slammed down the receiver, aware for the first time of the tension in his shoulders, the tightness in his jaw and the stiffness in his neck. Walking slowly across the kitchen, he gripped the window frame with both hands and wondered how he'd come to care so much about DJ and Marissa in such a short time. He'd met women in the two years since his divorce, but none that had made his heart yearn to fall in love again.

He stared out the window for a long time, but he didn't see anything until several minutes had passed. Slowly he became aware of the trees along the street and the cars in the parking lot at DJ's store.

She would be there, he knew. Dressed in some ridiculous getup and those god-awful boots. If he went to her now, she'd listen and ease his concerns with those deep brown eyes of hers. Without saying a word, she would make him believe everything would work out.

Closing the blind, as if blocking out the scene could remove DJ from his mind, he turned away. The last thing he needed was another woman in his life. He'd lost too much during his marriage to Victoria, and life with DJ wouldn't be any different.

She would want someone steady for Marissa. Someone she could count on to be home in the evenings and do daddy things. But he couldn't offer any guarantees.

Look at him now. He'd left home at a moment's notice to take this assignment, and he had no idea when he'd be free to go home again. DJ deserved much more than he could offer, and it would be unfair to lead her to believe otherwise.

He walked back to the table, lifted the screen on the computer and tapped the space bar. He would work on his damned report and he'd keep his eyes open whenever Galloway was around. And somehow he'd find a way to stop wishing things could be different with DJ.

CHAPTER EIGHT

ADAM WALKED SLOWLY behind Marissa's wobbling bicycle as she guided it down the sidewalk toward the corner. The sun had dropped low in the western sky, shadows fell across the concrete and the early-evening air had grown almost cold.

He'd been ready to call it quits and go back inside until DJ had come home from work a few minutes ago. Marissa had gotten her second wind, and even Adam had found the prospect of practicing for another half hour more interesting. After all, DJ needed to see what Marissa had learned.

When they reached the corner, he helped Marissa turn her bike around so she could start back toward her mother. The child gripped the handlebars and concentrated on steering back over an uneven spot on the sidewalk, then beamed at him.

He smiled back. He liked making her happy.

She turned away and waved to DJ. "Mommy, look!"

DJ pushed to her feet and started down the steps. "I'm watching, sweetheart."

Adam tried not to stare, but each time he saw DJ she seemed different. And each time, he had the sensation that he was getting his first glimpse of the real woman. At first, the sensation had bothered him. But he'd decided over the past week that it would take years to understand all the facets of her personality. He wished he had years to spend.

Tonight she wore jeans and sneakers and a long white sweatshirt that fell past her hips. Her dark hair reflected the last rays of the evening sun, and her sudden smile brought on the surge of longing he'd learned to anticipate each time he saw her.

Marissa slid down from her bike and raced toward her mother before Adam fully realized she'd stopped moving. "Did you see, Mommy? I rode all by myself."

He caught the bicycle an instant before it crashed to the sidewalk and watched while DJ wrapped her arms around her daughter and swung her into the air.

"I sure did. You're doing great, sweetie. Just great." She kissed Marissa's cheek loudly.

Squealing with delight, Marissa grinned at Adam for half a second, then started wriggling from DJ's grasp.

"She's a natural," he said. "A few more practice sessions and she'll be riding on her own."

DJ lowered Marissa to the ground, and the girl hurtled herself at him without warning. Wrapping her arms around his knees in a generous hug, she nearly knocked him over. She had more energy than Adam ever remembered seeing in one package before, but her joy in life delighted him. He'd found more pleasure in simple things during the past week than he had in the past five years.

He laughed as she released him, and tousled her hair.

"Can I ride once more?" she pleaded.

Adam would have let her, but DJ shook her head. "I think you've put Adam through his paces long enough for one night. He has work to do, remember? Besides, we've got a big day tomorrow, and you need to get to bed early tonight.''

Marissa almost pouted, but then she brightened again. ''Can I ride tomorrow?''

''Yes, if we get back from the zoo early enough. Now, put your bike away and feed Holly her supper.''

Marissa danced away again. ''Okay.''

''Right now,'' DJ warned.

As if on cue, the dog bounded out of a hedge and wagged the rear half of her furry black body at Marissa. The child laughed and dropped to her knees, wrapping her arms around the wriggling animal. ''Are you hung'y?''

Holly yipped.

''Okay. Come on.'' She started to run away, but DJ called after her.

''Take your bike with you.''

Marissa raced back toward them, gripped the bicycle by its handlebars and guided it around the corner of the house.

Smiling, Adam watched until they'd disappeared from view, then turned back to say something to DJ. But in the half-light of dusk, with the breeze carrying the musky scent she wore across the space between them, the air seemed too close, and he had trouble drawing a steady breath.

DJ smiled up at him. ''Thank you for helping her with her bike. I hope she wasn't too bothersome.''

''Not at all. I'm the one who's getting the best end of this deal.''

She laughed. ''What makes you say that? Are you using it for research?''

''No.'' He heard the gruff note in his voice and

wished he could take the word back. She couldn't know how guilty he felt each time she reminded him of his lie—the lie that might save her.

Her smile faltered a little. "Well, thanks anyway." She turned to walk away, but he didn't want her to go. He didn't want to stand here in the shadows alone.

Without warning, he was filled with an urgent need to belong somewhere. Worse, he wanted to belong here, with the woman standing before him, and the child who wanted him to be her make-believe daddy.

He tried to push the idea away, but he couldn't. He wanted her to stay.

He reached for her. His fingers touched her elbow, and a gentle warmth spread from his fingertips up his arm. He closed his eyes, afraid she'd pull away from him, but she didn't move.

He looked at her again, wishing he could ask her to stay with him, but he couldn't speak. He wasn't good with words. He'd never been able to easily express what he felt. Whenever he tried to say what was in his heart, it came out all wrong. But he needed her company. If only for the moment.

"I didn't mean to offend you," she whispered.

He found his voice. "Offend *me?* I thought it was exactly the opposite."

Her lips curved into a smile, but her eyes revealed a different emotion. Everything about her was open and giving and vulnerable, and he wanted her. He couldn't think about tomorrow or forever. He could only think about tonight.

He reached for her again and slowly pulled her toward him, still half expecting her to draw away. She shivered slightly, then melted against him.

Relieved, he cradled her in his arms. He could feel

the rapid beat of her heart and the softness of her breath through his shirt. She felt so good in his embrace, so right in his arms, the implications frightened him.

Her gaze traveled slowly across his face and silently answered the question he'd been trying to find words to ask. They'd gone too far already for him to walk away without hurting her. And when she found out the truth about him, what would she think then? How could he ever look himself in the eye again, knowing he'd hurt her?

He didn't want to think about it. He didn't want her to see the fear in his eyes, so he dipped his head and touched her lips with his as he'd imagined doing the night of the barbecue. They felt feathery soft beneath his, just as he'd known they would. Her breasts brushed against his chest, robbing him of his next breath, and he waited again for her to pull away.

She didn't.

He deepened the kiss and crushed her against him. All the passion he'd managed to ignore over the past few years erupted within him; all the need he'd been suppressing rose to fill him; all the hunger he'd denied consumed him. And he knew there would be no going back from this moment. He'd given a part of himself to this woman.

He groaned softly in the back of his throat. She responded to the sound, demanding more from the kiss than he'd given so far. The world reeled under his feet as she strained upward and sighed softly into his mouth. He pulled in the sound with his next breath and accepted what she offered in return.

"Hey!" someone shouted.

As if she'd been shot, DJ pulled away from his

embrace and the world screeched to a halt with an almost-audible crash.

"Hey!" Marissa shouted again. "Look who's over there!"

Adam tried to make sense of her words at the same time he cursed himself for giving in to his instinct while Marissa was nearby. How would they ever explain this to her?

To his surprise, she didn't seem interested in them at all. Instead, she pointed to something behind him. "Look!" she insisted again.

Adam looked, half expecting the dog to dart out at him from behind a bush or to drop a stick at his feet. Instead, he realized someone was standing in the deep evening shadows across the street. A second later, he recognized Larry Galloway, and his already fading passion evaporated.

Galloway must have realized they'd noticed him, because he stepped out of the shadows and started across the street. He tried to look casual, as if he'd just arrived, but Adam knew he must have been there a while. Just as he could tell by the ice in his expression that he didn't like what he'd seen.

Adam cursed himself silently and reminded himself once again of his reasons for being here. He'd lost sight of his objective. He'd let desire overshadow his duty.

He still didn't know what Galloway really wanted with DJ and Marissa. It might be true that he wanted nothing more than a chance to know his daughter and granddaughter. But most likely it was more than that. And Adam had exposed DJ and Marissa to needless risk.

Well, he couldn't let it happen again. From here on

in, he would have to ignore DJ's charms and close his heart to Marissa—at least until he knew they were safe from any possible harm. Obviously, he couldn't get emotionally involved and still protect them.

DJ stood beside Adam and struggled to calm her breathing as she watched Larry cross the street. Apprehension and anticipation seemed to war with each other, both in her relationship with Adam and in the idea of Larry Galloway being her father.

A week ago, she'd been so certain of her life, of her goals, of her dreams. Now she didn't even know who she was. From the minute Larry had appeared, she'd even lost herself, and she'd turned to another stranger—Adam—to ground her. She'd kissed him as if her life depended on it. And maybe it did. She just didn't know anymore.

Larry looked older than her mother. And hard, as if his life had taken him down difficult paths. It probably had. If her mother hadn't admitted the truth, DJ would never have believed his story.

She couldn't picture Christina Prescott in love with Larry Galloway. In her wildest dreams, she couldn't imagine the two of them together—even when he was as young and handsome as he'd been in the photograph.

She could sense Adam tensing at her side and realized she could still taste his kiss on her lips and feel the strength of his arms around her. She'd abandoned all reason the instant he'd touched her. She'd given herself to his embrace as if she expected it to go on forever. But the instant she'd pulled away, harsh reality had flooded back over her. How had it happened that two men—two total *strangers*—had so quickly taken over her life?

The instant the question formed, she knew the answer. Her mother. She rubbed her forehead with the tips of her fingers and tried to force away the resentment that filled her when she thought of Christina dashing about Europe while DJ dealt with the fallout of her decisions.

Until a week ago, she'd felt so close to her mother. Now, Christina seemed as much a stranger as Larry and Adam. And instead of running into Adam's arms, DJ should be concentrating on Larry—her *father*. She didn't know yet how she felt about him showing up after all these years. Or what she wanted, now that he had. Or even what she needed him to say or do to make up for all the time he'd been gone.

To her surprise, Larry touched her shoulders lightly when he reached her and pressed a kiss to her cheek. Unaccustomed to the display of affection, she drew back almost without thinking, then forced herself to relax.

"This is a nice surprise," she said with a smile. "I didn't expect to see you tonight."

Larry rolled his eyes. "Are you kidding? Now that I've finally found you, I'm not going to pass up a single chance to spend time with you."

Did that mean he was ready to tell her about the past? She studied his eyes, trying to find the answer there, but he gave nothing away. Instead, he glanced down at Marissa. "What are you doing, little one?"

Marissa buried her face in Adam's leg and refused to answer. Having two men vying for her attention after spending her entire life surrounded by women was obviously too much for the little girl to understand.

She gently touched Marissa's hair and filled the

space left empty by her daughter's refusal to speak. "She's been learning to ride her bike, haven't you, sweetheart?"

Marissa nodded without lifting her face from Adam's leg.

Larry hunkered down to Marissa's level and softened his tone a little. "You know, *I'm* pretty good at riding bikes. Do you want me to show you how?"

DJ silently urged Marissa to do something—to lift her head and smile, to accept Larry's offer, *something* to take away the sting of her rejection.

But the child only shook her head and sidled a step or two away.

Larry inched closer. "I could show you real good."

Marissa shook her head again and clutched the denim of Adam's pant leg with one hand.

DJ moved her hand to touch her daughter's shoulder. "Marissa's a little shy around strangers, but she'll warm up. Give her time."

Larry straightened slowly. His mouth tightened in a scowl and he looked almost challengingly at Adam. DJ knew that Marissa's attachment to Adam hadn't gone unnoticed.

"We're all through riding bikes for tonight, anyway," DJ said quickly. "In fact, we were just about to go inside."

Larry turned his gaze toward her and smoothed the back of his hair with his palm. "Good idea. It's getting cold out here."

As if she could feel Larry's attention waning, Marissa released Adam's pant leg. DJ smiled with relief and told herself again that Marissa just needed time to adjust to having Larry around. They both needed time, and if Larry would only be patient, everything would work out. But when Marissa raised her arms to Adam and Larry's face clouded with anger, DJ knew he wouldn't be content to wait for her daughter's attention as long as Adam was around.

Adam hesitated for an instant, then picked Marissa up. She buried her face in his shoulder and wrapped her tiny arms around his neck.

Larry's scowl deepened, but he turned a thin smile toward DJ. "Mind if I come inside for a while?"

She could see the effort it cost him to look pleasant, but she appreciated the attempt. "Of course not. I just got home from work a few minutes ago, so we haven't eaten yet. Do you want to stay for dinner?"

"Love to." He turned slowly to face Adam and lifted an eyebrow. "Unless *you* mind me hanging around."

Adam shook his head, but he didn't look as if the idea pleased him. "Not at all."

DJ suppressed a groan. Marissa's reaction to Larry would make the evening difficult enough. But two grown men arguing like children over a favorite toy wouldn't make things any easier.

Well, she wouldn't add to the mix. She forced a note of brightness into her voice and clapped her hands. "Good. Why don't I order pizza? Unless someone else is in the mood to cook—?"

To her relief, Adam grinned. "Pizza sounds great to me."

"It's fine with me, too," Larry said.

Marissa turned her face away from Adam's neck and spoke for the first time since Larry's arrival. "*I* like pizza, Mommy."

DJ's hopes rose a notch. "I know you do, sweetheart. Pepperoni, right?"

Adam pulled back and smiled down at Marissa with such a soft expression, DJ's heart melted.

"Pepperoni's all right," he said. "If we can add black olives. What do you think, DJ? Pepperoni and black olives?"

"And mushrooms," she agreed.

Raising one eyebrow in mock horror, Adam looked back down at Marissa. "Mushrooms? She likes *mushrooms?*"

Marissa giggled at the look on his face. "I like 'em, too."

"You do?" He pretended to scowl, which earned even more giggles from Marissa. "Well, all right, then. Pepperoni, black olives and mushrooms." But when he turned to Larry again, the light in his eyes dulled and his teasing expression vanished. "Anything else?"

Larry met the question with a scowl. "I'm allergic to black olives. Can't eat 'em."

He looked so argumentative, DJ wondered briefly whether he had an allergy to black olives or to Adam. At least Adam was making some effort to be pleasant. Larry didn't seem inclined to budge an inch.

DJ refused to let the selection of pizza toppings disintegrate into an argument. "I'll order two large pizzas. One with olives and one without."

Now that Adam had teased her out of her shyness, Marissa seemed more herself. "And we can have leftovers for breakfast, can't we, Mommy?"

"I don't see why not. We should have plenty left."

"Leftover pizza for breakfast?" Adam grinned at Marissa and wriggled his eyebrows. "How did you know that's what I like best in the whole world?"

Marissa giggled. "I didn't, silly. That's what my mommy likes."

Adam's lips curved into a lazy smile that made DJ's heart race again. "You like pizza in the mornings, too?"

She couldn't believe the effect he had on her. The mere sight of him brought her senses to life. The sound of his voice made her heart skip a beat. And even the whispery touch of his hand against hers made her breath catch in her throat. She tried to look away from his gaze and ignore the rising desire to kiss him again, but with no success.

He didn't look away, either. "Warm or cold?"

"What?"

"Do you like your leftover pizza warm or cold?"

"Cold."

Adam winked at her and hoisted Marissa a little farther in his arms. "I'm a cold-pizza man, myself. What about you, Marissa?"

"Cold."

"I knew it. A woman of taste and quality." He grinned at her and chucked Marissa under the chin.

"*Warm,*" Larry said, and the coolness in his voice instantly shattered the spell woven by the heat in Adam's.

For the second time, DJ had to push aside a flash of irritation at Larry's determination to challenge Adam.

Adam didn't seem to notice. "We're not going to have *any* pizza if we don't order it. Right?"

Marissa grinned. "Right."

"All right. Let's go order." He started up the steps toward the front door.

Marissa wriggled from his arms and ran toward the

door. "Will you play a game with me until the food gets here?"

Adam slowed his steps slightly. "What kind of game?"

"I want you to see how Holly chases her ball and how good I can throw it for her." Reaching for his hand, she tugged him through the door.

They looked so natural together that, for just a moment, DJ let herself imagine a life with Adam. Since her divorce, she'd half-jokingly maintained that it would take a very special man to make her willing to give up half her closet space and put up with whiskers in her bathroom sink. For the first time since Jeff had left, she was actually considering both. Or maybe she was doing exactly what she feared most—looking to someone else to make her problems seem smaller. If that was what she was doing, even inadvertently, she had to stop now. Adam was a good man—he deserved to be loved, not used.

She started to follow them into the house, but Larry touched her arm and jerked his head in the opposite direction. "Mind if I ask you a question before we go inside?"

"No. Of course not. What is it?"

He led her a couple of steps away and glanced over his shoulder, as if he thought Adam might come back to eavesdrop. "I took a little walk around your place the other day."

"You did? When?"

He waved the question away with one hand. "I don't remember. The point is, you've got quite the setup here."

"Thank you." DJ tried not to let his admission bother her, but she couldn't help wondering whether he'd looked around before or after he'd introduced himself, and why she hadn't noticed him.

"Big," he said. "Must be worth quite a little bit." He turned to look the place over again.

DJ forced a smile. "There are other places much bigger."

"Are you managing all right on your own?"

The question made her uncomfortable. She had no idea how to answer. "Yes," she said at last. "Fine."

"Do you need any help?"

She shrugged and struggled not to let her resentment show. "Not really. I've got a great staff—"

"No," he interrupted quickly. "I mean... Well..." He looked slightly uncomfortable, as if he didn't know how to say what was on his mind. "Sometimes men don't like taking orders from a woman, you know what I mean? And I got to thinkin' that maybe I could help you out with that aspect."

This time, she couldn't hide her reaction. She pulled back a little and stared at him in disbelief. "I don't have any trouble with my employees."

He winked at her and grinned. "Well, maybe not. None that you know about, anyway." He lifted his cap and scratched his head. "Think about it. Having me around to help might make things easier on you. Take some of the burden off your shoulders. Help keep your people in line."

She tried reminding herself that Larry came from a different generation, when comments like the ones he'd made had been acceptable—even expected. But she couldn't hide her growing resentment. "My 'people' aren't out of line, and even if they were, I'm perfectly capable of handling any trouble on my own."

He obviously heard the ice in her tone, because he studied her face for several seconds, and she watched as enlightenment dawned in his eyes. "I didn't mean *that*. I just meant—" His expression sobered and he darted a glance around, then leaned closer. "Look, the truth is, I'm a little short on cash. I'm not one to ask for a handout, but I figured maybe you could use an extra hand at the store, that's all."

"You want a job?"

He nodded quickly. "Yeah. Doing whatever you need. I was just kidding about the other. That's one thing you don't know about me yet—I'm a real kidder."

DJ struggled to catch up with the new twist in the conversation. How could she say no? But how could she say yes? She couldn't afford another employee on the payroll.

"Working together would give us a chance to spend more time together. We could talk. Catch up. Who knows…?"

DJ tried not to let herself read too much into the suggestion. She didn't want to set herself up for disappointment, but she had to take a chance, didn't she?

She drew in a steadying breath and smiled. "Of course I'll give you a job, Larry. And I *could* use help."

"Perfect. I *knew* it. You won't be sorry, you'll see."

She let him drape an arm across her shoulders and lead her up the steps, and she told herself the emotion in his eyes was relief, not triumph.

ADAM WORKED THE lid on the pizza box closed and watched Galloway through lowered eyes. The older man sat with his hands laced across his belly and his eyes closed. He looked relaxed and happy, totally unconcerned about the turmoil he'd caused DJ.

The more contact Adam had with the guy, the less he liked him and the less he trusted him. He'd been watching all through dinner, just waiting for Galloway to say or do something incriminating. But Larry had been more than careful. He'd given nothing away.

Holding up the pizza box, Adam asked, "Mind if I put this away now?"

Galloway opened one eye and focused slowly. "I guess not. But I might have another piece later."

Adam couldn't even pretend surprise. Larry had already eaten more for dinner than anyone else in the house. He forced a smile and worked the box into the refrigerator. Turning back, he caught a glimpse of DJ and Marissa in the hallway, arguing softly about bedtime.

He could tell Marissa didn't want to go, but he didn't know whether she was more worried about missing some of the excitement or about being alone. Whatever the reason, tears streamed down her tiny face and sobs racked her small body.

Adam tried to ignore her tears. He'd never been good at dealing with crying women and children. Instinct always told him to *do* something when problems arose. Tears left him feeling huge and clumsy and hopelessly inept.

"I w-w-want more p-p-pizza," Marissa sobbed. "I d-d-don't w-w-want to go to b-b-bed."

"Oh, sweetheart," DJ said with a sigh, "your tummy's already so full you'll probably be sick tonight."

Marissa sniffled and shook her head. "Uh-uh."

"You've had enough. And if you don't get into

bed now, we won't be able to go to the zoo tomorrow.''

"But, Mommy, I c-c-can't.'' The tears started all over again.

Adam stifled a groan and tried to look away, but he couldn't shut out the image of the child's tear-streaked face or ignore the sound of her sobbing.

As if she sensed Adam watching, Marissa glanced at him. Her big eyes filled with hope. "I can't go to bed until I say night to Adam.''

DJ glared at him as if she suspected he'd planted the idea in Marissa's head.

Shrugging, he lifted both hands to show his innocence.

DJ didn't look particularly impressed, but she patted Marissa on the back and scooted her into the kitchen. "All right, but say good-night quickly. No thinking of a dozen other things you need to do while you're out here." As Marissa scampered toward Adam, she added, "Say good-night to Larry, too.''

At the mention of his name, Larry sat up and opened his eyes again. He leaned forward and held out his arms as if he expected Marissa to turn to him. Instead, she darted away and skidded to a halt in front of Adam.

He stooped down and smiled. "Good night, Marissa.''

To his surprise, she launched herself at him and threw her arms around his neck. He touched one hand to the floor to keep his balance, and put the other arm around her. He hadn't been told good-night with such enthusiasm for a long time—if ever.

She pulled far enough back to look into his eyes. "Will you tell me a beddie-bye 'tory?''

A story? No. He couldn't remember any stories. Too many years had passed since he'd read to his brother's children—and even then he hadn't done it often.

To his relief, DJ stepped in to save him. "Oh, no, you don't," she said to Marissa. "I see what you're up to, but it's time for bed. Right now."

Larry leaned into the conversation. "You like stories, do you?"

At the sound of his voice, Marissa stiffened against Adam. Touching a finger to the tip of her nose, Adam winked, and she managed a trembling smile in return.

Larry went on, oblivious as always. "I used to tell *my* little girl stories all the time. I know a hundred of 'em. Come on over here. I'll tell you one."

Marissa shook her head almost imperceptibly, then raised her hands to cup Adam's face. "Tell me just *one* 'tory? P'ease?"

"Forget about him, missy," Larry said, his voice sounding stiff and a little loud. "He doesn't want to tell you a story. Come over here." He propped his elbows on his knees and reached for her.

She took another step closer to Adam and clutched the back of his shirt.

Adam looked up at DJ, willing her to do something. Marissa so obviously didn't like Galloway, and was so obviously frightened of him, Adam couldn't understand why DJ didn't tell Larry to leave the child alone. But she looked almost as helpless as Marissa, and even a little sad.

He reminded himself that DJ's childhood yearnings had probably blinded her to Galloway's faults, just as Adam's knowledge of the man's past probably made him more paranoid. "I don't know any good stories," he confessed to Marissa. "But I'll read you one."

Marissa scowled at him. "I don't want you to *read* a 'tory. I want a made-up 'tory."

"I don't know how to make up good stories."

The girl's frown deepened and her brows knit together. "Yes, you do."

"No, I don't."

"*Everybody* knows how to make up 'tories—'specially you. You're a book writer."

Caught in his lie, Adam flushed and glanced at DJ to gauge her reaction.

To his relief, she laughed. "Marissa's right. You're an author, for heaven's sake. Don't try to tell us you can't make up stories."

He stood slowly. "Not kids' stories."

But DJ grinned as if this were all a grand joke. "Are you going to tell me you've never made up any stories?"

That was exactly what he wanted to tell her. But he could only smile in resignation and hold out a hand to Marissa. He didn't want to call any more attention to his mistake.

Marissa grabbed one finger and tugged him toward the door. "Come on."

He racked his memory for any fairy tale he could remember from beginning to end. He had no idea how any story he could make up would satisfy this child, who had no doubt heard every story imaginable a thousand times.

Marissa led him down the darkened corridor into a small bedroom-turned-family-room. DJ had wedged a love seat, two comfortable-looking chairs and a few floor lamps between sets of overfilled bookshelves—

as if the books had come first and seating arrangements had been an afterthought. Almost forgotten, and certainly not the focal point of the room, a small television set occupied one corner.

In fact, as he studied the room, he realized books dominated every surface. They didn't stand in rigid rows on shelves the way he'd always imagined books should. These lay on their sides and filled every shelf in rows two deep. Paperbacks and hardcovers trailed into neat piles onto the end tables and the floor, as if they'd multiplied in the night when nobody was watching.

Adam could feel DJ in here, and he knew instinctively that the woman who lived in this room was as much a part of her as the woman in the plaid flannel shirt, the overalls and the work boots, the woman who was Marissa's mother and the woman who ran a business with one hand and a home with the other.

She had so many different sides to her, Adam realized he could spend a lifetime discovering her. And for a heartbeat, he wondered whether she found him even half as intriguing as he found her.

Almost immediately, reality pushed the thought from his mind. No. Of course she didn't. How could she? She didn't even know the real Adam McAllister; in fact, she had no idea he even existed. She knew only the pretense.

Adam cursed silently. He knew better than to let himself get personally involved in a case. He'd been wrong to let himself feel anything for DJ, and even more wrong to want her to feel anything for him.

Marissa tugged on his hand again and forced him to refocus on her. "Hurry, before Mommy says I have to go to bed again."

He smiled down at her. "Are any of these books yours?"

She scowled as if she suspected a trick. "Yes, but I don't *want* a 'torybook.'"

Well, no one could blame a guy for trying. Adam sank into one of the chairs while Marissa jumped onto the love seat and dragged a blanket back down with her. She crossed the room and climbed onto his lap as if she'd been doing it all her life. "I'm ready."

Adam didn't know how to react. She snuggled against his shoulder and looked into his eyes with her huge brown ones.

Without warning, his eyes began to sting and Marissa's face blurred in his vision. Oh, hell. Now *he* was crying.

Blinking rapidly, he cleared his throat and hoped his voice would sound normal. "Once upon a time," he said around the lump in his throat, "there was a beautiful little princess named Marissa."

She sighed with contentment, twirled a lock of hair around one finger and leaned her head on his shoulder.

He fixed the blanket around her feet and went on. "She was the most beautiful princess in the whole kingdom."

Tilting her face, Marissa looked into his eyes again and smiled. "I wuv you."

The next sentence of his story evaporated before he could even make it up. He tried to look away, but he couldn't. He struggled to think about something else so he could prevent the damned tears from spilling down his cheeks.

Marissa's trust reached deep into his heart, and her love pulled an answer from his lips.

"I love you, too," he said. And he meant every word.

He leaned his head back against the chair and tried to pull himself together. It would be so easy to get caught up in emotion and lose his heart to DJ and Marissa. Separately, each threatened his heart and soul. Together, they were as dangerous to him as a match tossed into a tank of gasoline.

He couldn't keep letting his guard down like this. He was on assignment. He was living a lie. If he let himself get involved with them, he'd only cause heartache for everyone; he'd be smart to remember that.

He had to regain control over himself, and he'd have to find some way to ignore his heart the next time it tried to speak louder than his head.

CHAPTER NINE

DJ STOOD IN THE doorway, watching Adam and Marissa together. She'd been surprised to find Marissa sitting on his lap and touched by the joy and contentment on her daughter's face. But the pain and tenderness on Adam's shocked her.

She backed into the hallway and pulled the door closed quietly behind her. But even then, she couldn't put the image of his face completely from her mind.

For the first time since his arrival, she saw Adam clearly. Not as someone to discuss her troubles with, or as a friend of her mother's, or even as someone who attracted her—but as a man, with hopes and fears and disappointments of his own. She'd been so worried about Larry, so concerned for Marissa and so hurt by her mother's lies, she hadn't spared a thought for Adam as a person.

Leaning her head against the wall, she closed her eyes. Exhaustion weakened her knees and made her long for a quiet moment alone so she could sort through all the conflicting emotions that warred within her. She'd never expected to feel this way about a man again, and she wasn't at all certain she liked it.

She hadn't wanted any of this—not *now*. She'd worked hard to reach a stable place in her life, and she'd finally grown strong enough that she didn't *need* someone to love her. And just when she'd grown content with the way things were, her entire world had started to tilt under her feet.

She felt as if her soul had been through an earthquake that had left everything slightly off-balance; as if everything had shifted and she no longer knew her way around inside her own head or heart.

She needed time. Time to decide what she wanted to do about Larry and her mother. Time to decide what she felt for Adam.

But before she could reflect any further, she heard Larry's footsteps coming down the hallway toward her. She couldn't even find time alone to *breathe,* much less make sense of her life. She thought about ducking into her room to avoid him—if only for five minutes—but Adam and Marissa looked so peaceful in the other room, she didn't want Larry to disturb them.

Sighing softly, she pushed away from the wall just as he rounded the corner.

He stopped short when he saw her in the shadows, and a flicker of surprise crossed his face. "There you are. I wondered where you'd gone."

"I was just checking on Marissa," she whispered, and started away from the family room.

Glancing at the family-room door, Larry hesitated, as if he intended to push past her and interrupt the story. But after a second, he shrugged and followed DJ back into the kitchen.

She studied him as they walked and tried again to find something familiar about him. She wanted desperately to *feel* something for him, to believe that this man was actually her father. But her mind stayed blank and her heart remained numb. She still couldn't imagine Larry and her mother married. But they had been—DJ was living proof of that.

Larry reached into his pocket and held out two wadded bills. "Since I'm going to be working again, let me chip in a few bucks toward the pizza."

She shook her head quickly. She didn't need his money, and she didn't want to take what little he had. "You don't need to do that."

"Take it," he insisted. "You already have *one* extra mouth to feed."

DJ didn't want to take it, but she didn't know how to refuse. She didn't know Larry well enough to even guess how he would react. "Adam helps out with the groceries," she said with a smile. "In fact, he's given me more money in the past week than I usually spend in a month."

Larry barked a rude laugh. "Really? What's he trying to prove?"

"I don't think he's trying to prove anything."

"Well, he wants *something*," Larry said. "Or maybe he's trying to *buy* something."

DJ could only stare. "What makes you say that?"

"It's obvious."

Had her attraction for Adam blinded her to something she should have seen? "What do you think he's trying to prove?"

Larry shook his head slowly. "I wish I knew. How long have you known him?"

"A short time." She couldn't admit aloud it had only been a week.

"What do you know about him?"

How could she answer that? Adam was a good man. Kind. He cared about Marissa, and about DJ, but DJ had to admit she knew very little else.

"You don't know anything about him, do you?" Larry asked.

"Not much," she said reluctantly.

Larry nodded in satisfaction. "Let me tell you something, Devon. You can't *ever* know enough about a person. You need to find out if he's hiding something from you. If he is, get rid of him—fast."

She bit back the first words that rose to her lips, but she couldn't force away the resentment that tensed her shoulders or the headache that throbbed low in the base of her skull.

Larry seemed oblivious to her reaction. "Is he going to the zoo with you and Marissa tomorrow?"

DJ nodded without speaking.

"Then I'm coming, too. I don't trust him."

"Nothing's going to happen at the zoo."

Larry stared at her for several long seconds, then gripped her shoulders. "Has he got you fooled or what? What are you going to do, let him come in here and take advantage of you?"

"No."

Larry snorted. "No? Well, that's exactly what's going to happen if you don't make it your business to find out who he is and what he wants."

All at once, DJ's patience snapped. She pulled away from his grasp and glared at him. "I don't think any of this needs to concern you," she said before she could stop herself.

"Of course it does. I'm your father."

DJ shook her head and took a step away. "You're a *stranger*. I know more about *Adam* than I do about you."

Larry recoiled as if she'd struck him. "I'm here,

aren't I? I'm trying to give us a chance to get to know each other.''

She took another step away. ''What chance? You appeared out of nowhere and turned my life upside down. You want me to start from here and move forward without even knowing how I got here. But I can't do that. I need to know what happened between you and Mom. I need to know who you are and where you've been for the past thirty years. *You're* the one who's being evasive.''

His face clouded and he started to turn away.

But she wouldn't let him shut her out again. ''Tell me about yourself. When is your birthday? Where do you live? Who were my grandparents? Did you get married again after you and Mom split up? Do I have any other brothers and sisters? What do you like to do? Who *are* you?''

He stared into her eyes. His gaze was cold. Icy. ''What do you want me to say?''

DJ's throat burned, her head throbbed and anger boiled up inside her. He didn't understand, but she didn't know how else to say it. ''Just *talk* to me. Tell me why you left me. Why you stayed away all these years. Tell me why I grew up without you and why my mother didn't ever tell me about you. Just tell me the truth.''

''The truth?'' He laughed harshly and took several jerky steps away from her. ''Whose truth? Mine or *hers?*''

Tears of outrage filled her eyes, but she wouldn't let herself ask again. Larry might want to treat this as a game, but she refused to play. Dashing tears away with the back of her hand, she waited silently for him to go on.

His eyes blinked rapidly as he studied her face. Some emotion darkened them, frightening her for an instant, but it vanished so quickly she wondered whether she'd only imagined it.

"What's past is past, Devon," he said at last. "It doesn't matter. Let's just worry about what's going to happen next."

"I *can't*. I'm too confused. I can't even think about the future until I know about the past."

"Then ask your mother. I can't go back again."

She folded her arms across her chest and forced herself to say the only thing she could. "Then you'll have to leave."

Larry's expression twisted with shock and anger. "You don't mean that."

"Yes, I do."

He drew in a deep breath and looked away. "You'll send me away because I won't talk about the past?"

Her heart drummed in her chest, and the ache in her head matched its tempo. But she couldn't back down. Not now. "I'm telling you to leave if you can't be honest with me."

Larry scratched his chin and closed his eyes. "Maybe you're right," he conceded after a long moment. "Maybe you do need to know what happened. I'm not trying to be difficult. I just don't want to hurt you. I thought it would be better for everyone this way."

"What way?"

He stuffed his hands into his pockets and shrugged, but he didn't respond to the question for several seconds. "You have to understand that I loved your mother. Nobody's ever loved a woman the way I loved her. I treated her like a queen and she had everything she needed or wanted.''

DJ didn't move a muscle. She didn't want to do anything to stop him now that he'd finally started talking.

"We didn't start out expecting to split up," Larry said. "I thought we'd be together forever. I didn't expect Chrissy to end up hating me or to take my deepest secrets and turn them against me. I thought I could trust her." Again he blinked rapidly and looked away. "I found out I couldn't. She betrayed me, Devon. She screwed me over royally.''

Her mother? DJ gulped air and tried to force away the sudden nausea that threatened to overwhelm her. In spite of everything, in spite of the lies her mother had told her, she wanted to believe that the past thirty years had been someone else's fault. But that illusion fell beside all the others. "What did she do?''

"She betrayed me. That's all you need to know.''

"No," she insisted. "You've gone this far, tell me the rest. What did she do? Have an affair?''

He met her gaze squarely. "An affair? No. I think I could have lived with that. What she did was much, much worse." He rubbed his face and let out a deep breath. "All right. The truth is, she stole you and hid you from me.''

DJ stared at him. "What do you mean, she stole me?''

"You shouldn't have spent the past thirty years with your mother. You should have been with me. She snatched you and ran. She *stole* you from me.''

The words ran together, then slowly separated and replayed through her mind, and she felt the foundation of her world slip out from beneath her. "Are you saying she kidnapped me?"

Larry's eyes filled with tears. "The last time I saw you, you were in my living room. I kissed you good-bye. I lifted you up and flew you around the room. You liked that. Do you remember?"

Some dim memory tweaked at her, but it vanished again. She didn't want to believe him. She *couldn't* believe him. Her mother couldn't have done something like that.

"She came home from work while I was gone and took you right out from under Mary's nose. Do you remember Mary?"

"I don't remember anything or anyone. Who was she?"

"A friend of ours," he said with a wave of his hand. "Long gone now."

DJ looked away and tried to find some memory of her childhood that might go along with this story. But it seemed impossible. Unthinkable. "What did you do? Call the police?"

Larry shook his head and made a face. "No. They wouldn't have done anything, anyway."

"But if she—"

He held up a hand. "Take my word for it. She'd just have twisted everything around to make herself look good. That's the way she's always been. Good with words." He opened his arms and beckoned to her. "See? I told you the truth would upset you, and it does, doesn't it?"

DJ's mind raced and her breath came in shallow gasps.

Larry closed the distance between them and pulled

her into his arms. "We're together again now," he whispered. "That's all that matters, right?"

DJ tried to nod but her head wouldn't work right. She felt numb inside. Overwhelmed. She could only stare at his shoulder as he held her, at the walls of her house, at the trees in her backyard swaying in the wind. Larry's tears spilled onto her shoulder, but she didn't cry.

She closed her eyes and tried to block everything out, but her heart was beating too fast, her mind racing. Horror and disbelief mingled together, clouding her judgment and confusing her totally. She couldn't tell fact from fiction anymore. She didn't know where to look for answers or even whom to trust.

DJ STROLLED ALONG the walk at the zoo, lifting her face to the sun for a moment, then lowering it to watch Adam, Marissa and Larry as they hurried through the crowd toward the hippopotamus display. The crisp fragrance of autumn blended with the earthy odor of zoo animals and the sugary scent of cotton candy and popcorn to create a distinctive aroma. Eau de Zoo.

She smiled as she watched Marissa clutch Adam's fingers. The child nearly had to run in an effort to match even his slowest gait. But DJ's smile faded when she looked at Larry.

He kept time on Marissa's other side and pointed out birds and small animals, desperately trying to get her to relax around him. But Marissa had little or no interest in Larry—she wanted Adam.

DJ had to admit that Adam was wonderful with her. He gave Marissa exactly the kind of attention she needed. And what Larry offered didn't satisfy the same needs. Maybe it was because he was older. Maybe it was because DJ had been so careful not to confuse Marissa with complicated relationships. Or maybe it was because Larry was as confused as DJ, although he didn't show it.

They stopped and waited for her to catch up. DJ walked a little faster and drew up beside them just as Marissa released Adam's hand and raised her arms to him. "Can you lift me up?"

Adam started to comply, but Larry stepped in front of him. "I'll do it, Marissa. Come over here with me."

Marissa hesitated and took a step closer to Adam.

Larry reached for her again. "Come *on*. I'll show you the fat old hippos."

Marissa leaned against Adam's legs and stuck one curled knuckle between her teeth.

DJ rubbed her forehead. She didn't want to force Marissa into anything, but Larry's growing frustration had taken on an almost-tangible quality. If DJ could feel it, she knew Marissa could, too. Which meant Marissa would pull even further away, Larry would get even more upset and DJ would be torn between concern and confusion.

Maybe she should encourage Marissa to go with Larry. Maybe Marissa was holding back because she didn't know if her mother approved. Still, DJ couldn't help wishing he'd calm down and give Marissa time to get used to having him around.

She understood his anxiety. He had no way of knowing that Marissa reacted to most men slowly and that her response to Adam was unusual. He only saw Adam, a newcomer like himself—and one with *no* claim to Marissa's love—getting the attention Larry wanted and believed he deserved.

She smiled at Marissa and touched her arm gently. "Marissa, sweetheart, Larry wants to show you the hippos."

"No."

DJ flicked an embarrassed glance at Larry. A muscle in his jaw worked, and he flushed an angry red. "Please, sweetheart," she begged. "Mommy and Adam will be right behind you."

Marissa shook her head again. But this time, she whispered, "I don't wanna. I don't like him."

Before DJ could frame a response to that, Larry planted both hands on Marissa's tiny waist and lifted her. He turned her toward him, no doubt trying to get a better hold on her, but she screamed and bucked against his grip and started to topple backward. DJ reached out, aware that Adam did the same.

But Larry gripped the girl tighter and pulled her to his chest. "Damn it!" he snarled. "I'm not going to hurt you." When Marissa cried out again, he clamped a hand over her mouth. *"Stop it!"*

For one horrible moment, DJ recoiled, held in place by an emotion she couldn't name as she watched anger flash across Larry's face and heard steel in his voice. In the next second, she lunged toward them and grabbed Marissa. "Let her go."

Larry glared at her for what felt like an eternity, but his grip on Marissa slowly loosened.

With trembling arms, DJ pulled Marissa close and soothed her. She brushed her hair with one hand and rocked her gently, speaking softly into her ear. Adam stayed at her side, alternately glaring at Larry and looking gently at Marissa. He appeared almost as angry as DJ felt—and almost as shaken.

DJ met Larry's gaze and held it. He looked different to her suddenly, and she felt uncomfortable being near him. Nevertheless, she forced herself to speak. "We need to talk."

"Fine." The word fell like a stone into water.

She refused to let him intimidate her. Glancing at Adam, she nodded down at Marissa. "Would you mind taking Marissa for a few minutes?"

"Not at all." He held out his arms and Marissa lunged toward him. He pulled her close and brushed a kiss on the top of her head.

DJ smiled at the picture they made, then forced herself to turn back to Larry. "Let's go over by the fence."

He stuffed his hands into his pockets and scuffed his feet on the sidewalk as he trailed her. "All right," he said when they were finally alone. "I'm sorry. I shouldn't have yelled at her."

DJ didn't think he sounded sorry, but she tried to keep her own tone from sounding accusatory when she responded. "She's not used to having men around. She's not used to your gruff voices and your rougher ways. You have to remember, we've been on our own for most of her life."

Larry used his chin to point at Adam. "She doesn't have any problem with *him*."

Again, DJ heard more in his tone than she wanted to hear. He sounded like a petulant child, but she refused to soothe him. "I know. I can't deny it, but I can't explain it, either."

His expression hardened, and a hint of a sneer curled his lip. "I can."

DJ didn't like this side of him, but she tried not to show it. "How?"

"It's you."

This time, she couldn't hide her reaction. "What?"

"She's reacting to you," Larry said. "She can tell you like that guy, so she likes him, too. And she can tell you don't like me, so she won't even give me a chance."

"That's ridiculous. What makes you think I don't like you?"

Larry folded his arms across his chest. "Have you told her who I am?"

"No," she admitted slowly. "But—"

He nodded as if she'd made his point for him. "How in the hell is she supposed to learn to like me if she thinks I'm a stranger? If she can tell *you* don't want me around?"

His assumption seemed to come from nowhere, and she struggled to remember some snippet of conversation, something she'd said or done that might have caused him to feel this way.

He laughed. "You're so much like your mother, it's pathetic. You want to blame me for what happened over there, but it's not my fault. If *you* won't even trust me, how's she supposed to?"

DJ took a step back, then forced herself to stand her ground. "It takes time for trust to build—"

"Time? I haven't got time. I've lost thirty years already, thanks to your mother."

"Larry—"

"Dad!" he snapped. "I'm your *father*, dammit, not your friend. Why can't you call me Dad?"

She started to respond, then stopped herself. Why couldn't she? She'd wanted a father all her life, and she finally had one. So what kept her from acknowledging him? She shook her head slowly. "I don't know."

"What's wrong? Don't you believe me? Don't you believe I *am* your father?"

"Of course I do." She couldn't make herself speak above a whisper.

"Then what's your problem?" he demanded.

She couldn't answer that.

"You know what it is? You don't *want* Marissa to love me, that's what it is. You don't want her to have a grandfather because I wasn't around for you. You're punishing us both because of my past."

"That's not true."

"Isn't it?" He glared at her for several long seconds. "Then what *is* your problem? You act as if you expect me to *earn* every little bit of affection you decide to toss my way."

Some small part of DJ wanted to deny what he said and tell him how unfair his accusations were, but she couldn't. She couldn't honestly say what he wanted her to say. Perhaps that was just what he had to do— earn their trust.

Larry turned away, then wheeled back to shove his finger under her nose. "Just don't blame me for scaring Marissa. You're the one who's making her afraid of me. I'm working my tail off trying to make up for what I've done wrong, but you can't see that, can you? Well, I'll tell you what. From now on, you tell me what you want from me, and I'll see if I can manage to give it to you. That way you won't try to blame me for your mistakes."

DJ couldn't speak. She couldn't even breathe. His anger and accusations tore through her like a storm and left her weak and shaking. Was it true? "I don't know what I want," she admitted at last. "I've never had a father."

He glared at her for another minute. All at once, his shoulders sagged and his eyes filled with tears. He closed the distance between them in two steps and pulled her close. "That's all right," he said. "It's not your fault, either. We're both paying for what your mother did. We're both trying to figure out what to do next. Right?"

She forced herself to nod.

"Just don't ever do that to me again," Larry whispered. "Don't make me angry like that."

DJ felt like a small child unfairly accused of starting an argument. She tried to pull away so she could see his face. "But I didn't do anything!"

He laughed harshly in her ear. "You accused me of things I haven't done. You tried to blame me for your mother's mistakes." He pulled away and looked deep into her eyes. "Just don't do that again, that's all I ask. Okay? Can you do that?"

Confused, DJ studied his face. Was he serious, or could he possibly be joking? His expression revealed nothing. She couldn't even remember how they'd reached this point, but she tried desperately to understand. She couldn't move. Couldn't react. Couldn't even force herself to nod this time.

He sighed heavily, as if the weight of the world rested on his shoulders. *"Okay?"*

This time, DJ nodded quickly, almost instinctively—a reflex to the apprehension she felt curling in her stomach.

Larry smiled, and his expression softened again. "Good. That's my girl." He clapped an arm around her shoulders. "Let's get back to the others, and we'll forget all about this."

As if in a dream, DJ allowed him to lead her back to Adam and Marissa. For Marissa's sake, she tried to force herself to smile, but her heart felt heavy and her mind swirled in confusion.

Adam would be able to see the turmoil reflected in her eyes. He would want an explanation, but DJ had no idea what she could say to him. For the first time in her life, she had no answers.

FROM HIS POSITION under the huge oak tree across the walk, Adam held Marissa and watched DJ and Galloway. He'd been horrified by Galloway's reaction to Marissa's obvious fear, and his disgust had quickly given way to heated anger. Now he tried to remain calm for Marissa's sake. But he'd have given almost anything to hear the conversation across the way and to add a few comments of his own.

If opening his mouth wouldn't have put his job on the line, he would have told Galloway exactly what he thought. He wanted to push Galloway up against the fence and show him what it felt like to be bullied by someone large and mean and full of hatred.

But he couldn't say a word. Rules and regulations kept him silent. Even though Galloway was coming dangerously close to breaking parole, he didn't want it—couldn't let it be—at Marissa and DJ's expense.

Marissa leaned against his shoulder and followed the direction of his gaze. "I don't like him," she whispered.

Adam wanted to say he didn't blame her. He wanted to say that he didn't like him, either. He wanted to promise he would never let Galloway

frighten her again. But he couldn't say any of those
things for her own sake, so he cuddled her closer and
tried to look reassuring. "Your mother's talking to
him. She won't let him act that way again."

Marissa sighed, then stiffened slightly as a leftover
sob worked its way through her tiny body. "Why
does he have to come with us? I don't want him
here."

What could he say to that? He couldn't explain the
relationship—DJ didn't want her to know about it.
And he couldn't bring himself to pass off Galloway
as a friend of the family. Shushing her gently, he
rocked her in his arms. "I know you don't, sweetheart."

She shuddered again and burrowed her head into
his shoulder. Her absolute trust in him made Adam
feel even worse. His feelings for DJ grew more intense each day, and with every passing hour, he became more attached to Marissa.

He hated the lies, no matter what the cause. He
detested being forced to stand still and witness episodes like the one he'd just seen. He loathed being
expected to keep his mouth shut while DJ fell further
under Galloway's spell and the jerk terrorized Marissa.

As he watched, Galloway pulled DJ into his arms
and held her there. Clutching Marissa against his
chest, Adam allowed his anger to grow—not just at
Galloway this time, but at DJ, as well. What was she
thinking? How could she believe anything that idiot
said?

He took a number of shallow breaths and tried to
get himself under control again. She didn't know
about Galloway's record. She had no idea what a vol-

atile person he really was. Everyone had conspired to keep her in the dark—and Adam was one of the offenders, though not by choice.

When Marissa shrank against him again, he looked over at DJ and Galloway. They'd started back across the walk, and Adam realized he'd have to spend the rest of the day interacting with him normally.

When he'd accepted this assignment he hadn't expected a problem—he'd always been able to separate his business and personal lives before. But not this time.

He couldn't let her go on this way. He didn't care what it did to the assignment, DJ deserved to know the facts. No matter what it took, he had to convince Chuck that keeping DJ in the dark was more dangerous than telling her the truth.

CHAPTER TEN

ADAM SAT AT A picnic table in Pioneer Park, waiting for Chuck to arrive. Growing anxious, he readjusted his position on the hard seat and leaned his elbows on the table. The moment he'd stepped inside the house after that episode at the zoo, he'd given DJ an excuse to leave and called Chuck from a pay phone. Chuck had sounded angry when Adam insisted on an emergency meeting, but he'd finally agreed.

Glancing at his watch for probably the tenth time in as many minutes, Adam felt his stomach churn as his anger grew. He tried to force himself to calm down by rehearsing the points he wanted to make when Chuck arrived. He had to make certain he sounded rational if he wanted Chuck to agree with him.

Evening shadows stretched across the lawn. Homeless people wandered through the park looking for handouts and digging into trash barrels for their evening meal. Adam could hear the bells for evening Mass in the distance, and the clock on the city-and-county building chiming the hour. Five o'clock. He'd been waiting nearly fifteen minutes already, and he was growing more and more impatient.

When a footstep sounded on the sidewalk behind him, he turned back and watched Chuck barrel toward him.

"What the hell's going on?" Chuck demanded. Even in the dim light, Adam could see the anger in his eyes.

"I need to clear something with you about Galloway."

"Yeah? Well, it had better be damned important to pull me down here like this." Chuck's eyes narrowed to slits in his round face.

"Galloway's getting dangerous. He could go off at any moment. DJ needs to know the truth about him. You need to let me tell her what kind of man he is."

"You brought me down here to ask me *that?*"

"I need you to untie my hands and let me do my job the right way."

Chuck propped his fists on his waist, looked down at his feet and shook his head as if he couldn't believe what he'd just heard. "What do you want to do, blow it?"

"I want to tell the woman the truth. Somebody *needs* to tell her or she's going to get hurt."

Chuck sighed as if Adam had tested his patience to its limits. "That's not your call."

"It should be, dammit! She needs to know about Galloway's history of abuse. Of the violence. About the time he's served in prison."

"What is this? Have you gone soft on me because your hormones have kicked in over some woman?"

"I don't want to see a woman and her child put in harm's way when there's no reason for it." He glanced away, then glared at Chuck again. "Galloway's getting aggravated. He's going to lose his temper. Last time he went down, it was for assault with a deadly weapon. The next time, it could be murder.

Do you want that on your conscience? Do you want to be responsible for DJ's or Marissa's death?''

"No," Chuck snapped. "But we can't take matters into our own hands. We can't override Christina Prescott's decisions. We have limits. That isn't what she hired us to do."

"I know how Christina Prescott feels," Adam shouted. "I've talked to her, remember? She doesn't want her child and grandchild to die or even get hurt—that's why I'm there in the first place."

"If you do your job right, nobody will get hurt."

"I *can't* do my job right if I'm bound by a bunch of half-witted rules and regulations."

Anger tightened Chuck's face, but Adam didn't care.

"I'm the one who's on the scene," he snarled. "I'm the *only* one qualified to assess the situation and make decisions. And I'm telling you, DJ needs to know about Galloway."

Chuck's face grew stony. "No."

"Are you crazy? What do you mean, no?"

Chuck flushed with anger. "I mean, no. You don't tell her anything, do you understand that?"

Adam clenched his jaw and gripped his belt to maintain what little control he had left.

"If you tell her, your career's shot and everything you've worked for goes down the tubes," Chuck shouted. "Is that what you want? Are you willing to risk that for a woman you've only known a week?"

Adam could only glare at him.

"Don't be stupid," Chuck continued. "*Think* about what you're doing. If you tell DJ who you are, Galloway will find out. If that happens, the whole assignment is over."

"I have thought about it. That's why I'm asking for authorization. That's why I asked you to meet me here."

"If Galloway finds out who you are and Mrs. Prescott pulls you out of there, who's going to keep DJ and Marissa safe? Galloway will still be free, and they'd be without protection."

"But they'd know the truth."

"Our client doesn't want them to know the truth."

"I'm not sure *what* our client wants," Adam muttered. Chuck's argument made sense, but he wasn't ready to abandon his own position yet.

Chuck shook his head and spoke through clenched teeth. "You're acting like a fool. No woman's worth it. You gave up your career once for a woman. Are you going to make the same mistake twice?"

Adam held back the reply he'd been about to make. *Was* he doing the same thing all over? Was he putting his career on the line again?

Yes. He supposed he was, but this situation was nothing like the demands Victoria had put on him. That time, he'd given away his life in exchange for nothing. And he'd been miserable and alone ever since.

DJ's situation bore no resemblance to his marriage, but if he put his job in jeopardy, he had no guarantee DJ would even want him to stay around. He could wind up alone again. And DJ would be left alone with Galloway.

"Well?" Chuck demanded. "Is that what you want? Is it really worth losing everything?"

Adam shook his head slowly and forced himself to speak. "I don't know."

Chuck paced back to face him. "If you can't tell

me yes without hesitation, then you're making the wrong choice.''

Adam growled low in his throat and looked away.

"Forget it, Adam. Do your job the way you've been briefed and quit letting the woman get to you."

Frustrated by his position, angry with Chuck for being so blind, and enraged by Galloway's very existence, Adam whirled around and smashed his fist into the picnic table.

"Dammit!" Almost immediately, his hand began to throb and he swore again, this time at himself.

"Well—?"

Adam shook his hand in a futile effort to relieve the pain. It didn't work. "This isn't about me," he managed through gritted teeth. "And this isn't about Christina Prescott. This is about protecting DJ and Marissa."

"Then protect them. But not by spilling your guts."

"You won't authorize it?"

"Hell, no, I won't authorize it."

"If Dodge knew—" Adam began.

"Dodge isn't going to know you even asked. Not unless you're willing to walk away from your job right now. Hell, Adam—" Chuck broke off and shook his head. "Will you look at yourself? What's that woman done to you?"

She'd captured his heart and pulled him back into the land of the living, but Adam couldn't explain that to Chuck.

"You've got your orders," Chuck snarled. "Now get back to your post if you're so worried."

"Right."

Chuck glanced around. "Where's your truck? Don't tell me you walked all the way over here."

Adam nodded toward Third West, over half a mile away. "I parked by Union Station."

"You want me to give you a lift back?"

"No. I'll walk." Even if he'd been five miles away, he wouldn't have taken a ride from Chuck at that moment. Besides, he could use the time and the fresh air to let his anger clear and the pain in his hand diminish a little. He made a noise Chuck could interpret any way he wanted, and turned away. Once Chuck made a decision, he never deviated from it. Adam should have known better than to even ask.

He shuffled through the park, listening to the crackling of the leaves and branches underfoot. But he felt no better when he reached his truck than he had when he and Chuck parted. If anything, he was even angrier—this time, at himself.

Revving the truck's engine, he peeled out of his parking spot. He gripped the wheel, not caring whether his hand hurt or not. He drove too quickly, rounded the corners too fast and sped over the viaduct toward home.

He'd been so certain of the best course of action when he'd left DJ. Now he was confused and unsure. He had two choices—tell DJ anyway or stay with her and continue to lie. Either option presented a risk. Either could easily be the wrong choice.

The responsibility for DJ and Marissa fell squarely on his shoulders. He just hoped he had what it took to choose wisely.

DJ WALKED SLOWLY through the rows of potted rose-bushes behind her customer, a wiry man in his late sixties who'd looked at every table of close-out annual and perennial bedding plants and then decided roses sounded better. Overhead, a flock of seagulls circled in the pale blue sky and a few lazy clouds drifted across the sun.

Her patience had already worn thin, but she knew her irritation came more from within than anything her customer had done. She'd been neglecting her business for nearly two weeks now, and she had to reassess her priorities.

She'd been teetering on the edge of financial disaster before Larry had made his appearance. She'd been in trouble before Adam had walked into her life. Like a fool, she'd ignored everything and let both men take over her mind, her heart and her every waking thought.

But no more.

True, she'd been unusually troubled for two days—ever since the incident at the zoo. She hadn't been able to concentrate on much since. She'd begun to wonder if maybe Larry was right. Maybe she had caused Marissa's hesitation with him. Maybe she should tell Marissa who he was. But something still held her back.

She was equally distracted by Adam. Every minute she spent around him brought her closer to losing her heart completely. But she didn't trust herself to make a wise choice where love was concerned—she'd already made one huge mistake by marrying Jeff. She couldn't afford another disaster, and neither could Marissa.

Her customer paused at the end of one of the tables and rubbed his chin. "What about these?"

With effort, DJ forced herself to concentrate on her

current task, but she almost resented the energy it required. She'd spent the better part of an hour helping the man, but he'd spent more time chatting than actually looking at the stock. Just thinking about the time being wasted made her even crankier.

The man scanned the bushes closest to him and stretched forward slightly, as if he intended to reach for one. Smiling over his shoulder at her, he shook his head. "I don't know. I'm thinking maybe a nice red one would look better in the front yard. What do you think?"

DJ bit back a sigh and forced a smile. She needed this sale, even though it meant putting in extra hours later. "We have some nice varieties of red over here." Turning toward the next table, she stepped back again to let him study the selection.

He took several seconds to ponder and made another couple of adjustments to his fishing cap before he nodded. "Well, then. I guess that's what I'll get."

Scarcely able to believe he'd finally made a decision, DJ lifted a healthy bush out of the cluster before he had a chance to change his mind. She reminded herself how badly she needed every customer if she hoped to keep the store open through the end of the season. If she couldn't, she would be working somewhere else by spring. Indoors. At a desk. She shuddered and made an extra effort to look pleasant as she directed the customer toward a checkout stand.

Once she'd turned him over to the cashier, she let out a sigh of relief. Determined to finish at least the first task she'd begun that morning, she started toward her office.

"DJ, wait up." Ramon's voice reached her just as she passed the soft-drink machine. He caught up to her a minute later. His eyes looked troubled and his mouth curved down at the corners. He looked so unlike himself, DJ grew immediately concerned.

She led him into her tiny office and closed the door behind them. Motioning him toward the only chair, she perched on one corner of her desk. "What's wrong?"

Ramon puffed out his cheeks and exhaled slowly. "It's that new guy you've hired. Where'd you find him, anyway?"

DJ's heart dropped. "Larry? Why? What's he done?"

"He's a jerk," Ramon said with a sneer. "He's coming off like some kind of big shot, and he's getting on everybody's nerves."

"He has a difficult personality," she admitted.

Ramon leaned back in his chair and shifted position slightly. "It's more than that. There's something weird about him."

DJ stiffened. "What do you mean, weird?"

"He's just…" Ramon searched for the right word. "*Weird,* you know? Spooky."

"No, I don't know," she said, but her voice came out harsher than she intended. Making an effort to soften her tone, she tried again. "If you have specific complaints, tell me what they are and I'll deal with them. But if you just don't like him, or you're having trouble getting along with him—"

Ramon shot forward. "It's not just me. He's a jerk with everybody. He and Manny nearly came to blows earlier this morning." He broke off and shook his head without averting his gaze. "He's trouble, DJ."

DJ let his comments sink in for a moment. Larry

did have an abrasive personality. "He's only been here two days," she began.

"No kidding. Tell *him* that. The way he acts, he's been here for years. He probably thinks he knows more than *you.*"

DJ didn't want to hear this. Not today.

Ramon shook his head in exasperation. "You know those perennials you wanted Joseph to move? Well, Galloway's out there bossing Joseph around like Joseph's too stupid to understand what you want."

"Let me talk to him."

Ramon fell back against the chair and gazed at her.

"I'll talk to him," she said again.

Ramon lifted one shoulder in halfhearted agreement. "Where *did* you find him, anyway? I thought you couldn't afford to hire anybody new."

She hesitated a second before answering. "He's an old friend of the family," she said at last.

Ramon's eyes widened a bit. "You're kidding."

She shook her head and managed a halfhearted smile to back up her lie.

He pushed the fingers of one hand through his hair and studied his knees for a few seconds. "You know, I came in here ready to tell you I was quitting—or maybe give you an ultimatum."

DJ's stomach tightened. "I'm glad you didn't. I need you here."

He looked at her anxiously. "You really think talking to him will do any good?"

She nodded, but she didn't feel even half as confident as she pretended.

"All right, then." Ramon relented with a shrug. "I'll give it another chance. But if things don't get better, I *will* leave." He gave her an embarrassed smile. "You're not paying me enough to put up with this kind of crap."

DJ's lips curved slightly. "That's true."

Sighing heavily, Ramon pushed to his feet. "You know what I'd do if I were you?"

"Tell me."

"I'd let Larry know who's in charge. I'd make it *real* clear he's not in charge of anything. If you don't, he's going to keep pushing people around until you lose your whole crew."

DJ couldn't even respond to that. If Larry had managed to upset her staff that much in two days, she'd have a disaster on her hands within a week. She didn't need anything else to worry about.

Ramon pulled open the door and, with one last glance over his shoulder, stepped through and let it shut behind him. Almost immediately, the voices of the other crew members reached her ears through the thin wall.

"What'd she say?"

Ramon answered too softly for her to hear. He must have given a condensed version of the conversation, because within seconds, someone moaned and someone else swore.

She sucked air into her lungs and released it slowly, then buried her face in her hands and tried not to listen. But her staff's disappointment and resentment reached her even through the wall.

She'd let them down. She'd let herself down. And she'd let Larry down, although he didn't know it. Faced with the chance to claim him as her father, she hadn't done it.

And for the second time, she began to wonder if

her reluctance had roots that reached deeper than confusion.

CURSING UNDER his breath, Adam bounded up the
stairs and into the kitchen. His clock must be wrong.
It couldn't be nine o'clock in the morning already.

He hurried to the window and peered outside.
Dusty gray clouds blocked the sun and darkened the
sky, a stiff breeze rustled the leaves in the trees and
he caught a glimpse of Brittany leading Marissa away
from the house. Where were they going on foot on a
day like this?

He glanced at the clock over the stove and cursed
again. His watch was right. He'd slept too late. He'd
missed hearing DJ leave for work and he'd slept
through Marissa's usual morning routine—in and out
of the bedroom, up and down the hall over his head.

He'd planned to wake early so he could catch DJ
before she went to work. She'd been quiet last
night—too quiet—and he'd started to worry about her
long before they'd finished dinner. She'd been re-
served with him, restrained with Marissa, and stand-
offish toward Larry.

At first, Adam had chalked her mood up to worry
and overwork. By the end of the night, he'd become
convinced she had something more serious on her
mind, but he hadn't been able to get her alone long
enough to find out what.

Shoving his fingers through his hair, he glanced
around the room and tried to get his bearings. One
empty cereal bowl sat in the sink, and a pot of coffee
warmed on the burner. The acid-bitter smell in the air
told him it must have been there for hours.

He went to the refrigerator and reached inside for

the leftover meat loaf from dinner. But he felt only a handful of air where the container should have been. He peered inside, but the meat loaf had disappeared.

Under normal circumstances, he wouldn't give missing meat loaf a second thought, but he knew instinctively where it had gone. Galloway had either finished it or taken it with him—either way, he'd sponged another meal from DJ, and Adam hated the thought.

After watching Galloway for the past week or so, Adam had become convinced the man was a lot more resourceful than Christina Prescott wanted to believe. He'd also grown certain that Galloway's only priority was Galloway himself.

Only a fool could fail to notice DJ's confusion or Marissa's fear. Only a self-indulgent jerk could close his eyes to the turmoil he left in his wake. Now that he'd found DJ, Galloway didn't care what he put her through. And now that he had a granddaughter, he didn't care that the child cringed every time he came near her. But self-indulgence was nothing compared to what Adam feared was Larry's real agenda. He felt sure he was a dangerous man who wouldn't hesitate to harm his own daughter to get back at his ex-wife.

Sighing heavily, Adam closed the refrigerator and crossed to the counter. He dumped the stale coffee and rinsed the pot, then refilled it.

After two weeks on the case, he still hadn't caught Galloway violating his parole, although the incident at the zoo had come chillingly close. In the meantime, he might not be able to warn DJ about the danger she faced, but at least he didn't have to sit and watch while the deadbeat took advantage of her.

Feeling a little better, he reached into the cupboard

overhead for a fresh filter and caught a glimpse of Galloway walking through the parking lot.

Adam stepped back to avoid being seen and watched until Galloway reached the store's front doors. There, he glanced around furtively and slipped inside.

He was up to something. Adam could sense it. Whatever it was, it couldn't be good. Not for DJ, anyway.

Adam raked his fingers through his hair and ran down the back steps into the rising storm. He jogged across the parking lot and slipped into the building only a few minutes behind Galloway.

Inside, he paused on the threshold, panting a little to catch his breath. He didn't have to look very hard to realize Galloway wasn't inside the store itself. The foul weather had obviously affected business—the only two people Adam could see were Heather and Ramon, and they were so engrossed in their conversation, he didn't think they'd even noticed his arrival.

Scanning the empty aisles, he hurried to the back of the store and looked through the sliding-glass doors. Joseph and Billy were working together, moving plants from the raised wooden benches to a flatbed truck, but Adam couldn't see Galloway anywhere.

He turned slowly and caught Ramon watching him.

Ramon jerked his head in greeting. "What's up?"

"I'm looking for Galloway. He came in a few minutes before me. Did you notice him?"

Ramon's face tightened. He used his head to point toward the south door into the fertilizer shed. "Out there."

Adam crossed the store at a near run. Galloway had

already reached the fertilizer shed. He turned the corner and disappeared just as Adam slipped outside. Smiling grimly, Adam hurried after him. Wind whipped at a layer of heavy plastic that protected the plants from the elements, and the fresh scent of ozone warned him it would rain soon.

The overhead lights flickered, urging Adam to hurry. He didn't like the thought of Galloway alone in the fertilizer shed. He'd heard of too many incidents on the news over the past few months involving someone like Galloway, raw chemicals mixed with other easily obtained ingredients—and death.

He rounded the corner and went into the shed as the lights flickered again. Galloway stood in front of a stack of large bags at the far end. He positioned his cart and started loading it with bags of some kind of fertilizer.

With his heart in his throat, Adam scoped out the area, looking for some kind of weapon in case he needed it. But he couldn't see anything useful.

Galloway climbed halfway up the stack and pulled another bag from the top with a grunt. He dropped the sack onto the cart as Adam closed the distance between them. Chemical dust billowed away from the bag, and its acid scent filled the air. When Galloway saw Adam approaching, he stiffened perceptibly and waited.

Trying to look casual, Adam strolled toward him, crunching crystals underfoot. He walked slowly, still looking for a way to defend himself or stop Galloway if he needed to.

When he drew close enough to see Galloway's face clearly, he nodded. But he cursed his rotten luck for being in a predicament like this without his side arm and vowed not to face Galloway again without one. "What's going on?"

Galloway nodded back. He looked wary—even hostile. "What the hell are *you* doing here?"

"Just checking things out. What about you? What are you doing?"

"What business is it of yours?" Galloway leaned one hip against the stack and squinted down at Adam.

"Just curious."

"You know, you're really starting to bug me."

Adam didn't mind that at all, but he smiled innocently. "Sorry."

"Yeah. I'll bet." Galloway's hostility crackled like sparks in the heavy air. The lights flickered again, and thunder rumbled close by.

Adam didn't want to get caught out here in the dark, but he wouldn't leave Galloway alone. He perched on a stack and tried to read the label on the bags on Galloway's cart.

"You know," Galloway said, "I think it's about time we cleared the air between us—got everything out in the open. What do you say?"

Adam shrugged. "If you want."

"For some reason, DJ seems to like you. Obviously, my ex-wife likes you. Me? I don't like you. I don't trust you. What are you really doing here?"

"Like I said, I'm just checking things out."

"No, dammit!" Galloway shouted, then made a visible effort to pull himself together. "I mean in general. What are you doing *here*." He gestured with both hands. "What do you want with DJ?"

The question caught Adam off guard, and he repeated it to make certain he'd understood. "What do I want with DJ?"

"Yeah. What do you want? Are you after her or what?" Galloway's face left no doubt what he meant, and his insinuation sickened Adam.

"No. I'm not 'after' her."

Galloway barked a laugh. "You're a rotten liar, McAllister. I saw you kissing her the other day. God only knows what you would have done if I hadn't come along."

"I never said I'm not attracted to her—"

"Yeah? Well, I don't want you to be 'attracted' to her. You only want one thing from her."

"You're wrong."

"Am I? I don't think so. DJ doesn't need someone like you hanging around."

"Don't you think that's up to DJ to decide?"

Galloway snorted in derision. "No. She's too soft-hearted. She'll take *anything* in."

Irritated beyond words, Adam let his gaze travel slowly over the other man. "Obviously."

Galloway's face froze in an expression of pure hatred. "I don't want you lying to her."

The words stopped Adam cold. Did that mean Galloway knew who Adam was or that he was bluffing? Adam didn't respond. He didn't want to tip his hand.

Galloway's eyes narrowed. "And you'd better not even *think* about hurting her."

Funny. Adam had been about to warn Galloway about the very same thing. This time, he answered. "I have no intention of hurting her."

"Right." Galloway snorted again and climbed partway down the stack. "If you even *try* to take advantage of her, you'll have to answer to me."

Adam couldn't tell whether he heard a threat in those words or a father's concern for his daughter's heart. But he couldn't honestly imagine Galloway being concerned for anyone but himself. "I won't take advantage of her."

Galloway's expression didn't soften. "You'd better not." He jumped the rest of the way to the floor and pulled another bag from a lower stack. He tossed the bag onto the cart and raised another cloud of chemical dust. "Well, I'm trying to do my job, so maybe you can 'check things out' somewhere else." Tugging the cart around behind him, he pushed past Adam and went on out the door, disappearing around the corner.

Arguing silently with himself, Adam followed Galloway's trail out of the fertilizer shed and through the greenhouse toward the nursery. Had he been wrong about Galloway? Maybe Galloway did want to change his life and mend his ways. Maybe he did want nothing more than to settle near his daughter and make up for lost time. Maybe he intended to give DJ exactly what she wanted—a father.

Maybe.

Instinct told him not to believe it. Galloway had spent his life living by his wits. He knew exactly what to say and when to say it to get what he wanted. He was smart enough to pick up on Adam's distrust and play off it.

Slowing his pace a little, he thought back over the events of the past two weeks. He didn't believe the fatherly concern. And the idea of Galloway questioning *Adam's* intentions toward DJ made him laugh.

He slowed his pace even further and stared at the ground, then snorted at the turn his thoughts had taken. *Intentions?* Sure, he found DJ attractive and he'd even indulged in a fantasy or two—but he had no intentions. That word implied change. Permanent change. And he'd never once thought of DJ as a permanent fixture in his life.

He stopped walking altogether and scowled down at a row of prickly red bushes with orange berries and realized that he'd thought about "permanent" once. Maybe twice. But he hadn't been serious.

Had he?

He lifted his head and stared at the rows of plants stretching away from him to meet the Jordan River. The breeze tugged at his hair and rustled the leaves in the trees overhead. The chemical-scented air carried with it the faint fragrance of roses. Somewhere nearby, a sprinkler ticked its rhythm as it sent water across a section of DJ's inventory.

Adam studied it all and wondered silently just what he wanted in his future. He'd grown used to all this in a very short time, but could he spend the rest of his days here?

He pictured DJ in the distance, lifting a tree onto a cart. He could almost see her dark hair gleaming in the sun, could almost smell her scent and feel the touch of her hand on his.

He imagined Marissa dancing around his feet and tugging on his hand to urge him to run in a direction he hadn't ever thought of going. He even saw the dog, Holly, scampering toward him and wriggling as if he were the most important person in her furry black life.

Closing his eyes, he held the moment for as long as he could. And he knew he couldn't lie to himself any longer. He wanted all this. This life. This place. This woman. This child. He loved it here. He loved Marissa.

And most of all, he loved DJ.

A chill ran down his spine and forced his eyes open

again. And he knew, in that moment, he'd been asking himself the wrong question all along. He didn't need to know whether he could spend the rest of his days here, but whether he could survive if he left.

But would DJ want him to stay? Could she love him? Could she forgive him for lying about his reasons for being here?

For less than a heartbeat, he considered the possibility that she might never need to find out. He could spend the rest of his life pretending to be a writer who never wrote. He could keep her from ever meeting his family and friends.

He drew in a deep breath and forced himself to face reality. Even if he tried living a lie, he'd worry every day that DJ would find out. He'd spend weeks, months or years agonizing about her reaction, fearing rejection and dreading the inevitable.

No. The only way he could have the life he wanted with DJ would be by telling her the truth—just as soon as he could. Telling her the truth would be the hardest thing he'd ever done—he'd be taking the chance of losing her forever. But every day he waited would only make the truth harder for her to hear—and harder for him to tell.

CHAPTER ELEVEN

FOR THE THIRD time in as many hours, DJ checked her watch and tried to calculate how long it would take Laura and Bob to drive from Lake Powell back to American Fork. The crisis at the store had only fueled her determination to find out all there was to know about Larry. She needed Laura's calming influence, her soothing voice and her stability.

Laura had always been her rock. Her port in the storm. And Laura had often had to serve as go-between for DJ and Christina. As a young girl, DJ had idolized Laura, and had longed to go everywhere and do everything Laura did. But with a twelve-year difference in their ages, they'd been from separate generations.

While DJ had been playing with dolls and learning to roller-skate, Laura had been experimenting with makeup and agonizing over boys. While Laura had been adjusting to marriage and her first pregnancy, DJ had been selling Girl Scout cookies.

After DJ left college to marry Jeff, the years between them had suddenly evaporated, and they'd been best friends ever since. And DJ turned to Laura with her problems almost as often as she'd turned to her mother. If her mother couldn't—or, more accurately, *wouldn't*—tell her the truth now, Laura would.

She glanced at her watch again and cursed herself

for letting precious minutes go to waste. After scanning the store quickly for unattended customers or potential trouble spots, she slipped inside the office and locked the door.

She walked to the desk and punched in Laura's home number. Almost the instant she finished dialing, her courage faltered.

She closed her eyes and waited through four endless rings before Laura answered. She sounded breathless and slightly harried, and DJ could picture her rushing down the stairs and leaning over the banister to grab the wall phone in the kitchen.

"Laura? Thank God you're there."

"DJ? Is that you?"

"Yes."

"What's wrong? Are you okay? Is Marissa okay?"

"She's fine," DJ said quickly. "So am I—I guess."

"What do you mean, you *guess?* Something *is* wrong. I can hear it in your voice. What is it?"

DJ tried to remember what she'd decided to say. But her mind was a blank and she could only manage to ask, "Have you talked to Mom yet?"

"Not since before we left," Laura said. "Why?"

"There've been some odd things happening around here lately, and I need to ask you some questions. I need you to promise you'll tell me the truth."

A hint of wariness crept into Laura's tone. "What kinds of questions?"

"All I want is the truth, Laura. Do you promise?"

Laura let out an exasperated sigh. "When have I ever lied to you?"

DJ laughed, but even she heard the anger and bitterness behind it. "I need your promise, Laura, or I'm hanging up."

"All right," Laura said quickly. "I promise. What's wrong?"

"I need you to tell me everything you know about Larry Galloway."

Laura sucked in a quick breath. "Where did you hear that name?"

"He showed up on my doorstep the other day."

"Larry Galloway did? My God. Are you sure it was him?"

"Positive."

"Dammit." The word sounded soft and faraway. Laura must have moved the receiver away from her mouth. Almost immediately, she put it back in place. "How did he find you? What does he want?" No denials. No questions. No confusion.

"He wants to get to know me. He wants to be a grandfather to Marissa."

"A *grandfather*—? Listen to me, DJ. Don't let him anywhere *near* Marissa."

Laura's reaction frightened her. "Why?"

"Would you, for once in your life, just do what somebody else tells you without asking a hundred questions?"

DJ shook her head as if Laura could see her. "Tell me *why* I should keep him away from Marissa."

Laura paused for a long time before she answered. "I can't. I promised Mom I wouldn't tell you."

DJ closed her eyes and tried to calm herself. "Mom knows he's here."

"She does?" Laura couldn't even hide her surprise. "When is she coming home?"

"She's not."

"Are you serious?" Laura demanded. "What did she say when you told her?"

The words still felt like rocks in DJ's stomach, but Laura would clam up if DJ let her anger and hurt come through in her voice. "She admitted everything."

"Everything?"

"Yes," DJ lied. "She told me he's my father, if that's what you're wondering."

"Don't call him that," Laura snapped. "He doesn't *deserve* to be called that." DJ heard footsteps through the line and knew Laura had started pacing. She always paced when something upset her. "What does he want?"

"I told you. He wants a family. He wants to make up for all the years I didn't even know about him. He wants—"

"Money," Laura interrupted angrily. "Has he asked you for a loan yet? Has he asked you for a place to stay?"

"No," DJ said, and forced herself to ignore the niggling reminder of Larry asking for a job and showing up for meals without invitation.

"Well, he will," Laura said. "Don't give him anything."

"Why?"

"Because you'll never get rid of him if you do. How long has he been there?"

"A little over a week."

"A week?" Laura muttered something under her breath. "When did he get out?"

DJ stared at the receiver in her hand and repeated, *"Out?"*

"Out of prison?"

DJ's stomach knotted and her heart skipped a beat. Larry had been in *prison?* She shoved the fingers of one hand through her hair and struggled to pull her scattered thoughts together.

Laura halted whatever she'd been doing and a stony silence fell between them. "I thought you said you'd talked to Mom." The words sounded more like an accusation than a question.

"I did."

"I don't believe you."

"You don't have to believe me," DJ said angrily. "I talked to her the day he arrived."

"Tell me exactly what she told you."

DJ answered truthfully this time. "Not much. I had no idea he'd been in prison. Why didn't she tell me? What was he convicted of?"

"Several counts of assault with a deadly weapon."

"Assault—?" DJ broke off and stared at the wall in front of her desk and tried to tell herself it wasn't true. She closed her eyes and rubbed her forehead. "What did he do?"

"What he always does," Laura said. "He got angry and decided to teach somebody a lesson."

DJ couldn't have mistaken the note of hatred in Laura's voice if she'd tried. She lowered her trembling fingers to her desk and gripped a pencil. "Is that why she lied to me about him all these years?"

"Not entirely."

"Tell me the rest."

"I can't."

"You *can,*" DJ insisted. "You just don't want to."

"No, I can't. I promised Mom."

DJ's patience reached its limit. "I don't care what you promised Mom. She's been lying to me my whole life. Everything I've ever known—everything I've believed about myself—has been a lie.''

Laura didn't respond.

"Put yourself in my place," DJ said. "How would you feel if you suddenly discovered you had a father you never knew about? And that the two people you trusted most had been lying to you as long as you could remember?''

Laura still didn't respond, but DJ could hear her breathing. "You've got to get rid of him," she said at last. "Send him away. *Don't* let him worm his way into your family. Don't let him get close to Marissa— she's the same way you were as a child.''

"What way?"

"Stubborn. Full of life." Laura paused again, then asked, "Where is he now?"

"He's stocking weed killer for a sale I'm running tomorrow.''

"You mean he's *working* there? My God, DJ. What are you thinking?''

DJ tried not to resent the question and the implication behind it, but she could hear the anger in her voice when she spoke again. "He's my father and he needed a job. What do you expect me to do?''

Laura sighed heavily. "Is he actually working? Or is he just collecting a paycheck?''

"He's working."

Laura laughed through her nose. "I'll bet he is. He's still on his best behavior.''

"You don't like him at all, do you?"

Laura laughed bitterly. "Like him? God, no. I hate him.''

"Why? What did he do?"

"What didn't he do. He's a dangerous man. He'll

hurt you and he'll hurt Marissa. Is that what you want?"

"No, of course not."

"Then get rid of him."

"I can't."

"Why not?" Laura's voice rose to a near shout. "Tell me why I should."

"I can't, DJ. I promised Mom—"

"If that's all you're going to say, then drop it."

"DJ—"

"I mean it, Laura. If that's your answer, I don't want to hear it again, because I'm already so angry with Mom, I can't stand it. I don't want to talk to her, and I certainly don't want to *see* her."

Laura sighed heavily. "That's not fair. You have no idea what Mom went through with Larry."

"You're right," DJ retorted. She could hear the hysteria building in her voice, but she couldn't seem to stop it. "I don't. But I'd love to understand, so *tell* me."

"I can't," Laura said once more.

This time, DJ couldn't even begin to hide her irritation. "You *can*. You can play this game all you want, Laura, but I am not going to send him away unless you give me a better reason than you've given me so far."

"All right!" Laura shouted. "Fine. Have it your way. Let him stay until he ends up hurting someone."

"How can you be so certain he will?"

"I know him. But if you insist on being so damned stubborn, at least find someone to stay at the house with you. I'll feel better knowing you're not alone."

DJ pushed the hair from her eyes and rested her

elbow on the desk. "Adam's already staying in the basement."

"Adam?" Laura's voice rose again. "Who's *Adam?*"

"He's a friend of Mom's. She promised him a place to stay while he researches a book, and guess whose place that was."

"She didn't."

"She did."

"So some old friend of Mom's is staying in your basement while Larry Galloway's hanging around?" Laura paused for a few seconds. "Tell me about him. Could he be of *any* help if Larry becomes dangerous?"

DJ couldn't help but smile at the image of Adam that formed in her mind. Broad-shouldered. Narrow-waisted. Long-legged. And arms that felt like bands of steel when he wrapped them around her. "Yes," she said. "I think he would be."

Laura groaned. "I can't believe this. What's Mom been doing, teaching writing classes again? I *hate* it when she does that and all those people start hanging around as if she's going to give them a free ride to the top."

"She likes to help. Adam needed a place to stay, I needed the money and he's here."

Laura indulged in another long sigh, and DJ could almost see her rolling her eyes with exasperation. "I suppose I should be glad of it this time. Just keep him there with you. And keep Larry Galloway away from the house."

"I can't make any promises," DJ said.

"Maybe you should tell this Adam guy about Larry so he's aware of what to watch for."

"They've met," DJ admitted.

"That's good. What does he think of Larry?"

"He hasn't said." It was the truth, even though his expressions and his actions left no doubt that he felt much the same as Laura and her mother.

"I wish you'd change your mind." Laura's voice rose a note, almost as if she'd asked a question, but DJ couldn't respond.

"Keep me posted," Laura said at last. "And *please* be careful."

"I will," DJ replied. She could promise that much. "I'll call you tomorrow."

"I'll be busy all day. We've got a shipment of weed killer coming in the morning."

"I don't care," Laura warned. "I'll call you, anyway." But she sounded more like herself, and DJ smiled.

"I'm sure you will."

"Call *me* if anything happens."

"I will," DJ said. "I'm hanging up now before you drag this out another half hour."

"Brat," Laura snarled, but DJ could hear a note of affection in her voice.

"I'm hanging up," DJ said with a laugh. But after she replaced the receiver, her smile faded and she stared at the top of her desk and let the conversation replay in her mind.

Laura's reaction to the news about Larry had surprised her. So had Laura's certainty that Larry posed a threat of some kind to DJ and Marissa. But her refusal to elaborate left DJ frustrated and angry.

Pressing the fingers of one hand to her forehead, DJ thought back over the times she and Marissa had been around Larry since he'd first appeared in her driveway. She'd seen flashes of temper and she had been more careful around him since that day at the zoo. Even she couldn't excuse the way he'd treated Marissa then.

Pulling her hand away from her forehead, she stared at it for a long time, as if she expected it to give her the answers. When she realized what she was doing, she laughed at herself and pushed away from the desk.

She had to admit Larry frightened her a little, and Laura's reaction had worried her more than she'd let on. But that only made it harder to tell Larry she wanted him to leave—not easier.

WHILE DJ TUCKED Marissa into bed and read her a story, Adam reworded a paragraph of his report and saved his document. He'd been pretending to write his book since dinner and hating every minute he had to spend on the computer. He didn't like computers. Never had. He didn't like making DJ believe he was working on his nonexistent book while he struggled with the report. He felt better since deciding to tell DJ the truth, and he planned to do it tonight. But even knowing he'd made the right decision didn't make him less uneasy about what he had to do.

He glanced at the kitchen doorway, wishing DJ would come back so he could get it over with. He'd apologize for deceiving her. He'd tell her he loved her. And then he'd hold his breath and wait for her to either send him away or forgive him.

The computer made a couple of grinding noises, then blinked the report onto the screen again and waited for him to type more. He held back a heavy sigh and bent over the keyboard again.

Even under the best of circumstances, completing a report in the painstaking detail Thomas Dodge demanded was a challenge. But tonight, with so many other things on his mind, Adam had to struggle for every word. He didn't know why he bothered. Chuck and Dodge would probably yank him from duty by morning. But he had to do *something* while he waited.

He stared at the screen for a few minutes, but he couldn't drag his mind back to the task at hand. Almost too soon, he heard DJ's footsteps in the hallway. A second later she came into the room.

Deep-toned and rich, her hair hung below her shoulders, and she stared at him with eyes dark as the night. She seemed different, somehow. More fragile. More guarded.

He dimmed the screen on the computer and tried to force a smile. "She's in bed, then?"

"Yes," she said. "Finally."

He let his gaze linger on her face and tried to read her expression. "You look tired."

She crossed the room and dropped onto a chair beside his. Lacing her fingers, she propped her elbows on the table and rested her chin on the bridge of her fingers. "I am. Today was a very long day."

"You were busy at the store?"

She lowered her eyes and looked away, almost as if she wanted to avoid his gaze. "Not really."

Adam studied her for another second, but she refused to look up. "What's wrong?"

DJ stiffened and glanced uneasily at him, but immediately returned her gaze to the table. "What makes you ask that?"

"It's written all over your face."

She touched one hand to her cheek and smiled, but

it didn't look genuine. She looked troubled. Concerned. Confused.

"What is it?" he asked again.

She hesitated for a long moment before she finally answered. "I talked to my sister today."

No wonder she seemed distracted. "She's back from her trip?"

DJ nodded. "She and Bob got home this morning."

"And you asked her about Galloway?"

She nodded again but didn't elaborate.

Adam tried to be patient and wait for her to give him the details. But when she hadn't spoken after a few seconds, he cocked an eyebrow at her. "And—?" he prompted. "What did she say?"

DJ shrugged listlessly. "Apparently Larry was in prison before he showed up here." She flushed a deep red.

Adam held back a relieved sigh. That made one less thing he had to tell her. One less reason for her to turn him away. "Did she say what he was in for?"

She nodded, but she still wouldn't look at him. "She said he was convicted of assault with a deadly weapon." She looked almost embarrassed—even worried—as if she expected him to hold Larry's past against her.

Her reaction touched Adam deeply. He longed to take her into his arms and reassure her. He ached to pull her close and kiss away her uncertainty. But he only touched her hand with his fingertips. "I see. And how do you feel about that?"

She gave a bitter laugh and looked at him. "I don't know. Betrayed, I guess. *Again*." She shook her head and looked away. "And incredibly stupid."

"Stupid?" Adam tightened his hold on her hand. "Why?"

Pulling her hand from his, she stood. "I should have expected something like this. I should have known."

"How *could* you have known?"

"I could have asked."

"You think he would have told you the truth if you had?" He smiled gently to take any sting from his words and added, "I think you're being too hard on yourself."

"I *could* have asked," she insisted. "But I didn't. I could have hired a private investigator to check him out, but I trusted him. I could have taken you up on your offer to find out about him—" She shook her head sadly. "I don't know. Maybe I didn't want to know the truth. Maybe I wanted to believe—just for a little while."

Her words hit Adam like a blow to the stomach. So much depended on this conversation, he didn't want to say or do the wrong thing. But she looked hurt and far too vulnerable. All at once this didn't seem like the time to unburden himself. He couldn't justify adding anything else to the list of problems she had to contend with.

He pushed aside the niggling thought that he might be using her emotional state as an excuse to avoid something unpleasant. "Maybe you needed to believe in him."

She laughed without humor. "The ironic thing is, if I'd been doing business with him, I'd have been *much* more careful. I'd have checked references and made sure I knew who I was doing business with."

Adam rose, as well. He couldn't let her beat herself

up over this. But he felt like a jerk going to her, holding her, offering comfort without removing the lie that stood between them. For a heartbeat, he considered taking a chance and telling her anyway. But when she met his gaze and he saw the pain in her eyes, he knew he had no right to soothe his conscience at her expense. He couldn't follow this latest betrayal with one of his own.

She paced away again and stared out the window into the night. Sighing, she leaned her head on the corner of a cabinet and sent him a sideways glance. "I want to believe he's changed, but I can't forget the way he treated Marissa at the zoo. I can't ignore his temper any longer. He's upset my whole staff and Ramon's ready to quit—"

Adam lifted one shoulder in a halfhearted shrug. "You're right to be cautious."

"How do I tell him I've changed my mind? How do I tell him to leave? You know how he is. He wants to be part of everything, and he doesn't even understand why I want to take things slowly. What do you think he'll do if I tell him I don't want him around anymore?"

Adam stuffed his hands into his pockets and forced himself to stay on his own side of the room. She'd run away from him twice—he wouldn't chase her. "If you're ready to send him away, I'll do what I can to help."

She gave him an anguished glance. "How do I do that?"

Adam had a few ideas, but none that would pass Chuck's and Thomas Dodge's scrutiny. "Start by telling him you need a few days when he's not around while you figure out how you feel about him coming back.''

She shook her head slowly. ''What good would that do? He'll just come back again.''

''If he does, I'll be here.''

DJ's eyes darkened but she didn't argue.

Again, the urge to pull her into his arms rocked Adam to his very soul, but he battled the urge and leaned one shoulder against the refrigerator. ''I'll be right here with you,'' he repeated.

DJ didn't look sad and lost anymore. Her eyes snapped with anger and her face was flushed. Standing there in bare feet, jeans and a T-shirt, she looked more beautiful than he'd ever seen her. ''Why can't finding my father be simple, exciting and beautiful? Why does it have to be ugly, frightening and confusing?''

Adam couldn't answer that, but neither could he tear his gaze from her. Abandoning the battle with his self-control, he walked toward her. He expected her to pull away again as he drew near; instead, she lifted her chin and stared into his eyes.

Silently, hesitantly, he wrapped his arms around her and pressed a kiss to the side of her cheek. ''You don't have to do this alone, you know. We'll get through tomorrow together, and we'll get Larry to back off a little and give you some time.''

''I can't ask for your help.'' She spoke so softly, he could scarcely hear her.

''You're not asking, I'm offering.''

She tried to smile, but her lips trembled and he could see what the effort cost her. ''Laura wants me to ask you to stay so you can protect us.''

''I can do that.''

''No.'' She shook her head again. ''I can't ask that of you and I won't hide behind you.''

''*You?* Hide behind *me?*'' He worked his arms a little tighter around her waist. ''In my wildest dreams, I can't imagine you hiding behind anyone.''

She looked away quickly, but not before he caught the gleam of unshed tears in her eyes.

He hated seeing her hurt, and hated even more knowing he was partially responsible. Tilting her chin until their eyes met again, he whispered, ''You *could* try letting someone stand beside you. That wouldn't hurt too much, would it?''

She swiped at her eyes with the back of her hand. ''I don't know. I've never tried.''

''I haven't, either,'' he admitted. ''Not really.''

This time, he drew a genuine laugh from her, but she sobered instantly and studied his face for one heart-stopping moment. ''How do you do this to me? How do you make me smile—even laugh—in my darkest moments?''

He lifted one shoulder in what he hoped looked like a nonchalant shrug, but his heart pounded and his senses were filled with her. ''I guess that's the kind of guy I am. Amazing, isn't it?''

He tried grinning at her, but his smile wouldn't stay in place. Cupping her chin with one hand, he searched her eyes and tried to tell himself he shouldn't take advantage of her vulnerability. But logic had no power over his thoughts. He lowered his lips to hers and brushed a kiss across her mouth, then another.

She leaned into him and slid her arms around his neck, and she offered more with the touch of her lips than he'd ever dared imagine. Her kiss robbed him of breath and filled him with hope.

When he ran his tongue across her lips, she opened her mouth to him and moaned softly. Desire swept through him, and he deepened the kiss. He pulled her closer until the soft swell of her breasts pressed against his chest. He wanted her. He needed her. And in this moment, he believed she needed him just as much.

Tightening the embrace, he crushed her against him. Every nerve tingled as if his body had been asleep for a long time and had just awakened. He used his fingers to trace the curve of her spine and the swell of her hips, and he reveled in the luxury of holding her in his arms.

He trailed kisses along her jawline, then buried his face in the hollow of her neck and let his mouth play across the skin there. With her eyes closed, she tilted her head back and moaned again. A fresh wave of desire rolled through him, tightening his loins and sending fire through his veins.

He captured her mouth again and nipped softly at her lips with his teeth. Her lips curved into a smile, and she let her hands run down his back and settle around his waist. He pulled her solidly against him and held her there for a moment while he studied her face—her eyes, her chin, her throat—and realized how much he'd give to spend the rest of his life with her. He wanted to possess her—to make her his. But no man could possess a woman like DJ; to try would destroy everything fine and wonderful about her.

He leaned forward to kiss her again, but this time she pushed him away gently with the palms of both hands. Struggling to catch her breath, she managed an apologetic smile. "If you kiss me like that again, I'm going to trip you and beat you to the floor." Her grin widened, but she shook her head slowly. "But I can't. Marissa's in the next room, and—"

Adam touched two fingers to her lips and pressed a kiss to her cheek. "I know. I don't want to take any chances, either." At this moment it felt like a lie, but he knew that when reason returned, he'd be glad they'd waited, if only for DJ's sake.

He couldn't let desire rob him of reason or take them somewhere DJ might later regret. He couldn't allow their relationship to reach a new level with a lie standing between them.

He didn't want to risk DJ's eventually resenting him for trapping her when she was most vulnerable. He'd survived many things during his life, but just the thought of losing DJ made his stomach clench in fear.

She'd never know how much he wanted her or what effort it took to release her. His world felt empty without her in his arms, and letting her go was one of the hardest things he'd ever done. He wanted to hold her forever. He wanted to feel her silky softness pressed against him. He wanted *her*.

For the first time in his life, he'd found someone from whom he couldn't remain detached on some level. The realization frightened and exhilarated him at the same time. And he knew, deep in his soul, that he couldn't risk losing her or he would never survive.

CHAPTER TWELVE

CLUTCHING HER FIRST cup of morning coffee in one hand, DJ held open the front door for Marissa and Holly with the other, then followed them outside. She blinked rapidly as her eyes adjusted to the sunlight and stifled a yawn as she lowered herself to the steps.

She'd spent most of the night awake reliving Adam's kiss and agonizing over her family. Sometime during the night, she'd stopped playing games with herself about her feelings for Adam. She wanted a life with him, a future. She'd even come to terms with her conflicting feelings toward Larry. And for the first time in two weeks, she felt as if she had her life back on track.

Leaning her back against the step behind her, she looked out over her yard and savored the cool, clean air and the bright morning sunshine. The trees had already turned red and gold, a layer of leaves lined the street and the chill from the concrete crept through the denim of her jeans.

She loved autumn with its warm days and cool nights. But this fall had been so different, she hadn't had time to enjoy the season. She hadn't taken Marissa for a drive through the Wasatch Mountains to look at fall leaves. She hadn't planted any new fall bulbs in her garden. She hadn't even thought about decorating for Halloween. But with her life on a more even keel, she would be able to do all that and more in the weeks ahead.

Sighing with contentment, she watched as Marissa raced Holly across the lawn. At the street, the girl pivoted back to face her. "Can we go to the park, Mommy? P'ease?"

DJ sipped coffee and smiled. "All right, if that's what you want to do on my day off."

"It is, it is. Can we take Adam, too?"

Just the mention of his name made DJ smile. "We can ask him, but he might need to stay home and work."

"No he won't. He doesn't like to work."

He didn't seem to—at least not with the same zeal her mother put into her writing. DJ had to admit, she found Adam's more laid-back approach to his career easier to live with than her mother's near obsession. "We'll ask him."

"Can I ask him right now?"

"I think he's still asleep. Let's wait until he wakes up."

"He might be awake right now. I could go see." Without waiting for DJ's permission, Marissa started up the steps.

"Oh no, you don't." DJ snagged Marissa by the waistband of her pants and held her in place.

Marissa's face puckered into a frown. "But there's nothing to *do*."

"Play with Holly a while longer. We can go to the park after breakfast."

Marissa's face fell, but she stopped struggling against DJ's hold. "I hope he wakes up soon."

As if on cue, the front door opened behind them and Adam stepped onto the porch looking as if he'd just climbed out of bed. He wore faded jeans and an untucked, unbuttoned thermal shirt. His hair stood up in soft spikes, and a night's growth of beard darkened his cheeks and chin. He looked incredible. More seductive than any man should so early in the morning.

DJ's pulse raced and her heart gave its now familiar leap at the sight of him.

Marissa shouted with delight and bounded up the steps toward him. "Goody. You're awake. See, Mommy? He's awake. Will you come with us to the park?"

"Let him wake up first," DJ said.

He met her gaze, and a slow, sexy smile crossed his face. "Tell you what, squirt. Let me talk to your mom for a few minutes. We can play in a while." He ruffled Marissa's hair, but kept his gaze firmly riveted on DJ as he spoke.

Marissa scowled, but Adam's promise seemed to satisfy her. Slapping her thigh, she called Holly and skipped down the steps to the lawn.

Adam watched her race away, then grinned at DJ and seated himself on the step behind her. When their eyes met, everything inside her seemed to liquify. His knees touched her shoulders as he sat, and desire coursed through her. Leaning slightly forward, he brushed a quick kiss across her lips. "Good morning."

She grinned up at him, content in his presence, secure by his side. "Good morning. Do you want coffee? It's fresh."

"I'll get it in a minute. First things first." He kissed her again, longer and more passionately this time. When he pulled away, his eyes seemed to bore into her, as if he could see through to her soul. "How are you feeling?"

"I'm fine." She leaned against his legs and smiled. "More than fine."

"Are you still planning to ask Larry to leave?"

The intimacy of the contact left DJ flushed and breathless, but she managed to speak and hoped she sounded halfway normal. "Yes. I have to. You've seen how he treats Marissa. I can't let that continue."

"No, you can't."

"He's upset everyone at the store. I'll lose my staff if he stays."

Adam nodded slowly, but he searched her face. "What about you? How do you feel about him leaving?"

She sighed softly. "I'm fine. I thought about it all night, and I realized I'd built up a fantasy father in my mind. I can't let everyone around me suffer because of a dream."

He nodded and squeezed her shoulders. "Have you been thinking about what your sister said?" The intensity of his gaze and the gentleness of his touch made her shiver with anticipation.

"Among other things."

Adam didn't speak for a long time. He watched Marissa scamper across the grass in front of the dog and his expression softened.

DJ studied his profile, the set of his jaw, and her heart lurched in her chest. When he turned to her again, she lost herself in his eyes. He pulled her into his orbit and robbed her of the energy and the will to resist.

Sighing softly, she surrendered to the moment. She

wanted to forget the past and concentrate on the future. And she wanted that future with Adam.

To her surprise, his hands stilled and his features sobered. "DJ, we need to talk."

He looked so serious, her heart slowed and dread took the place of anticipation. She sat up and turned to face him. "All right."

"There's something I need to tell you."

"All right," she said again. "What is it?"

He looked away and swallowed. She watched his throat work, his mouth tighten and his eyes dull. "When I came here, I didn't have any idea what you were like. I—"

When he broke off and looked away, her throat clenched with fear. She'd grown used to having him here—to the feel of his arms around her, the taste of his lips on hers, the insistent brush of his whisker-stubbled chin on her cheek. But what if he didn't feel the same way? What if he wanted to leave?

As if he could read her mind, he pulled his hands from her shoulders. He shielded his eyes and stared at something behind her. "Is this someone you know?"

Frustrated by the interruption, DJ turned just as Laura's blue Chevrolet pulled into the driveway. "It's my sister."

"She looks upset."

She did, but at this moment, DJ didn't care. She wanted to know what Adam had been about to say.

He pushed to his feet and held out a hand to her. "Let's see what she wants."

Biting back a sigh, DJ let him pull her to her feet and started down the steps as Laura slid out of the car.

Her eyes looked dark and angry, her shoulders tense, her jaw set and ready for an argument. She slammed the car door behind her and took Adam's measure quickly. "Who's this? Mom's friend?"

A little embarrassed by Laura's uncharacteristic rudeness, DJ nodded. "Adam McAllister—my sister, Laura Oliver."

Laura's eyes tilted down at the corners, and her mouth thinned. "Did you tell him?"

"Yes, I told him what you said about Larry." DJ had seen Laura in this mood before. She didn't like it. "He knows as much as I do."

Laura glanced at him again. "Good. You can help me talk some sense into her." She turned back to DJ with a tight frown. "I've been thinking about our conversation all night, and I'm not going to sit back with my mouth shut while you make the biggest mistake of your life."

"I've already—" she began.

But Laura waved a hand and interrupted. "You don't know what kind of man Larry he is. Trust me— you don't want him anywhere around."

Her attitude grated on DJ's already sensitive nerves. She laughed harshly. "*Trust* you? You've been lying to me my entire life, and now you expect me to *trust* you?"

Laura leaned close to DJ and spoke through gritted teeth. "Larry Galloway is a horrible, angry, violent man. He's vicious and hateful, and he'll do anything to get what he wants."

"Oh?" DJ snapped. "What do you think he wants?"

"He wants Mom!" Laura nearly shouted. "He's *always* wanted Mom. He's never forgiven her for leaving him, and if he's here now, it's because he thinks he can get to her through you."

"He's never said anything about Mom," DJ argued.

"He's not *stupid*. If he lets you know how much he hates her, you'll keep your guard up against him."

"Why does he hate her? What happened between them?" DJ demanded for what felt like the hundredth time in two weeks.

"Maybe you ought to tell us what you know about their divorce," Adam suggested. And when Laura acted as if she didn't want to answer, he added, "The more we know, the better chance we'll have to protect DJ and Marissa."

Laura eyed him for a long moment, then nodded slowly. "Larry's a very controlling person. I'm sure you've already figured that out. Mom realized almost immediately after DJ was born that he wouldn't be able to control her the way he did us. She has a different personality." She turned to DJ and tried to force a laugh. "You're too stubborn for your own good. You always have been."

Adam's eyes met DJ's and his lips curved into a ghost of a smile that took away some of the sting of Laura's words.

"Mom knew he'd lose control with you the first time you told him 'No' or disobeyed him," Laura said. "And she knew he'd be harder on you than he was on anyone else, because he thought you were his perfect little princess—his only child. He hated me for not being his." Her voice caught, and she dashed a tear away impatiently.

Laura's version of the story left DJ confused. Larry had never talked about Laura as if he hated her, but then, she didn't trust him to tell her the truth—not anymore.

"I was only five when Mom met him," Laura said. "She wasn't like she is now. She was quieter. Shy. Unsure of herself. You don't remember Grandpa, but he used to treat her horribly. Even *I* used to get angry with him for the way he talked to her. And my dad wasn't any better. I still remember the horrible fights they had and the things he said to her. Anyway, I guess she was so used to being treated like dirt by the men in her life, Larry had an open door to walk through. Only with Larry, things grew worse—much worse."

"Did she know he was like that when she met him?" Adam asked.

Laura shook her head and leaned against the porch rail. "No. She thought he was so nice at first. But then, men like Larry usually act that way. *I* didn't like him, though. I guess kids have a better sense for people than adults do."

DJ glanced at Marissa and thought back over all the times Marissa had shown her dislike of Larry. With a sinking heart, she realized how many times she'd ignored Marissa's reaction or excused it as something else.

"Anyway, I resented Mom for a long time," Laura admitted. "He was mean, and I hated her for staying with him. And then, when you came along—" She broke off and looked at the trees across the street. "Even though she wasn't able to leave for *me,* she finally left for *you.*"

DJ let out a breath she hadn't been aware of holding. "If you were that angry, why did you keep her secret? Why didn't you tell me the truth?"

"Because if you'd known who Larry was—if you'd even known he existed—you'd have tried to find him. If you had, he would have manipulated you into staying with him, and that would have broken Mom's heart. Besides, you're my little sister. I couldn't let him do to you what he did to me."

"What did he do to you?" DJ asked.

Laura's lips thinned and her eyes clouded. "Just what I told you. He controlled everything. He had to have everything his way. And when things didn't go the way he wanted, he 'punished' us. But Larry doesn't think he's ever been at fault for anything—even the crimes that got him sent to prison. I'll bet he even told you the divorce was Mom's fault and that Mom's a terrible bitch for leaving him."

DJ could feel Adam's eyes on her, but she couldn't say anything. Laura's words struck too close to home.

"That's what he did, isn't it?" Laura demanded. "He blamed Mom."

DJ's throat constricted, but she managed a weak nod.

"I shouldn't be surprised," Laura said with a brittle laugh. "He'll always find some way to make himself look good. That's what worries me about him being here with you."

"If it makes you feel any better," DJ said, "I've already decided to ask Larry to leave."

"You have?" Laura's eyes lit up with hope, and she managed the first genuine smile of the morning. "I can't tell you how glad I am to hear that. But he won't go quietly, I can promise you that."

"I'll be here," Adam said. "She won't have to tell him alone."

"He'll be angry," Laura warned. "And that's really why I came. I think you should let me take Marissa home with me so she's not anywhere near when he blows up.''

''You think he'd hurt her?'' DJ asked.

''He'd do whatever he thought would get him what he wants,'' Laura said. ''He might even take her, just like he took you from Mom. He obviously knows how much you love her. She's your weakest spot, and that's where he'll hit you.''

An image—a dim memory—suddenly flashed through DJ's mind. It disappeared before she could identify it, but it left her cold and almost frightened. ''What do you mean, he 'took' me?''

Even Adam looked stunned. ''Tell me about it.'' His voice sounded gruff. Harsh.

Laura considered for a moment, then nodded. She dragged in a deep breath and let it out slowly. ''When Mom filed for divorce, the judge granted her temporary custody. Larry was allowed visitation twice a month, but only in the presence of a court-approved supervisor.''

''Supervised visitation?'' Adam asked. ''Why?''

Laura's gaze faltered a little. ''Because he took DJ away from Mom when they separated, and he made some threats....''

DJ took a step closer to Laura. ''What are you talking about?''

''It was all such an ugly mess. They were supposed to settle on a supervisor, but they couldn't ever agree, so Larry never saw you. But that was *his* choice—it wasn't Mom's fault.''

Adam leaned forward, obviously fascinated by the story, and DJ wondered for half a second whether it was concern for her or the scent of a story that held his attention. She forced herself not to worry and to focus on Laura's face.

"He never paid child support," Laura said. "He said he wasn't about to pay for some kid he never saw." Laura's voice changed, almost as if she were mimicking Larry's own words. "He thought holding out on the money would bring Mom running back, but he didn't know the new Mom. No matter what he said, no matter how many times he threatened her, she didn't give in. Anyway, the divorce dragged on for a long time, and Larry tried everything to get Mom to come back, but you know Mom—once she makes up her mind, nothing changes it. In the end, he offered to forfeit his parental rights, and Mom took him up on the offer without hesitation."

DJ's head reeled. It was all too much to take in. "The court just let him give me up?"

Laura nodded. "Yes. It isn't common, but because of the kind of man he is and the things he'd done during the divorce, the judge thought it would be best for you. Larry had a record even then, and Mom finally revealed the things he'd put us through. He denied everything, of course, but the judge believed Mom and terminated Larry's paternal rights. Legally, he's not your father anymore."

For an instant DJ wondered if she'd heard right. Her own divorce had made her familiar with custody issues. If the court had allowed Larry to give her up, the judge must have believed he was a dangerous man.

She tried to block out Laura's voice, but she heard every word. She took a step backward to escape, but she ran into the solid wall of Adam's chest. She tried to rub the pain from her forehead with trembling fingers. For the first time, she was horribly afraid.

Adam stood behind DJ, wishing he could say or do something that would help. But everything he thought of would have sounded weak and useless. And she was wound so tight, she'd probably jump out of her skin if he touched her.

Laura closed the distance between them and pulled her sister into an embrace. DJ responded like a rag doll—limp, unseeing. But before he could make a move toward her, Marissa cried out, almost as if she'd been hurt.

Torn between them, Adam hesitated for only a second. DJ had Laura; she didn't need him right now. Jogging down the steps, he scanned the yard, but before he could locate Marissa, he heard Laura's shocked voice.

"Oh, my God! I don't believe this." She sounded strange. Frightened.

Adam's heart twisted in his chest as images of an injured Marissa filled his imagination. He followed Laura's gaze and looked past the girl cowering beside a tree near the road to Larry Galloway standing a few feet behind Laura's car.

Adam battled an almost-irresistible urge to use his fists on Galloway. He wanted the jerk to know what he thought of his decision to abandon DJ and then waltz back into her life thirty years later. He wanted to defend Marissa by frightening Galloway. He wanted him to see how it felt to be defenseless and at someone else's mercy. But he forced himself to remain in control.

Once Galloway realized they'd seen him, he pasted on an unconvincing smile, swaggered toward the steps and tried to act as if nothing were out of the ordinary. "Good morning."

Nobody spoke.

Galloway's smile faded a little. "What's going on?"

Laura looked away. "What's *he* doing here?" she demanded of DJ.

"I don't know—" DJ began, but she couldn't say any more.

"What's going on?" Galloway asked again. "Havin' a party?"

DJ struggled to return the smile, but her effort came out as forced as Galloway's. "Laura stopped by—"

Larry's expression shifted so suddenly, it caught even Adam by surprise. "Laura? No kidding?" He peered at her and tried to look friendly. "What the hell are you doing here?"

Laura didn't even look at him, but her jaw tightened and her face grew red.

"Well? What is it? What's going on?" Galloway paused with his foot on the bottom step and his smile faded. "Oh. I get it. You're talking about me, aren't you?"

DJ glanced uneasily at Laura, but Laura still refused to acknowledge Galloway.

"*Plotting* against me?" Galloway asked with a stiff laugh.

Adam didn't like the look on Galloway's face or the gleam in his eye. He positioned himself between Galloway and the women, but he forced himself to wait. He couldn't take any action unless Galloway did something threatening, but he had no intention of leaving Laura and Marissa unguarded so close to him.

Before he could completely block Galloway's path,

Laura pushed past him. "Get out of here before I call the police."

Galloway stepped back and held up both hands to ward off the attack. He looked supremely innocent. "What's the matter with you?"

"I said, get out of here."

"Why? What did I do?" Galloway looked around as if he'd missed something.

"It's no use pretending," Laura snapped. "I'm telling her the truth about what happened."

Galloway's innocent expression changed to one of open hostility. "What truth?"

"I was there, remember? I saw it all."

He shook his head. "What did you see?"

Laura's nostrils flared and tears of anger glinted in her eyes. "I saw you beat my mother."

DJ gasped and stepped back. She clutched her stomach as if she were about to be sick, and Adam's own stomach knotted in sympathetic pain.

Galloway's face paled, but he recovered quickly and leaned closer to Laura. "I didn't beat your mother. I just dealt with her when she needed to be taught a lesson. She asked for what she got."

"I saw you slam her face into the radio." Laura's voice shook with rage. "I saw you kick her down the stairs. How the hell did she ask for that?"

Larry sighed as if Laura tried his patience. "She talked back. I had to teach her—"

DJ stared at him, obviously horrified by this latest revelation.

"What about *me?*" Laura demanded. "What did *I* do to deserve getting thrown down the stairs?"

"You didn't learn, either," Larry said. His voice rose to match Laura's. "You were hardheaded like your mother. Women who don't want to listen have to be taught.''

Sickened, Adam moved his hand to the back of his waistband and touched his side arm. He didn't intend to unholster it—if he did, he'd probably kill Galloway. But it made him feel better knowing he had it there. He moved into Galloway's path and straightened to his full height. "I think you'd better leave. DJ doesn't want you here anymore."

Galloway's gaze flicked from Adam to DJ. "What? You don't want me here? Is he kidding?"

DJ shook her head. "He's right. You frighten Marissa, and you've offended almost everyone on my staff—"

"*I* frighten Marissa?" Galloway touched his chest with both hands in a gesture of helpless innocence. "She's my granddaughter. I love her. I love *you*, Devon. Just like I loved your mother and Laura.''

Laura snorted. "Yeah. You loved us so much, you beat us."

Galloway held out both hands as if he wanted to pacify her. "I do love you—"

"*Love?*" Laura pointed at DJ. "Then why did you give her up? Your money—your precious child support—was more important to you than *she* was."

"I didn't care about the money," Larry insisted. "Remember, your mother walked out and took Devon away from me. *I* was the one who was supposed to be hurting, and Christina used Devon to get even with me. I was given no choice. I had to give Devon up because your mother had everyone so convinced I was some horrible creature—"

"Yeah? Well, it was true."

Galloway glared at her. "You haven't changed a

bit, have you? You didn't learn then, and you're still not learning. So what are you doing here—turning Devon against me?''

"I don't need to," Laura said. "You've already done it yourself.''

"Don't start with me, you stupid bitch." Galloway slapped the side of the house with an open palm. Flesh hit wood with an almost-sickening pop, and Adam unsnapped his holster as a precaution.

DJ flinched, Laura's face tightened and across the yard, Marissa let out a wail that seemed to jerk DJ back to reality. DJ searched for her with frantic eyes, and to Adam, she looked like a startled bird ready to take flight.

He hesitated only an instant. He didn't want to leave Galloway alone with DJ and Laura, but he had to get Marissa to safety. He didn't want DJ to go to her or Galloway would follow, and he had to keep Marissa from crossing the lawn and putting herself in harm's way.

Racing down the steps and across the lawn, he scooped the child into his arms and cradled her against his chest for an instant. She felt small. Vulnerable. Fragile. And the absolute trust she offered threatened to bring tears to his eyes.

She wrapped her quivering arms around his neck and hung on for dear life. "I want Mommy," she sobbed.

Adam rocked her gently and spoke so low only she could hear. "It's okay. Mommy's going to be all right. See her? She's okay.''

Marissa buried her face against his shoulder. "I don't like him. He's mean. I want him to go 'way.''

Adam tightened his arms around her and kissed the

top of her head. "I do, too," he said honestly. "If I put you down by this tree with Holly, do you think you could stay right here and watch her?"

Marissa looked up at him with a tiny frown. "I don't want to stay here by myself."

Adam lowered her to the ground and then hunkered down to her level. "I know you don't, but I need you to stay safe right over here—okay?"

Marissa looked uncertain.

"I won't be gone long. I'll be right over there where you can see me. And I won't let anybody get hurt. Okay?"

She studied him with dark, baby's eyes. "Will you make him go away?"

"Yes," Adam promised.

Marissa didn't question how. Or when. She just leaned her head against his shoulder again and sighed.

She trusted him to keep her safe. She believed in him. And DJ believed in him.

He'd faced dangerous men before. He'd handled angry, violent people more than once. But he'd never had so much to lose.

CHAPTER THIRTEEN

DJ WATCHED ADAM rush across the lawn and Marissa lift her arms to him as he approached. When Marissa buried her face in his neck, DJ tried to fight a sudden rush of guilt. *She* should be the one comforting her child, but she couldn't make herself move.

When Larry swore violently and Laura shouted something back at him, DJ knew she couldn't let this go on any longer. Someone would get hurt. Marissa didn't need to see or hear any more.

She started toward them, surprised by Laura's lack of control. Laura had always seemed so together, DJ had a hard time connecting the sister she'd always known with the woman standing before her now.

Without warning, an image of a much younger Laura filled her mind. She stood with her head bowed and her shoulders quaking as she cried, and DJ could sense cold anger in the air around her—the same cold anger she felt radiating from Larry now. The picture vanished almost instantly, but the fear and sadness remained.

Blinking rapidly, DJ tried to convince herself it had been imagination—not memory. But she knew she'd seen Laura like that before.

She drew abreast of Larry and forced herself to look into his eyes. "I remember now. I remember how you hurt my mother and Laura."

He stared at her in stony silence for several long seconds. "What if I did? You got a problem with that?"

"Why can't you just leave and stay gone?" Laura shouted.

Larry glared at her. "Why should I? This is my daughter's house. I belong here. And I want my family together, no matter what it takes." He pivoted back to DJ and tried to look kind. "I lost you once. I won't lose you again. From now on, I'll keep you next to me. I'm holding on to my family."

Laura pushed between them. "We're *not* your family!" Her voice shook with the force of her emotions and her face grew an angry red. "You gave her up, and I never was part of your family."

Larry pushed her shoulder, and without warning, Laura struck his hand away. "Don't *touch* me. Don't you *dare* touch me." She lashed out at him again, then shoved his chest with both hands hard enough to make him stagger backward.

He worked up a cold, hard smile and jabbed her shoulder. "What's the matter with you?"

Adam worked his way past DJ and planted himself in Larry's path. "Don't touch her again," he warned.

Larry glared at him. "What the hell—?" He stabbed his fingers at Adam. "Keep your nose out of this. It isn't any of your concern."

"It is my concern," Adam insisted. "Don't touch her again."

Larry lifted both hands in a gesture of surrender, but DJ could see anger simmering in his eyes. "All right. You want to play big man, go right ahead. But you don't know *squat* about what's going on here." He used his head to point at Laura. "This one's been jealous of Devon from the minute she was born. Jealous and spiteful. Jealous because she didn't think I loved her as much as I loved Devon, and she looked for *any* excuse to hold against me.''

''That's not true!'' Laura shouted, and she came toward him as if she intended to strike him again.

DJ wrapped an arm around her and tried to hold her back while Adam kept himself directly in Larry's path. ''Laura, please,'' DJ said. ''Let's just get rid of him. Let it be over.''

But Laura didn't want to listen. She strained against DJ's hold and battled tears of rage. ''It's *not* over. It's *never* going to be over. I still have nightmares about him.'' She tugged one arm from DJ's grasp.

Terrified that Laura would do something to make the situation even worse, DJ clutched the material of her blouse, but Laura pulled so hard, the fabric gave way in her hand.

Catching Adam off guard, Laura darted around him and struck Larry across the face with the palm of her hand. As if in slow motion, Larry clapped one hand to the side of his face, and for one awful moment, DJ thought he'd hit back.

Thankfully, Adam stepped farther into his path. ''Don't even think about it.''

But Larry's temper had grown too hot for Adam to present much of a deterrent. He shoved Laura's shoulders and swore again.

Laura looked terrified, but she didn't cower under the force of his rage. She pummeled him with her fists and struck his chest, his sides, his arms. Adam pivoted toward her and tried to stop her, but she pulled away from him and struck out at Larry again.

She landed a blow to his neck and another to the side of his chin. "Go away!"

Again, Adam pushed between them. "Laura—"

She wheeled away from him, and her anger frightened DJ. She had no idea how best to react. After checking on Marissa, she forced herself to move closer and prayed for sudden inspiration if the need arose.

Larry caught Laura's hands in his and grinned. He turned to DJ. "Your mother thought she could take you away from me," he said. "She thought she could keep you from me. But she didn't win. She'll *never* win. I'll see her dead first."

DJ's heart beat high in her chest and her throat burned dry. She'd never been so frightened, but she couldn't let this go on any longer.

She took another cautious step toward them, but Adam got there first. "All right, Galloway. That's it—"

Laura interrupted with a howl of rage and fear. "I hate you!" she screamed. "I want *you* to die!"

Without warning, Larry released her hands and hit her across the face with the back of his hand. Blood spurted from her mouth and trickled from her nose. She covered her face and head with her arms. Her knees buckled, and she sagged to the ground.

Adam lunged at Larry, but Larry avoided him neatly and drew back his hand as if he intended to hit her again.

Forcing herself into action, DJ used her weight as a weapon and lunged at him. She caught his hand with her shoulder just before he struck Laura again, but she did nothing more than deflect the blow. His hand caught Laura on the side of the head and hit DJ in the shoulder.

Laura cried out in pain, and DJ stumbled backward toward the edge of the steps. When she landed the wrong way on the top step, her ankle twisted and threw her off-balance. Pain shot up her calf, and her ankle gave way beneath her.

Frantically, she grasped for the porch rail, but she was too far away to reach it. She plunged down the steps and landed on one knee with a sickening pop. The pain blazed a trail up from her knee to her thigh, and her ankle throbbed with every heartbeat.

Only Marissa's cry from somewhere behind her on the lawn kept her from closing her eyes and giving in to the pain for a moment.

While DJ tried to stand, Laura threw herself at Larry again. "You hurt her!" Laura cried. "I knew you would someday."

Larry grabbed her by the wrist again, but Adam intervened. Grasping Larry's wrist, he wrenched his arm behind his back and forced it up toward his neck. From across the porch, he locked eyes with DJ. "Can you walk well enough to get inside?"

"I don't know."

"Can you try? I need you to call 911. Get the Salt Lake Police Department over here."

"*I* didn't do anything!" Larry roared. "*Laura* brought this on—not me!" Eyes wide with surprise, he tried to pivot toward DJ. "Tell him, Devon. I was trying to defend myself. You could see that, couldn't you?" When she didn't answer, he shouted again. "Are you *blind?*"

He wrenched free of Adam's grasp and turned to

DJ with a wild look in his eyes. "Can you see now why I had to keep them in line?"

DJ couldn't see anything but a bitter, hate-filled man who hurt the people she loved most. Gritting her teeth, she gripped the porch rail for support and pulled herself to her feet. Pain seared her knee, and for a moment she didn't think she could remain standing.

In the background, Marissa's cries grew louder and the dog's angry barking pierced the morning air. A second later, Holly bounded past her and up the steps. Before DJ realized what the dog had in mind, Holly attacked, but she succeeded only in fastening her teeth into the denim near Larry's ankle.

Swearing, Larry tried to pull the dog from his pant leg, but Holly refused to let go. He swore aloud and kicked several times, but still the dog maintained her grip. At last he connected with the dog and sent her flying into the railing.

With a whimper of pain, Holly let go. But Larry aimed another kick at the dog's small body.

Marissa screamed and started across the lawn. "Don't you hurt my dog! Don't hurt my mommy!"

Adam hit Larry squarely in the stomach, and he staggered backward as Marissa started to climb the steps. DJ grabbed her around the waist and pulled her into her arms. "Stay with Mommy, sweetheart. Stay right here."

Holly lifted her head and tried to pull herself closer to Marissa, but she gave up after only a few inches and lowered her head to her front paws with a whimper.

"Mommy? Is she all right?" Marissa spoke softly, and circled DJ's neck with an arm.

"I hope so, sweetheart." Praying the dog hadn't

been seriously injured, DJ extended a hand and rubbed Holly's furry head.

Adam lunged again and struggled to pin Larry to the deck, but the older man used his feet as weapons. He struck out wildly and connected several times.

Marissa buried her face in DJ's shoulder. "Make him stop," she demanded. "Make him go 'way."

DJ held on to her, but she felt too frightened herself to offer much comfort.

Then Adam managed to hit Larry with an uppercut to the chin and a left jab to the stomach. Larry doubled over in pain and gasped for air. He struck back at Adam, but his few blows didn't carry much force.

With the advantage on his side for a moment, Adam fought harder and nearly pinned Larry to the floor. But Larry didn't give up. He thrashed and kicked and twisted under Adam's weight. He swore brutally and lashed out at Adam again and again. "You'll pay for this, McAllister," he snarled. "You'll be sorry you ever messed with me."

"I don't think so." Adam's voice sounded harsh and unfamiliar as he worked one knee into the center of Larry's back, pushing him against the cold wood.

Larry twisted again, reaching behind him and gripping Adam's shirt as he tried to roll away. Adam pulled back, but Larry didn't release him. The movement hoisted Adam's shirt up and exposed a handgun tucked into the waistband of his jeans.

At the sight of it, DJ's stomach revolted and her senses reeled. Adam had brought a gun into her home! He'd kept a weapon around Marissa without even discussing it with her!

Larry swore again and tried to dislodge Adam from

his back. "You think you're big enough to keep me down? You think you're *man* enough?"

Adam's expression tightened. With one last effort, he forced Larry's head to the floor and pinned his hands behind his back. "I'm both big enough and man enough to detain you until SLPD can arrive to take you into custody."

"For *what?*" Larry shouted. "You can't do that."

"I sure as hell can," Adam said. "You're going down. Two counts of assault. Parole violation—" He broke off and shouted again to DJ. "Call 911."

DJ couldn't move. She could only stare at his gun. She tightened her hold on Marissa and prayed Adam wouldn't pull the weapon, that it wouldn't discharge accidentally or that Larry wouldn't do something so stupid that Adam would think he had to use it.

"DJ?" Adam fixed her with his gaze. "Make the call, please."

DJ still couldn't make herself move. She pointed at the gun and glared back at him. "What are you doing with that?"

His face mirrored confusion for half a second, then he touched his back and flushed a deep crimson as he met her gaze again. "I can explain. I'm licensed to carry a concealed weapon if that's what you're worrying about."

She shook her head. "I don't care about that. I want to know why you have it in the first place."

"I promise you no one will get hurt." He looked confident. Sure of himself. "I'll lock it in my bag again as soon as the police get here."

Laura stood slowly. "Don't be ridiculous, DJ. You ought to be glad he's got it."

DJ felt sick to her stomach. Larry frightened her.

She didn't want him around Marissa any longer. But she'd seen a side of Laura she hadn't known existed. And Adam— If she were honest with herself, she would have to admit she didn't know Adam at all.

Maybe she shouldn't be surprised by the weapon. Maybe he did this sort of thing all the time. Maybe he wasn't the man she thought she knew, after all. She pulled in a shaky breath and stubbornly refused to look at Adam when he said again, "Call the police."

"You can't do this!" Larry roared. You're my daughter—my *baby!*"

"Do it," Adam said.

"You *can't* send me back to prison, Devon," Larry shouted. "You're not the vindictive type."

"Well, *I* am," Laura retorted. "If I have my way, you won't be free again for the rest of your life. In fact, if *I* had the gun, I'd shoot you myself."

"Shut up, you stupid *bitch*," Larry growled.

Determined to stop this nightmare before the unthinkable happened, DJ hobbled the rest of the way up the steps. She needed to get Marissa inside where she'd be safe and call the police before someone got seriously hurt or killed.

Adam jammed his knee farther into Larry's back. "Keep your mouth shut," he warned again. "If it wouldn't cost my job and Laura's freedom, I just might let her do it."

DJ froze midstride and stared at him. "Your job? What do you mean, your job?"

As if in slow motion, he raised his eyes to hers. He didn't say anything, but resignation mixed with apprehension on his face. "I can explain everything— I promise."

DJ's heart raced with dread. "What *job?*"

"I was trying to tell you when Laura showed up this morning. We can talk about it after Larry's in custody."

"Talk about it *now*. *What job?*"

Marissa tugged on the shoulder of DJ's shirt. "Mommy? Don't be mad at Adam."

That didn't even begin to describe how DJ felt. Numb. Apprehensive. Frightened. Furious. A combination of all four.

Adam still didn't speak for what felt like an eternity, but DJ refused to look away. "I'm not a writer," he said at last. "And I'm not a friend of your mother's, either. I'm a private security officer your mother hired after Galloway's release from prison to keep you and Marissa safe. That's why I'm here, and that's why I have the gun."

For half a heartbeat, DJ thought she'd heard him wrong. In the next second, she prayed she had. Her stomach lurched and everything inside her turned to stone. "She hired you?"

He nodded. "My primary objective is to catch Galloway in violation of his parole and return him to custody."

"You lied to me about that, too?"

He lowered his gaze, then lifted his eyes to meet hers again. "Not by choice."

"You *lied* to me!" she shouted. Tears filled her eyes and her breath came in shallow gasps.

"DJ, listen to me—"

But she didn't want to listen. She didn't want to look at him or even hear his voice. She backed away. "Don't. Don't talk to me. Don't give me excuses. Just leave."

Adam's heart sank, even though he'd expected just such a reaction.

"Mommy, no!" Marissa stiffened in DJ's arms, and for a moment, Adam feared she would try to get away from her mother and come to him. Luckily, DJ held her tightly.

Lifting her chin in a gesture of defiance, DJ stared into his eyes. "You knew who he was all along, didn't you?"

"I had his picture and a report from the agency, but I didn't know he was your father until he told you."

Galloway chuckled low in his throat and tried to lift his head. "Didn't I tell you he was hiding something?"

Anger tightened Adam's shoulders and constricted his chest. He wanted to shut Galloway's mouth—permanently. He needed a chance to make DJ understand.

She took another step away, but her face twisted in pain. "Stop it!" she shouted at Galloway. "Don't say another word."

Adam held out a hand to her. "DJ, please. Wait until I can turn Galloway over to the police. Then we'll talk."

"There's nothing to say."

"Oh, for heaven's sake," Laura said. "The man was just doing his job."

Galloway tried to lift his head again. "Don't listen to her, Devon. The guy's a jerk. I've been trying to tell you that since I got here."

"Stop it!" DJ glared at each of them in turn. "I don't want to hear another word—not from *any* of you."

Marissa cupped DJ's face with her hands. "Mommy, please don't cry. Let Adam stay. He'll make you smile."

Adam's heart felt as if it would break. His stomach clenched and twisted.

DJ kissed Marissa on the forehead, but she shook her head. "No, sweetheart. He can't stay."

"But Mommy—"

"Marissa, I said *no*."

Tears welled up in Marissa's eyes, but in the next second her little mouth set in the stubborn lines Adam had already learned to recognize. Before he could react, Marissa stiffened, twisted in DJ's arms and launched herself at him. "I want Adam."

DJ struggled to hold her, but Marissa fell straight toward the deck like a rock. Left with no choice, Adam turned from Larry just long enough to catch her before she hit the deck and then push her back toward her mother. But in that half second, Galloway scrambled out from under him and lurched to his feet. Before DJ could pull Marissa back to safety, Galloway kicked Adam in the groin.

Searing pain tore through his body and knocked the wind out of his lungs. He doubled over, gasping for air. He told himself to stand straight and take Galloway back into custody, but his body wouldn't respond. A second later, pain exploded in the back of his head and he felt himself falling toward the deck.

Even through the throbbing haze, Adam could hear Laura shouting and the sound of her footsteps as she ran after Galloway. "Call the police, DJ! He's getting away!"

Adam tried to pull himself together, but the pain

wouldn't subside. He could hear Marissa crying, but he couldn't focus well enough to see anything.

If he could only stand— He tried, but the throbbing tore through him again. All the sounds and voices mingled together until, at last, he heard Laura's feet climbing up the steps, panting as she struggled to catch her breath. "I couldn't catch him. He's gone."

At long last, the pain subsided enough to let Adam roll onto his back. He opened his eyes and stared straight ahead into the cloudless sky while DJ rushed inside and closed the door behind her. He'd failed Chuck, Thomas Dodge and Christina Prescott. He'd failed Marissa and Laura.

And worst of all, he'd failed DJ.

CHAPTER FOURTEEN

SLOWLY, STILL IN PAIN, Adam struggled to his feet.

Laura came up behind him and touched his shoulder. "You should have killed him."

He glanced back at her without speaking.

A sad smile curved her lips, and the light in her eyes told him she was only half serious.

"Are you okay?" he asked.

She nodded slowly and touched her fingertips to the bruise on her cheek. "He's hurt me much worse than this, before. The question is, are *you* okay?"

Adam nodded. He'd be fine. But he didn't want to think about the damage Galloway had done to the women in his life. He put an arm around Laura's shoulder and drew her against his chest. She relaxed against him for a second or two, then pulled away again and looked up at him. "So—? What are you going to do about my sister?"

"What about her?"

"Are you going to try talking sense into her or not?"

Adam studied her expression, but she gave nothing away. "What kind of sense?"

She pushed away from him with a soft chuckle. "If you don't know, you're in worse shape than I thought." She grinned up at him, leaving no doubt about her meaning this time.

"She doesn't want anything to do with me."

Laura sighed as if he were incredibly slow-witted. "She's in love with you, you idiot. I know her well enough to see *that*."

He allowed himself a glimmer of hope.

"Go on," she urged, and pushed him toward the house. "Talk to her." When he still hesitated, she nudged him forward again. "Go *on*. She's stubborn. Pigheaded. Unreasonable. *All* the women in our family are. One of these days, Bob can tell you how hard I made him work to win me over."

In spite of his apprehension, Adam smiled. "You think she'll talk to me?"

Laura rolled her eyes at him. "Of course she will. She's standing in there right now, wondering what's taking you so long to come after her."

Encouraged, Adam climbed the porch steps again. But when he reached the front door, he hesitated. What if Laura was wrong? What if DJ didn't want him? What if she sent him away?

Drawing in a deep breath, he forced himself to knock. He would never know unless he tried.

With his heart in his throat, he waited for DJ to answer. When a full minute went by without a response, he knocked again. With every passing second, his anxiety grew. He'd never had so much at stake— not only his heart, but his entire world stood behind that locked door.

"She'd better answer," Laura said softly in his ear.

She *had* to answer. Adam's life depended on it. He lifted his hand to knock again just as the door creaked open. DJ stood there in its shadow, looking lovelier than ever.

Adam's heart pounded in his chest, and he wondered how he would ever manage to get the words out. "I need to talk to you. Please let me explain why I didn't tell you the truth."

She lifted her eyes to meet his, but she didn't move away from the door. "There isn't anything to say."

"Please." He couldn't remember the last time he'd pleaded with a woman for anything.

"Oh, for heaven's sake," Laura said. "Let the poor guy inside."

He waited for DJ to respond, but she remained silent. "I need to talk to you," he said again. "I need to explain."

DJ lifted one shoulder in a listless shrug. "All right. Explain."

Not *here*. Not standing on the porch like some door-to-door salesman. "Do you mind if I come inside?"

DJ waited a long time before she stepped aside to let him pass, and even then she didn't meet his gaze.

Laura took Marissa from her arms and disappeared with her into the kitchen, leaving them alone. He followed DJ to the couch and sat on one end.

He looked deep into her eyes. There were so many things he wanted to say, he didn't know how to start. "All right," he admitted at last. "I lied to you. I'm sorry." The words sounded weak and useless, but he couldn't force any others from his parched throat.

She didn't answer.

Well, what had he expected? That she'd leap up and shout for joy? That she'd forgive him just like *that*? "I've wanted to tell you who I am and what I'm doing here almost from the beginning, but I couldn't. I was under orders not to tell you anything. Your mother didn't want you to know—"

She started to speak, but he held up one hand.

"Please. Let me finish or I'll never be able to say it."

She pressed her lips together and nodded. "Fine. Go ahead."

"Telling you the truth about myself would have cost me my job. Until today, I didn't realize how little my job means without you in my life. I love you, DJ. I want to spend the rest of my life loving you."

She shook her head slowly. "You expect me to believe you?"

Yes. He expected her to believe him. He *needed* her to believe him. But he could only say, "I hope you will."

"You lied to me."

"If I could undo that, I would. I'd start over this minute. I'd give *anything* to go back to the beginning, but I can't."

"No," she said. "You can't."

"I can't imagine life without you and Marissa in it."

She didn't speak for so long, he began to hope she'd relent. But she only shook her head again and stood. She tucked a stray lock of hair behind her ear and looked away. "I think it would be best if you packed your things and left now. Laura and I can keep Marissa busy while you leave. I don't want her to have to see you go. You've already hurt her enough."

Pushing to his feet, he thought frantically for some way to reach her. But his mind remained a stubborn blank. All his hopes and dreams crashed around him, and the heart he'd been so anxious to offer her grew cold.

DJ CARRIED THE LAST of her kitchen chairs into the living room, grabbed the broom and dustpan from the closet and limped back into the kitchen. In spite of her throbbing knee and ankle, she'd already polished every piece of furniture she owned, cleaned tile grout in her bathroom and scoured the refrigerator and stove until they gleamed.

She'd kept herself busy all day, pausing only long enough to feed Marissa and tuck her into bed. But she hadn't been able to work off the restless energy that had kept her moving since she'd watched Adam disappear around the corner the day before.

Her hair fell across her shoulders and down her back, damp from exertion. The last time she'd passed a mirror, she'd seen two huge dust smudges on her face, and her T-shirt and jeans definitely needed to hit the laundry the minute she took them off.

She took an almost-perverse pleasure in her appearance—as if it would prove how miserable she was if anyone cared enough to look at her. The ironic part was, there was no one left in her life who cared enough. In one horrible morning, she'd lost everyone but Marissa.

She forced away the tears that stung her eyes and attacked the kitchen floor with the broom. She supposed she ought to wait until morning to clean the floor—she would certainly be able to see better in the daylight. But if she stopped moving, she'd start thinking. And she didn't want to think.

Dumping the contents of the dustpan into the garbage, she replaced the broom in the closet and pulled out a scrub brush and bucket. She turned on the hot-water tap and stuck the bucket beneath it. Standing on tiptoe, she rummaged through the cupboard for the floor cleaner.

The telephone rang into the silence, startling her. She glanced at it, hesitated and decided to ignore it. She didn't want to talk to anyone—not Adam, not her mother, not Laura, and especially not Larry. None of them had anything to say she wanted to hear. But she couldn't stop her heart from wishing she would hear Adam's voice when the answering machine picked up the call. He'd already called her twice.

The machine clicked on after the fourth ring. She poured floor cleaner into the hot water while she listened to her own voice reciting her recorded greeting. But when the message came, it was her mother's voice, not Adam's.

"DJ? Sweetheart? If you're there, pick up the phone." She paused, waiting for DJ to answer. "DJ? I'm at Laura's right now, and I need to talk to you. Please? I'm sorry. I only did what I thought was best. I never meant to hurt you."

Tears burned DJ's eyes and her throat tightened. She knew her mother loved her—Christina's pain came through clearly in her voice.

She took a step toward the phone, but she had no idea what she would say if she answered. In the end, she hesitated too long. The answering machine reached the end of its time limit and beeped loudly as it disconnected.

Guilt and despair mixed with anger, and she didn't know which made her feel worse. On top of that, she felt an inexplicable disappointment when she realized Adam had given up trying to reach her.

Damn him. She didn't need him. She glared at her reflection in the kitchen window. Why did she care

whether or not he called? The only difference between Adam and everyone else was that she'd allowed herself to fall in love with him.

No, she insisted silently. She didn't love him. The
Adam she loved didn't even exist. He'd been a lie,
like everything else. Just another lie.

ADAM PACED the length of the tiny kitchen in his
apartment from the door to the window and back
again. Outside, clouds covered the moon, the wind
howled and icy raindrops pattered against the glass.

He'd spent the past two days thinking. About DJ.
About Marissa. About his career. And he'd taken a
good, hard look at himself.

By this morning, he'd come to terms with the mess
he'd made of everything. By midday, he'd slipped
into a blue funk. Now that evening had rolled around
again, the extent of his mistake hovered in front of
his eyes.

He'd cursed himself a thousand different ways and
thought of a dozen different things he should have
said to DJ. But in his heart, he knew that nothing
would have made any difference.

DJ would never forgive him.

He'd spent hours thinking about Marissa and wondering how she'd taken the news that he'd gone. Just
the thought of her deep brown eyes filled with tears
made his own eyes grow misty.

He was restless. Anxious. Troubled.

Maybe he was deluding himself. Maybe Victoria
had been right all along. Maybe he'd never be able
to hold a family together. Maybe he *would* make a
lousy father.

He stopped by the kitchen window and stared out

into the night. He swore aloud and started pacing again.

He'd lost everyone he'd ever loved—and for what? His career. Big deal. A career couldn't keep him company on a cold winter night. A career couldn't make him laugh or warm his heart. A career couldn't soothe his temper when he lost it or hold his hand when he needed it.

And the worst thing about it was, he couldn't blame anyone else for this one—not even Galloway, although the temptation to find some way to do so overwhelmed him at times. No. He'd brought this on himself.

Shaking his head in disgust, he went to the refrigerator and yanked open the door. He hadn't eaten all day, and he still didn't have any food in there. His mother's salad had deteriorated almost beyond recognition, and the odor emanating from the mystery dish made him a little ill. Tomorrow, he promised himself. He would get rid of that dish tomorrow.

Holding his breath, he scanned the shelves. Both cans of beer still sat there, just as they had the night Chuck had called to tell him about the assignment at DJ's. And tonight they had Adam's name written all over them.

He picked up one can and popped the top. But he didn't drink immediately. Instead, he slammed the refrigerator door shut and began to pace again. Floorboards creaked under his feet, and the silent apartment seemed to growl with every step he took.

He tried telling himself he didn't care whether DJ forgave him or not. He tried convincing himself he'd just been affected by watching her struggle to accept Galloway into her life; that he'd confused love with some other emotion—pity, perhaps. But he couldn't lie anymore. Not even to himself.

He loved her. And he'd lost her.

He lifted the can to his lips, but the smell of the beer only made him feel worse. Glaring at the can, he abandoned it on the counter and walked away.

He'd only gone halfway across the kitchen when the front doorbell rang. Who in the—?

Glancing at his watch, he started for the door. It felt like midnight, but his watch said it was only a little past eight o'clock. Maybe DJ had found his address. Maybe she'd come to him, ready to forgive him....

Hoping against hope, he hurried to the door and yanked it open. But instead of DJ, he found his brother Seth standing there, leaning against the doorframe and grinning. Under normal circumstances, Adam couldn't think of anyone he'd rather see. But not tonight. Tonight he wanted to be alone with his misery.

Seth's eyes narrowed as he pushed away from the doorframe. "Where have you been? I've been trying to call for two weeks."

An icy blast of air blew in through the door and wrapped itself around Adam. "On assignment."

"For two weeks?"

"Yes, for two weeks." Adam stepped away from the door. "Get inside. It's cold out there."

One of Seth's eyebrows arched as he entered. "What's wrong with you?"

"Nothing," Adam lied.

"Yeah. Right. I can see that." Seth paced behind Adam into the kitchen, lifted the beer can from the counter and sniffed it. "Beer? Do you have another one?"

Adam nodded toward the fridge. "Help yourself. There's one left."

Seth crossed to the refrigerator and pulled the door open, then stepped back and made a face. "Man! Smells like something died in here."

Adam glared at him. "I don't need any editorial comments about my housekeeping. What do you want, anyway?"

Seth lifted his eyebrow again. He took out the remaining can of beer and slammed the refrigerator door. "I came to find out if you're still alive. Believe it or not, I was worried."

Adam held out his arms to let Seth inspect him. "I'm still alive."

Seth leaned against the counter and studied him for a long moment. "All right, what is it?"

"What's what?"

"What's wrong with you?"

"I've already told you—"

Seth stepped away from the counter and shook his head. "Cut the crap, Adam. I'm your brother, remember? I've known you all my life. If you want to lie, try it on somebody who doesn't know you like I do." He popped open his beer and took a swig. "What happened? Did something go wrong on the job?"

Adam lifted a shoulder and turned away again. "You could say that, I guess." He had no intention of telling Seth about DJ.

"What?" Seth followed him. "Did you get passed over for a promotion or something?"

Adam just shrugged and snorted his response.

"Then *what?*" Seth took another long drink and

studied Adam for a minute. "You know what you're acting like? You're acting just like Luke did when Julie left him."

Adam glared at him. He most definitely was *not* acting like his other brother. Luke had been a basket case when Julie walked out. He'd been angry with the world, and he'd taken every opportunity to show it. "You don't know what you're talking about."

Seth stared at him for another minute, but instead of walking away like Adam expected, he laughed aloud. "What's her name?"

"Whose name?"

"The woman you're so upset about. Who is she and what's her name?"

Adam growled at him and strode into the living room. He picked up the stereo's remote control and turned it on. Immediately, K.T. Oslin's husky and melodious voice filled the room as she lamented a lost love. Swearing, Adam flicked the stereo off again.

Seth leaned against the door and took another drink. "Oh, yeah. You've got it bad." He closed the distance between them. "So? Tell me."

Adam tried looking away, but he couldn't. He tried keeping his mouth shut, but suddenly the need to tell someone about DJ overwhelmed him. And Seth, despite his annoying persistence, cared. Even Adam couldn't deny that.

"Her name's DJ Woodward," he said softly.

"Where'd you meet her?"

"On assignment."

"The one you just finished?" Seth lowered himself onto the sofa and leaned back.

Adam nodded.

"And—?"

"And I'm in love with her."

"Great! It's about time."

"Not great. She doesn't want anything to do with me."

"Well—" Seth cocked his head and grinned "—I can understand why she wouldn't."

Adam scowled at him, but he sat on the opposite end of the sofa and leaned forward with his elbows on his knees. Starting slowly at first, he told Seth everything. About Galloway. About Christina Prescott and Marissa. About DJ's reaction when she'd learned the truth. Talking soothed something inside. And Seth's obvious concern lifted his spirits a little.

"Well, well, well," Seth said, shaking his head and staring at his empty beer can when Adam finally finished. "You want my honest opinion?"

Adam nodded.

"She sounds perfect for you."

"She would be if she were even speaking to me."

"Have you called her?"

"Twice. She didn't answer the telephone."

"Did you leave messages?"

Adam nodded again. "Yes. I even left my phone number for her to call back if she wants. But she probably erased everything the second she heard my voice."

"What about flowers?"

Adam frowned at him. "She owns a nursery, for God's sake—"

"Candy?"

"She's not the candy type."

Seth rubbed his chin thoughtfully. "Jewelry?"

"She'd never accept it. And she already has a dog."

Seth laughed. "Okay, so a puppy's out. I don't know what to suggest, then. Unless you go see her."

Adam let out a huge sigh and shook his head slowly. "I might as well face the truth and get it over with—she'll never forgive me." But that wouldn't stop him from loving her. Or from worrying about her. "Right now, I'd be content to know she and Marissa are safe. That the new guard Chuck's assigned understands how serious the situation with Galloway really is and that she has someone there with her."

Seth shrugged. "Who did Chuck assign to take your place?"

"I have no idea."

"Can you find out? It might make you feel better."

Adam started to shake his head, then stopped himself. Why couldn't he?

He glanced over his shoulder at the cordless telephone on the kitchen table, and his lips curved into a smile. Surely he could find some way to convince Chuck to tell him that much.

Pushing to his feet, he crossed the room and snagged the receiver from the table. With unsteady fingers, he dialed Chuck's home number.

To his relief, Chuck answered almost immediately.

"Yeah?"

"Chuck? It's Adam."

"What now?" Chuck didn't sound at all pleased to hear from him.

Adam didn't care. "One quick question. Who have you assigned to guard DJ and Marissa?"

"Why?"

"Let's just say I'm curious."

"Let's not," Chuck growled.

"Who's the officer on duty?" He only needed a

name. He had a list of pager numbers for everyone on the crew. He willed Chuck to name Don Meier or Johnny Nitzel—both good men. Both friends who would return a page if Adam called.

"You blew the assignment, Adam."

Adam held back the response that rose to his lips and tried to keep his voice steady. "Thanks for pointing that out. Will you just tell me who the officer on duty is?"

Just when Adam had about given up hope, Chuck said, "Kenny Masters."

"Kenny?" Adam stared at the mouthpiece of the receiver. "Why the hell would you put Kenny on that job? He's just a kid."

"That doesn't concern you. You're not on the case anymore, remember?"

"You mean you left DJ and Marissa down there with nobody but Kenny to guard them? With Galloway still roaming the streets?" Adam's hand trembled, and his head felt as if someone had tightened a clamp on it.

Chuck's tone hardened. "Kenny's a good officer."

"Kenny's an idiot." Adam tried and failed to calm down a little. He'd caught Kenny sleeping on duty more than once and he'd had to warn him on several occasions not to get too lost reading his "Star Trek" magazines. Galloway could sneak right past him without even trying.

Adam drew in a deep breath and forced himself to release it slowly. It didn't help. "I'm going back."

"You're what?" Chuck demanded.

Seth sat up straight and stared at him.

"I said, I'm going back."

"Don't be a fool," Chuck warned. "Dodge is already furious with you."

"I don't care. I'm going back."

"If you do, you'd better not count on having a job with Dodge much longer."

Adam was tired of Chuck's threats. Tired of his sarcasm. Tired of Chuck, period. "Fire me if you want. I'm going back to make sure they're safe."

"What the hell's the matter with you?" Chuck said. "What are you thinking?"

"I'm thinking clearly for the first time in my life," Adam snapped, and before Chuck could say anything else, he flipped off the telephone, grabbed his keys from the hook on the wall and raced out the door.

He took the steps to street level two at a time and jumped the last three. He unlocked his truck and jumped inside, cranking the engine to life and squealing his tires as he peeled out of the driveway.

He passed Seth halfway to the street and pretended not to see him waving frantically. Whatever happened next, he would face it alone.

He'd created the mess; it was his responsibility to take care of it.

CHAPTER FIFTEEN

DJ SANK TO HER knees and wet the scrub brush, wincing a little at the temperature of the water and the pain in her leg. She'd used her muscles so much during the past two days, first at the nursery, then at home, they protested when she started scrubbing, but she kept going. The physical pain matched the pain in her heart.

At least she was free of Kenny, who only made her think of Adam. She'd sent him into town on an errand just to get him out of the house for a while.

She sat on her heels and pushed the hair from her eyes, but the instant she stopped working, tears welled up again and her throat tightened.

Angry with herself, she dashed the moisture away with the back of her hand and glared at the scrub brush. Two weeks ago, her life had been running along smoothly. She'd known what she wanted and where she was going. Now, she felt uncertain and alone. She'd lost her relationship with her mother, she'd lost Laura—and she'd lost Adam. All because Larry Galloway had walked into her life.

She let herself grow angry with Larry for an instant, but honesty forced her to admit she couldn't blame him, either. Larry's appearance in her life had been the catalyst, but he hadn't destroyed anything.

She reminded herself she still had Marissa. They'd

been fine before Adam walked into their lives, and she tried to convince herself they'd be fine with him gone. But Marissa hadn't stopped asking for him for two days, and DJ hadn't stopped thinking about him or missing him. The ache hadn't subsided even a little. If anything, the emptiness inside her had grown.

She dropped the scrub brush into the soapy water and sat back on the floor. Covering her face with her hands, she gave in to the tears as they burned their way down her cheeks.

She couldn't lie to herself any longer. She'd fallen in love with Adam. No matter who he was or what he did, she wanted to build a life with him. Marissa loved him and needed him as much as DJ did—and she was angry and hurt that DJ had asked him to leave.

DJ reached for the scrub brush and attacked the floor again, telling herself that Marissa would get over it in time. She'd forgive and forget, and within weeks everything would be back to normal again.

A nagging doubt formed in the back of her mind, but she pushed it away. Of course Marissa would get over Adam's absence. DJ had made the only decision possible.

At least she'd never told Marissa the truth about Larry. At least she didn't have to deal with losing Adam *and* a grandfather.

Holding back another sob, DJ pulled the scrub brush from the water, and the thought replayed itself in her mind. *At least she'd never told Marissa the truth about Larry.*

Suddenly nauseous, she dropped her hand into her lap and stared at the bucket. It couldn't be true! She hadn't been as guilty as everyone else, had she? Had she hidden the truth from Marissa and justified her lies the same way her mother and Laura had? The same way Adam had?

Another unwelcome thought nagged at the back of her mind. This time, she felt distinctly uncomfortable. She tried pushing away the self-doubt, but she couldn't ignore the similarity between her present situation and her mother's.

She sat that way for what felt like forever, taking an honest look at herself and the people she loved. Her mother, Laura—and Adam. Maybe they'd made mistakes, but was she any better?

She thought about what Laura had said that day on the porch in front of Larry. DJ was too stubborn for her own good. And just now, in the harsh glare of her empty kitchen, she wondered if Laura might be right. Suddenly DJ's reasons for isolating herself from everyone didn't sound nearly as convincing as they'd seemed at the time.

Tears filled her eyes. She felt foolish. Childish. Ashamed of herself for being so angry with everyone and so stubborn. She had to apologize. To explain. She needed to let Adam know she understood. She had to break down the wall she'd erected between herself and her mother and set things right with Laura.

She abandoned her bucket and brush and went to the answering machine. Replaying Adam's first message, she jotted down his number on a scrap of paper. She began to dial it, then stopped.

What could she possibly say to him? How could she apologize for behaving so foolishly? What if he'd changed his mind? What if her stubborn refusal to listen to him had killed his love for her? What if he didn't want her anymore? How could she survive hearing that?

Again, she caught herself and pulled herself up sharply. How had *he* felt when she'd sent him away? How could she be so selfish? How could she protect her heart after what she'd done to him?

Summoning all her courage, she dialed again and waited while the telephone rang once. Twice. On the third ring, someone answered.

"Adam?"

"No, this is his brother Seth."

Her heart dropped. "Is he there?"

"No, he's gone out for a while. I'm just waiting for him to come back. Can I give him a message?" His voice, so like Adam's, soothed her a little.

"Yes. Thank you. Would you just tell him... Tell him DJ Woodward called."

"DJ?" Seth laughed softly. "This is great! He was just telling me about you."

Her heart lurched. "He was?"

"All good, don't worry. As a matter of fact, I think he's on his way to your place now."

"He is?" She smiled. Her heart pounded and her hands grew clammy. "Are you sure?"

"Pretty sure. In fact, he ought to be there any minute."

He was coming back to her. She would have a chance to explain. He hadn't changed his mind. Her smile grew, and her mind flew this way and that as she tried to decide what to say.

She turned and caught a glimpse of herself in the kitchen window. Dirty face, messy clothes, stringy hair—she looked horrible. She couldn't let him see her like that. "Thank you. I...I appreciate it."

"No problem."

She hung up quickly and ran from the kitchen into her bedroom. She had to change her blouse, wash her hair, clean her face. Did she have time?

She raced to the closet and rummaged through the blouses hanging there. Which one? Nothing too fancy. Her black sweater. Perfect. She tore it from the hanger and started toward the bathroom just as the back doorbell rang.

She jumped a little and stared at herself in the mirror. He was here already. She didn't have time to clean up or make herself look presentable. Checking her reflection, she tried to do something with her hair, but it defied her efforts. She rubbed at the smudges on her cheeks, but they seemed to grow larger instead of smaller.

The doorbell rang again. Her heart thudded high in her chest and her fingers trembled. She didn't want to miss him. She didn't want him to think she wasn't home or that she didn't want to see him.

Tossing the sweater onto her bed, she hobbled past the kitchen, limped down the stairs as quickly as her leg would allow and pulled open the door.

But instead of Adam, she found herself staring into Larry Galloway's cold eyes.

He propped a hand against the door and pushed it all the way open until it banged against the wall. "I di'nt think you were home." He reeked of alcohol, his eyes looked bleary and unfocused and his speech sounded thick and slurred.

Dread replaced anticipation in the pit of DJ's stomach and her heart raced for an entirely different reason.

He took one drunken step toward her, as if he intended to come inside. "Well?" he demanded. "Aren't you glad t'see me?"

She gripped the door with both hands and tried to close it, at least partway. "What are you doing here?"

Larry shoved the door back open. "I've come home."

"This isn't your home. I told you to leave the other day. I don't want you here."

"You can't stop me from coming home." He leaned close. Too close for safety. "This is my house."

Instinct told DJ to step away from him, but she couldn't let him bully her. She stood her ground and blocked the doorway. "This is *my* house, not yours."

"Whaddaya mean? You're my daughter, aren't ya? This is my house." He gestured drunkenly. "I can come when I want to."

"No, you can't." She tried to keep her voice level as she again attempted to close the door between them. She'd seen him angry once—she didn't want to provoke that anger now.

But he pushed the door back again, this time with enough force to knock it out of her hands. Snarling, he shoved her hard, making her stagger backward into the step. Fresh pain shot from her ankle to her knee.

"I can come here any time I want," he repeated. "*Nobody's* goin' t' stop me." He swaggered inside and glared around him. "Where's your wannabe boyfrien'?"

DJ pressed her back against the wall, trying to stay as far from him as she could in such a small area. She lifted her chin, looked him straight in the eye and lied through her teeth. She didn't want him to know she and Marissa were alone. "Adam? He's outside in the front yard.'' She prayed furiously that Seth had been right—that he *would* be here soon.

''Well? Bring the SOB in here. I wanna kick his royal ass for what he did t'me.''

DJ backed up the first step without taking her eyes off him. She couldn't believe he expected her to deliver Adam to him. But he was drunk and angry enough to believe anything. ''I'll have to go get him.''

''Well, then, *go*. What the hell's takin' you s'long?''

She backed another step away and tried to think of some means of getting rid of him before he discovered the truth and harmed her or Marissa. But the pain in her leg had grown so severe, she had trouble walking.

Larry pushed past her and slammed his fist into the wall near the kitchen door. Pieces of plaster fell to the floor and a hole gaped where the wall had been. ''Get me a beer and get that boyfrien' of yours in here. *Now!*'' His voice rose steadily until the last word almost thundered into the silence.

DJ's hands grew numb and her heart felt as if it were beating in her throat. ''I don't have any beer.''

He looked thoughtful. ''Whaddaya have?''

She thought quickly. ''Wine.''

''*Wine?* What's that, yer boyfrien's drink?'' He laughed bitterly. ''Wine's for prissies, not men. You got a prissy boyfrien'?''

She shook her head and tried to sidle past him. She couldn't let him get to Marissa. She had to keep her child safe, no matter what the cost to herself.

''Tha's what it is, i'nt it?'' he taunted. ''He's a prissy boy, not a man. Only prissies drink wine. Only prissies let a girl order 'em aroun' like you did th' oth'r day.'' His eyes seemed to focus suddenly. "Jus' like your damned mother. Orderin' a man aroun'. She wanted t' order *me* aroun', but I wouldn't let 'er. I taught 'er who the boss was. I taught her t' respect me.''

DJ's hands trembled. Her mind raced as she tried to think of some way to distract him so she could get Marissa to safety. But she couldn't form a coherent thought.

''Y' know what ya need, Devon? Y' need a real man to teach ya who the boss is.'' Larry grabbed her by the shoulders and shoved her through the kitchen door.

She lost her footing and fell to the floor. Ignoring the searing pain in her leg, she scrambled backward on all fours and tried to put some distance between them. When she reached the cabinet, she grabbed it and pulled herself to her feet.

If she could distract him for a few minutes, she'd have time to get to Marissa's bedroom and sneak her out the sliding-glass door. She tried to keep her voice steady and to paste a smile on her face. ''Sit down for a minute while I get you something to drink.''

He glanced around the empty room and lifted his shoulders. ''On *what*?''

''I'll get you a chair.'' Hoping to buy time, she started toward the dining room, but he followed her. ''Forget the damned chair. Where's the prissy boy? Take me to 'im.''

''He's outside in the front yard,'' she said again.

But Larry shook his head. ''No, he's not. You're lying, aren't ya? Just like all women. Lyin', cheatin' whores, all of ya.'' Without warning, he lunged toward her.

Leaping sideways, she started to run. But now he was too close on her heels for her to take a chance on getting to Marissa. Instead she raced down the hallway toward the living room. The pain in her ankle and knee had all but disappeared in the face of her fear.

She prayed desperately that he'd follow, that she could draw him away from Marissa. Before she reached the front door, she heard him thundering after her.

She shoved a lamp out of her way and into Larry's path, but it didn't slow him down. Frantic, she grabbed the doorknob, but she'd already dead-bolted the door, and the knob twisted uselessly in her hands. She struggled to unlatch the lock, but her fingers felt awkward and stiff.

Larry's hands landed on her shoulders. She jumped and tried to pull away, but he yanked her around to face him. His face looked dark and angry. Twisted and ugly.

Her heart felt as if it had leaped into her throat and then dropped into her stomach.

''You need t' be taught a lesson, girl. You need t' learn respect for a man. Ya don't treat men like dogs and get away with it.'' He thrust her across the room as if she were nothing more than a rag doll. She landed on the arm of the couch, and her neck twisted when her head hit the cushions. She held back a whimper and tried to pull herself upright. But her arms trembled too badly to give her any leverage.

Galloway crossed the room and reached for her again. This time, she couldn't hide her fear. Screaming, she threw her arms across her face to protect herself and kicked furiously, trying to land a blow anywhere—his knees, his thighs, even his groin. But he slapped the blows away as if they were mosquitoes.

One hand hit her in the side. She gasped, more in fear than in pain, and tried to roll away from him. But he caught her shoulders again and pushed her onto her back.

"Don't touch me!" she screamed. "Don't you *ever* touch me again."

Anger filled Larry's eyes. He looked angry enough to kill someone. He raised a fist and glared at her, and DJ knew with dreadful certainty that if she didn't do something, he would take her life.

ADAM SHIFTED IN his seat and leaned against the door of his truck. He'd been out here for over an hour now, with no sign of Larry. He hadn't dared approach DJ or let her know he was out here watching. She would try to send him away again, but this time nothing would make him leave.

He pulled the travel mug from the dash and took a sip of coffee, but it had cooled while he'd sat here, and the lukewarm liquid tasted like hog swill. Tomorrow he would bring a thermos. And the next day. And the next, until he knew DJ and Marissa were safe forever.

Shifting again, he tried to work the kinks from his neck. Where the hell was Kenny? He hadn't seen any sign of him. Just then, he caught movement behind the curtains of DJ's house. He leaned forward, gripping the steering wheel. Was it her? Could he catch a glimpse of her?

The shadow moved across the room quickly. Too quickly. And in horror he watched as another shadow followed it. She wasn't alone. Galloway was in the house.

Dammit! How had Adam missed him? He hadn't taken his eyes off the house for even a minute.

Shoving open the truck's door, he touched the gun in the holster on his back as he ran, reassuring himself that he had what he needed to take Galloway down this time. He raced across the lawn, clearing the distance in seconds, and bounded up the steps just as a woman's scream tore through the night.

He hit the porch at a dead run and threw all his weight into the door. The wood frame splintered around it. He hit the door again and it fell into the room.

Galloway stood over DJ with his fist raised. He spun around when the door hit the floor. His eyes widened with shock, then an ugly smile took its place.

"Well. It's the prissy boy. The wannabe prissy boy." He seemed to forget about DJ as he turned toward Adam.

Adam moved into the room carefully, determined to keep Galloway's attention focused on himself. "Well," he replied in the same tone of voice Galloway had used, "it's the woman beater. Not big enough to take on a man."

An ugly expression crossed Galloway's face. "You wan' a taste of this, prissy boy? Come try me."

Adam didn't even hesitate. He crossed the room until he was close enough to do whatever he had to to take Galloway down.

Galloway took a swing at him, but he was obviously too drunk to control the punch. His fist flew wide of its mark. Adam took a step back, then another, hoping to draw Galloway away from DJ.

"Come on, tough guy," he taunted. "What's the matter? You don't know how to fight a man? Why don't you imagine I'm a woman? See what you can do then."

Galloway's eyes filled with hatred. "I'll kill you. You've done everything you can to turn my family against me. And now, you're going to pay the price. You're a dead man."

Behind him, DJ struggled to her feet. She looked weak and pale, but thank God she was alive.

Adam taunted Galloway again. "Think you can kill me? Come on. Try." He took another step away and used his hands to motion Galloway toward him. "Come on."

Without warning, Galloway pulled a knife and lunged toward Adam, but again his swing went wide.

Using both hands, Adam shoved Galloway's shoulders and let the force of the older man's own weight carry him to the floor. But Galloway rolled and lurched back to his feet. He lunged at Adam again, this time, aiming for Adam's chest.

Adam jumped back to avoid the blade, but the knife grazed him. A hot flash of pain followed it and blood flowed from the wound, although it hadn't gone deep.

To his surprise, DJ screamed and hurled herself on Galloway. Galloway must have been as shocked as Adam. His grip on the knife loosened and the weapon flew uselessly across the room. Pummeling him with her fists on the face and chest, DJ pushed him backward, straight into Adam. Fury propelled her and she didn't let up, even when Adam wrapped his arm around Galloway's neck and threw him to the floor.

Adam pulled the gun from his holster and forced it against the side of Galloway's neck. He cocked the hammer and nestled his finger on the trigger. He had him. He could pull the trigger and claim self-defense. The man had broken into DJ's home and used a weapon to threaten both their lives. He could take him out with one shot.

He lifted his gaze for a moment and looked into DJ's face. Her eyes, deep and wide were like a wounded doe's. Her breath came in shallow gasps and her body trembled. She would have bruises in the morning—bruises inflicted by this man now in Adam's control. Adam wanted nothing more than to see him dead.

But he couldn't make himself shoot. He might not go to prison for killing Galloway, he might not ever win DJ back, but he couldn't do anything to hurt her. If he shot this man in front of her, she'd be hurt.

Easing the weapon away from Galloway's neck, he held her gaze. "Call the cops, DJ. *Now*. No second chances."

She scrambled to her feet without argument and hobbled from the room. She was injured, and he wanted to hold her and take her pain away. He wouldn't leave here again without telling her how much he loved her and asking her once more to let him try again.

He forced his attention back to Galloway. He couldn't relax even for a second.

Galloway gasped for air and struggled halfheartedly to get away, but the fight had taken the power from him. For the first time, he looked exactly like what he was—a pathetic, weak old man.

Adam leaned into Galloway's back with his knee

and held him, suddenly aware of the pain in his chest and the amount of blood he'd lost. He willed the police to respond to DJ's call before he collapsed.

His head grew light as he watched the doorway for DJ to return. He imagined her standing there, smiling at him, loving him, the way he longed for her to do. He envisioned her walking slowly toward him, arms outstretched, willing to forgive him.

His eyelids flickered closed and the image of her vanished. In the distance, the faint wail of sirens cut into the night; the police would be here any minute to take Galloway away. He had to hold on until they arrived. He had to keep Galloway under control. He had to keep DJ and Marissa safe.

Gritting his teeth, he forced his eyes open and willed himself to hold on a little longer. He could do it. He had to. There was so much he still had to say to DJ—so many things he had to ask.

He focused on her face, her eyes, her hair—anything to keep himself conscious. He thought she moved closer, almost near enough to touch. He imagined her sitting on the floor beside him and letting her fingers graze his shoulder with a touch so gentle it could only have been a dream.

"I love you," he whispered.

In his dream, a smile crossed her face. She pressed a kiss to his cheek and trailed a finger along his jaw. And she answered him. "I love you, too."

Outside, tires squealed around the corner and flashing lights lit the windows of DJ's living room. He looked away from her for a second—surely no longer than that—and when he looked back again, she'd disappeared.

Footsteps thundered onto the front porch, voices

shouted, but Adam couldn't make his eyes focus any longer. Across the room, he could hear someone asking questions and DJ's voice as she answered.

"Get the paramedics in here," a voice called out near his ear. "This guy's lost some blood."

A second later, too weak to fight any longer, Adam felt himself slip into the black clouds, and even the sound of DJ's voice faded to nothing.

DJ PACED THE waiting room, clutching a single red rose in one hand and sending frequent, anxious glances toward the door into the emergency room. She checked her watch and sighed. Only a few minutes past midnight, but she felt as if she'd been waiting forever to see Adam.

Pivoting, she passed the nurses' station, walked to the end of the waiting room and stared at the fish tank. A television played softly—presumably to give relatives or loved ones something to keep them occupied.

The aromas of medication, disinfectant and illness stung her nose. And although she knew her reaction was unreasonable, the occasional burst of subdued laughter from the health-care professionals behind the counter irritated her.

She wanted to see Adam up and walking again, not weak and helpless the way he'd looked when the paramedics strapped him to the stretcher and carried him away. She needed a chance to tell him she loved him. A chance to explain and to apologize for letting stubborn pride stand in the way of reason.

At the other end of the waiting room, a door opened. DJ wheeled around, hoping the doctor would be coming to talk with her. Instead, she saw her mother standing there.

"DJ?" Christina hesitated, almost as if she were frightened to approach. "DJ? Sweetheart, are you all right?"

DJ took a step toward her. Apparently, that was all the signal her mother needed. She closed the distance between them and pulled DJ into her familiar embrace. Her scent, warm and familiar, surrounded DJ and comforted her the way it always had.

She looked so worried, DJ let herself relax. "I'm fine, Mom."

Sighing with relief, Christina pushed her to arm's length and studied her face for a second, then hugged her again so tightly, DJ had trouble drawing a deep breath. "Thank God you're all right," she said, more to herself than to DJ, then glanced around the waiting room. "Where's Marissa?"

"She's at home with Brittany. Adam's brother said he'd stop by on his way down from Ogden later this morning and bring her to see Adam. We're just waiting to find out whether he's all right."

Christina loosened her grip, but she kept both hands on DJ's shoulders. "Sweetheart, I can't tell you how sorry I am about everything. If I'd just been honest with you, poor Mr. McAllister wouldn't be in there—" She gestured toward the emergency room. Her face, her eyes and her voice told DJ more than she could ever have said with words. "Laura told me what happened with Larry. And then, when Tom Dodge *finally* called me to tell me about last night—" Christina broke off with a shake of her head. Her eyes narrowed and her brows knit. "Tell me about Mr. McAllister. How is he?"

DJ glanced again at the closed door to his room.

"I don't know. They tell me he's stable, but I haven't seen him yet."

Christina followed the direction of her gaze, studied DJ's face intently and looked down at the rose in her hand. Her expression softened. "Laura said she thought there might be something between you two. Is that for him?"

"Yes."

Christina squeezed her shoulder and smiled gently. "Do you love him?"

DJ nodded. "Yes."

"Well? Tell me everything. Does he treat you well? Is he good with Marissa? Does *he* love *you?*"

DJ smiled into her mother's eyes. In spite of everything, nothing had changed between them. "Yes. Yes. And yes."

"Does he know how you feel?"

"I don't know," DJ admitted. "I don't think so."

Christina started to respond, but when something behind DJ caught her attention she stopped abruptly.

DJ turned to look. The emergency-room physician stood just inside the door, speaking to a nurse. He looked up and caught DJ's eye. Smiling a little, he nodded and gestured to her.

Swallowing hard, DJ glanced at her mother.

"Go," Christina whispered, and gave her a gentle shove. "You and I can talk later."

DJ didn't have to be told twice. She walked quickly forward to follow the doctor toward Adam's room.

"Your friend's a lucky man," the doctor said to her with a tight smile. "He'll be stiff and sore for a few days, but he'll survive." He paused outside a closed door and pushed it open with one hand. "He's in here—waiting for you."

Relief washed through DJ. She hadn't consciously let herself think about the alternative, but now that the danger had passed, she realized the fear that had been there all along.

She peered inside and took a hesitant step forward. He lay with his head to one side, looking out the window into the night. She watched him for a moment, relieved to see that some of the color had returned to his face and that the bandage on his chest looked clean and fresh.

She longed to put her arms around him, but she didn't dare. Her heart hammered in her chest, and it seemed to take an eternity for him to realize she was there.

When at last he saw her, a weak smile flashed across his face but his eyes looked dark and she could see the question lurking behind them.

She crossed the room and touched one of his hands with her fingers. "How are you feeling?"

"Sore." He half smiled, but his expression sobered again immediately. "I'm glad you're here." He lifted his head slightly and touched his lips to hers.

She melted against him, then pulled back when she remembered his wound. "I'm sorry. Did I hurt you?"

He shook his head. "Never."

She drew in a steadying breath. "I came to apologize. I understand why you did what you did—"

He lifted his head again and pulled her back against him. This time his kiss was more insistent. Moaning softly, she opened herself to him. He used his tongue and lips to caress hers, but too much remained unsaid between them. She needed to tell him why she'd sent him away the first time and to beg him to forgive her. She pulled away from his embrace slowly, reluctantly.

"Listen to me, Adam. Please. I need to know you forgive me for being so stubborn and proud—and for sending you away."

One eyebrow flew up in that expression of surprise she'd learned to love. "Forgive you? I thought I was the one who needed to apologize. I'm the one who put you in danger by not telling you the truth." He struggled to sit and reached for her. "I won't do it again."

"I know."

He grinned back and pulled her into his arms. With his mouth against hers, he whispered, "I love you."

She managed to whisper back, "And I love you." But the words had no time to move across the space between them before he lowered his lips to hers again. He kissed her softly, carefully, until she wrapped her arms around his neck and wound her fingers into the hair on his nape. Nothing existed but Adam and the thunder of her heart.

"So, what's next?" he asked much later.

She settled carefully on the bed beside him. "I suppose we need to make a few decisions."

He shrugged lightly, but she could see a spasm of pain dart across his face. "I'm afraid I'm not very good at waiting. I want to marry you, DJ—right away. I want to build a life together. I want to be a husband and a father."

She grinned. "I'm not exactly patient, myself."

His expression sobered. "The problem is, I may not have a job after what happened—"

"You could always work with me at the store."

"Gardening? You know how good I am at that."

She pretended to consider. "You could take up writing."

He laughed, coughed a little and sank back on his pillow. "Not a chance."

She brushed a kiss to his lips. "Adam, no matter what happens to your job, we'll make it as long as we're together." Behind her, she heard someone enter the room.

"He doesn't have to worry about a job," Christina said. "Tom Dodge has already been on the phone with What's-His-Name." She smiled at Adam and held out her hand as she approached the bed. "Tom's intelligent enough to recognize what you did, and he's not the type to fire you for going beyond the call of duty." Her expression sobered. "You saved my daughter's life, Mr. McAllister. And my granddaughter's. Tom knows that. *I* know it. But making you put up with me for a mother-in-law may not seem like much of a reward."

Adam took her hand and worked an arm around DJ's waist. "I'll chance it."

DJ leaned into his embrace and smiled into her mother's eyes. For just a moment, she thought of Larry Galloway. If it hadn't been for him, she would never have met Adam. She marveled that the worst thing she could have imagined in her life had brought about the best thing ever to happen to her.

Adam tightened his arm around her waist and brushed a kiss across her lips. Her mother gently touched her hand with her fingers. And slowly, surely, DJ's world tipped back into balance.

And the Winner Is...
You!

...when you pick up these great titles
from our new promotion at your
favorite retail outlet this June!

Diana Palmer
The Case of the Mesmerizing Boss

Betty Neels
The Convenient Wife

Annette Broadrick
Irresistible

Emma Darcy
A Wedding to Remember

Rachel Lee
Lost Warriors

Marie Ferrarella
Father Goose

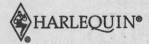 

HARLEQUIN SUPERROMANCE®

Come West with us!

In Superromance's series of Western romances
you can visit a ranch—and fall in love with a cowboy!

In June 1997 watch for
The Truth About Cowboys

by award-winning author
Margot Early

Erin Mackenzie considers herself a candidate for the Dumped
by Cowboys Hall of Fame. One in particular—rodeo cowboy
Abe Cockburn, who's also the father of her baby daughter. And
then there's Erin's *own* father, rancher Kip Kay, who's never
acknowledged her.

Erin does a risky thing: she goes to Colorado to tell Abe about
his daughter. And to tell Kip about *his*. She goes to Colorado to
find the truth about cowboys—and about fathers.

Look for upcoming HOME ON THE RANCH titles wherever
Harlequin books are sold.

And look for Margot Early's next Superromance novel,
Who's Afraid of the Mistletoe?, available in December.

Join bestselling author

Laura Van Wormer

in East Hampton, Long Island,
where old money meets new money

Just for the Summer

or until murder gets in the way.

In East Hampton, sex, money and power really do make the world go round. And when the ride stops at this elite summer playground, the vultures swoop.

Famous Hollywood producer Alfred Hoffman has died in a plane crash. Now everyone wants a share of the estate—his son from a previous marriage, his partner, the IRS. Hired by Hoffman's wife to complete an inventory of the estate, Mary Liz Scott uncovers dark secrets kept hidden until now. Too late, Mary Liz realizes she knows too much—because now someone is trying to kill her.

Available June 1997, wherever hardcover books are sold.

MIRA The brightest star in women's fiction

MLVWJS

Look us up on-line at:http://www.romance.net

HE SAID

SHE SAID

Explore the mystery of male/female communication in this extraordinary new book from two of your favorite Harlequin authors.

Jasmine Cresswell and Margaret St. George bring you the exciting story of two romantic adversaries—each from their own point of view!

DEV'S STORY. CATHY'S STORY.
As he sees it. As she sees it.
Both sides of the story!

The heat is definitely on, and these two can't stay out of the kitchen!

Don't miss **HE SAID, SHE SAID.**
Available in July wherever Harlequin books are sold.

HARLEQUIN®

It's hot...and it's out of control!

Beginning this spring, Temptation turns up the *heat.* Look for these bold, provocative, *ultra*sexy books!

#629 OUTRAGEOUS
by Lori Foster (April 1997)

#639 RESTLESS NIGHTS
by Tiffany White (June 1997)

#649 NIGHT RHYTHMS
by Elda Minger (Sept. 1997)

BLAZE: Red-hot reads—only from